LAKE ERIE MONSTERS

A STORY OF THE CLEVELAND IRISH

Lake Erie Monsters
Copyright © Ashley Herzog, 2019

ISBN-10: 1702362078

ISBN-13: 978-1702362078

*For my grandmother Regina Masterson Gorie, my
great-aunt Mary Jane Masterson, and my great-uncle
Grover Masterson, whose research into our family history
made this novel possible. And for Phil, and all the other
true Mastersons, may they rest in peace always.*

Introduction

The indigenous people of the Great Lakes states, especially the Ojibwa, tell a legend about a lake monster called the Mishipeshu, which loosely translates as "The Great Lynx." The Ojibwa believed this underwater panther guarded the substantial troves of copper and other precious metals in the Great Lakes from intruders. The Mishipeshu has been blamed for the death of many on the Great Lakes. In the early 1800s, a French Jesuit missionary named Claude Dablon relayed the story of four Ojibwa men who went hunting for copper in the lake. "The water panther came growling after them, vigorously accusing them of stealing the playthings of his children. All four of the Indians died on the way back to their village, the last one surviving just long enough to tell the tale of what had happened in his final moments before he died."

Beginning in the mid-1800s, Great Lakes steamboats began ferrying thousands of immigrants to the port cities, including Cleveland, Ohio. In the fall of 1887, my great-great-grandmother, Mary Chambers, was one of them.

6

One

Mary Chambers wasn't dead, but she was inside a casket, listening to the mourners sing a death song. As her seventeen-year-old sister, Katie, got up to eulogize her, the crowd fell silent. Mamie struggled to stay still in the cramped coffin, her arms crossed over her chest.

"Mamie was like a second mother to us all," Katie told the crowd. "When our dear sister Bessie first started walking, she would run after Mamie calling, 'Mama, mama, mama…'"

The guests laughed. Their laughter was punctuated by the squalling of Mamie's newborn sister, Norah, who was only a week old. Mamie closed her eyes.

The Irish, it was said, "Did death well." But on a personal level, Mamie Chambers had a deep hatred of wakes.

Including her own, apparently.

"Mamie takes care of our own mother," Katie Chambers continued. "Ah—*took*. So much so, we thought she might never leave home. Until she fell in love with the quiet and bookish Peter Sweeny…"

More laughter.

Peter Sweeny was Mamie's husband-to-be. Peter *was* intelligent, and bookish, and not too many years older than she: he was twenty-five and she was twenty. Peter had agreed to make Mamie his wife after Mamie's father, William Chambers, gave him a dowry payment for their life in America.

7

The lid of the casket creaked open, and Mamie saw Katie's face in a bright stream of light.

"You can come out now," Katie said, offering her hand to help. Mamie's brothers, Tom and Johnnie, emerged from their caskets, too. As the Irish did at real wakes, they'd placed their shoes at the foot of their caskets for the journey to the Great Beyond, and candles burned above their heads to guide them through Purgatory. In a moment of triumph, the Chambers siblings blew out the candles.

The crowd erupted into cheers.

This was their "America Wake." The Chambers siblings weren't dead, but it might be their relatives' last chance to see them alive. Tomorrow, they were leaving for the port city of Cobh, where they were catching a steamship to New York City. From New York they would travel to their new home.

Cleveland, Ohio.

It was November, 1887. A freezing wind whipped the town of Roskeen North in County Mayo on the west coast of Ireland, making the door on the Chambers' cottage rattle.

"We'll meet again, Mamie," Katie said, rubbing Mamie's arm. "I'm sure we will. Ships sail faster than ever, and letters take only weeks, not months. This isn't goodbye forever."

In the opposite corner of the room, their younger brother Johnnie was entertaining a semi-circle of giggling lasses.

"I lament the day I leave you lovely Irish roses, but I'm goin' to America first thing in the morn," he was telling them, putting his hat over his heart.

"And what will you do there?" one of the young girls asked.

"Whatever I want," Johnnie answered. "If I'm lucky, I'll get initiated as a Dead Rabbit."

The Dead Rabbit comment caught their father's attention. William Chambers motioned for his son to come over to him immediately.

"What did I say about that Dead Rabbit talk?" he asked Johnnie.

Johnnie looked up at their father, who was a head taller, a serious look befalling his face. "To never speak of it as long as I live," he replied with deadly earnestness.

"That's right," William Chambers replied. "I'm not sending you across the sea to join a gang. You're to stay out of trouble and be a man. And for God's sake, no more mentioning the Dead Rabbits, you *idiot.*"

The way William Chambers pronounced "idiot" made it sound like *"eejit."* But he and Johnnie smiled at each other, and Mamie knew they had an understanding. No one—least of all their father—would call Johnnie an idiot. A hoodlum, maybe. But not an idiot.

Peter Sweeny, now standing beside Mamie, shook his head. "I curse the day I agreed to make the journey with that boy," he grumbled.

"Peter," Mamie said, her eyes begging him for patience. "He's just a child."

But not for long. Johnnie was fifteen, on the verge of full manhood.

"Aye, that. But he thinks he's grown, and he has the mouth of a drunken sailor," Peter said. Peter watched Johnnie with narrowed eyes as he resumed holding court with the girls. "I swear, he causes any trouble on that ship, I will chuck his arse into the North Atlantic."

The men began passing out ales. Some of the men drank poitín, rumored to be the strongest alcohol on Earth, and a custom at Irish wakes. The women mostly stuck to tea. Someone handed Mamie a pint of ale, and she drank from it.

Mamie could feel the widow Sweeny's eyes on her. Peter's mother and brothers had deigned to attend the America Wake, but refused to participate in the revelry. They found it sacrilegious.

"Peter was to be my Irish Bachelor," Mrs. Sweeny had lamented earlier in the night. "He was my favorite son, the one born to care for me in my later years. But now…"

Peter apparently felt his mother's eyes on them, too. He reached out to try to take Mamie's glass of ale.

"Drinking the Creature now, are you?" Peter said with a raised eyebrow.

"Just this once," Mamie said. "I need to clear my mind, so please…"

As soon as Peter was distracted, Johnnie came by and clanked his glass against hers. "Smile, Mamie," he said. "And ignore those Sweeny people, those high-falutin' Lace Curtain ninnies…"

"Johnnie, stop," Mamie hushed him. "*We're* Lace Curtain, and you know it."

The so-called Lace Curtain Irish were the middle class, the people who eked out a modest living as shopkeepers and professionals. They were the people who could afford little luxuries like lace curtains—unlike the Shanty Irish, who toiled on farmland owned by British landlords. The Chamberses owned a tailoring shop, which was apparently Lace Curtain enough for the Sweenys, who had a small law practice.

"Well, I put a big scratch in Lord Browne's carriage, and 'tis Shanty enough for me," Johnnie said, and Mamie laughed. Lord Browne was the British landlord who owned the farmland around Roskeen, and he was deeply despised across three parishes.

Against her better judgment, Mamie took another sip of the ale. She was unsure whether the flutters in her stomach were the byproduct of excitement or fear.

Two

"What does Cleveland look like, anyway?"

Mamie sat on the edge of her parents' bed. Her mother, Bridget Chambers, was helping her fit her smallest belongings into her little trunk. Ma insisted on packing small trinkets on top of Mamie's chemises and wool skirts.

"I know they seem frivolous," Ma said of the items. "But you'll not regret having a bit o' home when you get to Cleveland. I should know; I made that journey to Ohio many moons ago."

Mamie knew Cleveland as a dot on a map, situated along one of many large inland lakes. It was in the Ohio territory, but Mamie didn't know a thing about Ohio, either.

William and Bridget Chambers had lived in Cleveland once. Mamie's parents had met there when her mother was still a teenager and her father was a young man in his early twenties. They were among the small number of Irish immigrants who packed up and came home. They rarely spoke of it, and Mamie never had reason to ask. But now…

Ma ignored her question about what Cleveland looked like, instead holding up a white kerchief that she had sewn herself. Mamie came from a family of tailors. Her parents had spent their adult lives operating a tailoring shop in Roskeen, and Bridget Chambers prided herself on her sewing skills.

"You'll carry this in your pocket at your wedding," Ma explained. "When you and Peter are expecting your first baby, a few stitches will turn this into your babe's christening bonnet."

Mamie's newborn sister, Norah, was asleep on her parents' bed. Mamie stared at the baby, watching her make suckling motions with her mouth in her sleep. Mamie still thought of herself as an oldest sister, not as a woman ready to bear children herself.

"You didn't answer me, Ma," Mamie replied. "Tell me, what is Cleveland like?"

"Yeah, what is Cleveland like?"

They both looked up to see Mamie's young sister, Elizabeth, called Bessie, padding into the room. She hopped onto the bed, playing with Mamie's hair.

"I don't want you to go," Bessie said mournfully.

Mamie sighed, her chest heavy with sorrow. "I don't want to go either," she said, pulling Bessie closer.

"But she must," Ma said, keeping her composure and refusing to cry. "There are few jobs to be had in County Mayo, and even fewer in Roskeen. But in the States, the factories and mills create jobs faster than men arrive to fill them. 'Twill be a better life for Peter and Mamie, and Tommy and Johnnie, too."

"How big is the city?" Mamie asked. "Will I get lost?"

"Nah, because you won't walk alone," Ma said. "As I said, it's no Roskeen North. But let me tell you something about Cleveland. It was my place of dreams. No one tells you what you'll do with your life when you reach the States. You create your own life. And you'll never be idle, Mamie. Women work if they choose. I worked."

"Where?" Mamie asked.

Ma paused for a long moment, rearranging the items on the top layer of the trunk. "I was a domestic," she said. "I've told you before."

"You never told me much," Mamie said.

"What's a domestic?" Bessie asked.

"A domestic is a maid," Ma replied. "I worked in a big mansion at the top of the hill, a short walk from my church. I worked for a wealthy man and his wife. The man's daughter lived there too, with her two wee children."

"Did she have a husband?"

Ma bit her lip. "Yes, she had a husband," she said, almost reluctant to mention him. "His name was Mark."

"Why did you leave them?"

Bessie had a habit of asking rapid-fire questions. Mamie decided to interrupt her, knowing Ma wanted to finish the packing.

"It's well past your bedtime," Mamie said. "Come with me, and I'll tell you a bedtime story."

Mamie took Bessie to the bed they shared with Katie and their other sister, Bridget, who was ten. All four of them huddled under a handmade quilt in one bed. By tomorrow night, Mamie would be gone, and only three Chambers girls would sleep here. Soon enough, baby Norah would grow big enough to take her spot.

"Mamie, tell me a story about faeries," Bessie said. "Please."

Being the oldest girl, Mamie had endless faerie stories to tell. She spun a good tale until Bessie's breath was deep and even.

Mamie slept hard for the next few hours. But in the dead of night, she awoke to a bone-chilling wail. She leapt to her feet, groping the walls to find her way to her parents' bed.

"What was that?" Mamie hissed in the darkness. "Did you hear that?"

"Hear what?" Ma whispered. "By God, daughter, it was just Norah."

Of course. The baby awakened at least twice every night. She wasn't shy about demanding to feed at Ma's breast.

"I'm sorry, Ma," Mamie said, slinking back to her own bed. "I'll see you in the morning."

As she drifted off to sleep, Mamie couldn't shake the thought that the wail hadn't sounded like Norah's at all. It sounded like the wail of a *bean sídhe*. The bean sídhe—pronounced "banshee" in English—was a small creature that stalked the Irish countryside, resembling a faerie. But unlike a faerie, the banshee was a terrifying sight to behold—or hear.

She was going to America, but Mamie was still Irish. And the Irish believed that when one heard the wail of a banshee, someone was about to die.

Three

Peter, Mamie, Tom, and Johnnie left Roskeen first thing the next morning. They traveled in a horse-drawn wagon operated by a man who made extra money shuttling people to Cobh.

In normal circumstances, a huge crowd of people would gather to see them off. But the Chambers siblings' exit from County Mayo would be a quiet one. They didn't want to attract the attention of the Royal Irish Constabulary.

It had "Irish" in the name, but the RIC was a British institution to its core. Mamie's brother, Johnnie, was supposed to go on trial in the spring for vandalizing the hated British landlord's carriage. No one was supposed to know he was leaving the country.

It was a cold and misty morning, and the ride out of Roskeen was bumpy. Mamie was sure she'd have a constellation of bruises on her back when they finally made it. Still, she knew she was lucky to have a ride at all. The famine generation had walked to the port cities to board their coffin ships, after the British landlords expelled them from their homes and turned them out on the road. They trudged days without shoes, eating grass and seaweed. Mamie had a wool sweater her mother knitted for her. When she thought of the starving Irish walking this path, she was grateful for her sweater.

They passed the cottage owned by Sully Mulchrone, an elderly neighbor who had many horses. He used to have many, anyhow—before he fell short on the rent and Lord Browne took them. Only a few horses remained. Mr. Mulchrone came hobbling up to the carriage, passing his stone pasture fence to the road.

"A horseshoe for you, Mary!" he called to Mamie, thrusting a real horseshoe at her. "Take it with you and carry it down the aisle. And luck be to the married couple!"

Irish brides had a custom of carrying a horseshoe down the aisle as a symbol of good luck. Mamie hadn't given a thought to where she'd get a horseshoe before her marriage to Peter. But now she had one, courtesy of her beloved old neighbor. She waved to him and gave a blessing in Gaelic.

Mamie turned the horseshoe over, feeling its heaviness in her hands. As Mr. Mulchrone and his beloved horses faded into the distance, Mamie felt an onslaught of sadness that she would never again walk this ancient road with the old stone walls.

Four

Tom and Johnnie didn't speak the whole way to Cobh. They were deep in thought about what would happen if Johnnie got turned away from the ship because of his arrest.

They were traveling on a ship named the *Britannic*, owned by a British company called the White Star Line. No self-respecting Irishman gave the English credit for anything, but White Star had a good reputation. The company treated its third-class passengers well and offered clean, comfortable accommodations.

Mamie's parents had heard horror stories about the filthy conditions aboard other ships. So they gave Tom strict instructions to buy tickets from White Star only.

"Let's hope they're not booked already," Tom said as the carriage bumped away toward Cobh. "We'll be stuck there until the spring."

That wasn't even a fathomable option, Mamie thought. Johnnie would go on trial before then, to face down Lord Browne and his minions for the petty crime of vandalizing a carriage.

"Few people travel in late November," Peter replied. He was still bitter about the timing. He had wanted to wait until April, but the Chambers' foremost concern was getting Johnnie out of Roskeen, and fast.

"We're a stone's throw from Queenstown," Peter said, noting the first signs of a city on the horizon.

"Cobh," Johnnie corrected him. "I'll jump from the Cliffs of Moher before I call it Queenstown."

Mamie and Tom laughed. The British had renamed Cobh to "Queenstown" out of spite.

"I second that," Tom said. "I'll call this town by its true Irish name. Not the name that honors that lumpen monarch and her horde of swishy inbred children."

Queen Victoria was a villainess, the scourge of the Irish. She'd allowed the Irish famine to unfold before her eyes and did nothing about it. Mamie could forgive Tom for his crude insults—even laugh at them a bit.

At the ticket counter, Tom slid the cash to the ticket officer.

"Three adults, steerage," he said matter-of-factly. "Two men. One lady."

The ticket officer looked them up and down. "Any head lice?"

"No," Tom replied. They'd get examined before boarding to prove it.

"Any arrests or convictions?" the officer asked, his steely eyes sweeping over them and landing on Johnnie. Mamie braced herself for the lie that was about to come out of Tom's mouth.

"No," Tom said. The ticket officer didn't respond but began counting their cash.

"Very well," he said at last. "Three tickets to New York."

Peter Sweeny shot Johnnie Chambers a cold look as he stepped forward to buy his own ticket with William Chambers' money. He made it clear he resented the boy for his presence here, as he narrowly escaped his due punishment.

Five

The Irish passengers were the last of the steerage passengers to board the *Britannic*. Hundreds of others had boarded in Liverpool, including lots of Swedes and Norwegians. Also on board was the Irishman's hated enemy: the British.

The Irish poured into the common area, awaiting further instructions. A large group of British boys crowded near the railing on the deck above, looking down at them.

"Fockin' Micks."

The voices rang down from above as Irish passengers milled around, finding their places in the dormitory-style rows of bunk beds. That was the English way—always looking down.

Johnnie whipped around, the luggage sack on his shoulder swinging with him.

"Who you calling a Mick?" Johnnie called up to them. He pushed his shirt sleeves up, revealing his arms, which were well-muscled for a boy his age. "Why don't you come down here and we'll scrap?"

The English boys laughed. But behind their laughter, they looked nervous.

Another Irish boy came alongside Johnnie. "Aye, come down here and fight us!"

"I wouldn't waste a fist on yer face."

Johnnie started to clap his hands, drawing attention from all corners of the common area.

"Some say the devil is dead…" he began to sing, loud and slow.

Other boys began to laugh and clap. "The devil is dead, the devil is dead," they chanted, growing louder.

"Some say the devil is dead, and buried in Killarney! Some say he rose again, rose again, and joined the British army!"

A big group of Irish boys were clapping and chanting the song, amid calls for the English boys to fight them. The English boys scurried like rats.

"What did I tell you?" Peter said to Mamie. "Nothing but trouble, that lad."

But it was the last time the English bothered any of the Irish immigrants on the *Britannic*. It made Johnnie a hero on the ship.

Every night after dinner, the Irish passengers gathered in the common area to play music and dance. The fact that their music and laughter bothered the British passengers made it all the more fun for them. Some of the Scandinavian passengers joined in, letting the Irish boys twirl them around.

As the band began to play a familiar tune, Mamie searched for Peter, hoping he'd dance with her.

"As I was goin' over the Cork and Kerry Mountains, I saw Captain Farrell, and his money, he was countin.' I first produced my pistol and I then produced my rapier. I said, 'Stand and deliver or the devil he may take ya.'"

"Where's Peter?" Mamie asked, growing concerned.

"Don't worry, Mamie, I'll dance with you," Johnnie said, whirling her around. She laughed and clapped along to the music.

Mamie spotted Peter Sweeny staring at her from across the commons. She halted and made her way to him.

"Having fun out there?" he asked.

Then he grabbed her hand. "Come with me," he said.

He was leading her into the men's part of the ship.

"Peter, am I allowed here?" she asked, looking over her shoulder for the stewards.

Peter led her into the men's dormitory, where the beds were empty. It was quiet here...too quiet.

"I thought we needed some time alone," Peter said, pushing her closer to his bunk. "Future husband and wife, aye?"

Before she could speak, his fingers were at her buttons, searching for a way to unhook them. He pulled her against him, kissing her roughly.

She kissed him back. But the thrill of the sensual was outweighed by the fear of getting caught...and by the power of her conscience.

"I'm not your wife yet, Peter," she said gently, reaching up to touch his cheek.

"Who are you afraid of finding out? Your da? He's not here."

Mamie laughed a little. Every man in Roskeen, even Peter Sweeny, harbored at least a tiny bit of fear of Will Chambers.

Peter kissed her again, and this time, she pushed him away.

"Peter," she said, glancing around at the rows of bunk beds, the bare, bright lights, the open doorways. "Not here. Not now."

It wasn't that she didn't have the desire; she did. But she had no desire to indulge it here, in the men's bunk on the *Britannic*.

He pulled away from her. "If you say so," he mumbled. "I'll be off to bed."

"Don't you want to dance?"

"I'm tired."

Mamie looked at her boots. "Do you mind if I return?"

"Do what you wish."

But Mamie's mood had dampened. She decided to take a breather on the rear deck, the only place the steerage passengers could get fresh air. Heavy iron locks prevented them from entering the first class area. It was international law. Steerage passengers were assumed to be dirty and diseased, especially the Irish. The ghosts of the famine generation still haunted the high seas, it seemed.

"God, if you delivered Jonah from the belly of the whale, you can deliver me from the belly of this ship," she sighed, watching the propellers create a ghostly white trail of churning seawater in the ship's wake.

Mamie tossed and turned with the North Atlantic that night, wishing this eight-day journey to New York could be over already.

Six

"Do you see that?"

Mamie shook Peter, who was asleep in a bunk on the Lake Erie steamboat packed with immigrants. Many of them were Irish. Others spoke back and forth in their singsong languages and wore strange clothing.

This morning, though, they all spoke the common language of joy. They smiled and shed tears of relief. They had spent weeks traveling by sea and land and had finally reached their destination.

"That's the city of Cleveland," Mamie said to Peter.

The *Britannic* reached New York Harbor last week. The passengers came out on deck to watch as they glided past the Statue of Liberty, holding her lamp beside the Golden Door. The French had gifted it to the Americans a few years ago, Tom explained. Mamie watched a magnificent humpback whale crest above the harbor's surface and dive back down, leaving a trail of seawater droplets and mist in her wake. It seemed, to Mamie, like the good omen she'd been waiting for.

The immigrants disembarked the ship and entered the processing station at Castle Garden. Rumor had it the Americans were building a new place to process immigrants, on an island in New York Harbor—but it wasn't open yet. So they went through the rigmarole at Castle Garden, which took an entire day.

From New York City they took a train to Buffalo. This overcrowded steamboat had departed Buffalo, New York, at nine last night. The journey across Lake Erie had taken all night through December fog and high winds. Mamie pointed out the window, which was dirty and streaked with smudgy handprints. But through it, she could see the burning fires of morning, the black silhouettes of tall buildings.

Peter flipped over and glared at her, looking annoyed by her presence. Technically, the men and women on this steamboat slept in separate quarters. But unlike the *Britannic*, no one on this cramped little boat seemed to care about rules.

"Dammit, Mary," Peter said. "Can't a man sleep? No rest for the weary, it seems."

Mamie shrunk away from him, withdrawing her hand from his shoulder. "You can start calling me Mamie now," she said softly.

In the other bunk, Johnnie shot Peter a dirty look.

"Ignore him," he said in Peter's general direction, although Peter didn't stir. "The layabout is always weary. Makes one wonder how he'll keep a job."

Tom Chambers sat up, looking half-amused and half-annoyed with Johnnie. "Well, you succeeded in your plot to fight with Sweeny from port to port," he said. "Fighting like Kilkenny cats."

"He sure makes it easy," Johnnie replied.

"I'm going outside on the deck," Mamie announced, securing her woolen shawl over her head. On her shoulders was the old sweater she'd brought from Ireland.

"In this cold?" Tom asked.

"I want to see a dolphin," Mamie told Tom. She also wanted to get some air. The crowding made this steamboat dreadfully hot and malodorous on the inside.

"There're no dolphins in Lake Erie, Mamie," Peter scoffed. He'd been listening to the Chambers siblings all along. "It's fresh water."

He finally sat up and shook his head. "Silly girl," he said with a small laugh.

Johnnie narrowed his eyes. "You didn't know that yourself until we left Buffalo and a seaman told you so, ya nitwit," he said.

"Johnnie!" Mamie hissed. "Not another word."

Mamie made her way to the deck. She welcomed the chill that set into her bones as she breathed the cold air blowing off the lake.

Seven

"Do you think our uncles will know who we are?" Mamie asked Tom as they stood at the railing, watching the steamboat chug into the port of Cleveland.

None of the Chambers siblings had ever met their uncles: Joseph, Dominick, and Michael McGlynn, who had fled Ireland for Cleveland more than twenty years ago. Ma had gone with them, in tow with a baby cousin named Agnes. Ma spoke with great fondness and more than a little melancholy of Agnes. In fact, she mentioned her far more often than she spoke of her time in Cleveland generally. Mamie did some simple math in her head and figured that Agnes would be about twenty-three now.

Mamie wondered if she would meet Agnes, too. She tried to imagine what her cousin looked like as a young woman. Perhaps she was a fine-boned, petite red-haired woman with big blue eyes, like Ma. Or maybe she took after her father's family—whoever he was.

"Ma described us in a letter to Uncle Joseph," Tom told Mamie. "The Irish newspapers in Cleveland print the passenger lists so the families know who's arriving every week. I don't worry, Mamie, and neither should you."

She nodded, leaning into Tom's broad, supportive shoulders.

"Don't worry about this gloom, either," Tom reassured her. "Uncle Joseph wrote that in the summer, you'll be able to see the sunrise over the lake from your boarding house."

Tom pulled a ragged piece of paper from his coat pocket. He leaned in to show Mamie the crude map Uncle Joseph had drawn.

"This is our new church, St. Malachi," he said, pointing to a square with a cross on top. It was at the junction of two streets. One street was labeled "PEARL" in big capital letters, the childish handwriting of an adult who had learned to write late in life. The area near the junction was labeled The Angle.

"They also call it Irishtown Bend," Tom said. "The boarding house is here..."

His finger wandered to another square, down a hill from St. Malachi. It was across the road from a peninsula labeled Whiskey Island.

"Whiskey Island?" Mamie asked.

"That's where the first wave of Irishmen laid down their roots, when they first arrived after the Hunger," Tom replied.

"Whiskey Island," Mamie repeated. "There's no question what goes on there."

"There was a whiskey distillery before we arrived," Tom said with a shrug. "But you're right. It's full of saloons and shanties. Uncle Joseph said you're never to walk there alone."

"Peter will look out for me," Mamie said.

"Like hell he will," Johnnie snapped, appearing behind them. "He can hold his whiskey, but he can't hold his own in a scrap."

"Shh!" Mamie hissed. "John, why are you always spoiling for a fight?"

"Fight?" Johnnie repeated, looking bemused. "That Billy Bones is not gonna fight me."

Johnnie relished calling Mamie's thin, lanky husband-to-be Billy Bones. Johnnie himself was shorter than most men, and stocky. He had a boyish face and a thick cap of wavy brownish-red hair, and mischievous dimples when he smiled. But he gained muscle easily, especially in his arms and chest.

He was going to land a hard punch when full grown, Mamie thought as the steamboat approached the dock.

A rush of immigrants eager to disembark this wobbly steamboat pushed forward. Mamie went back inside to find Peter.

On her way, she bumped into Annie Joyce, a girl from Roskeen who was her same age. Annie was always cool, never friendly, toward Mamie. She was traveling with her siblings too, but she had met a gaggle of girls on the train she took from New York City, who were also aboard this steamboat. Annie Joyce went everywhere with her new clique. She was giggly and boisterous around them. But alone, she clammed up around Mamie.

"Good day, Mary," she said in a stiff tone.

"Good morning," Mamie said, reminding herself to smile warmly. Maybe Annie was just shy, although she had been stiff and standoffish since she was a child. Their families attended the same church in Roskeen all their lives.

"Have you seen my Peter?" Mamie asked, trying to make conversation.

"Your Peter?" Annie repeated with a hint of a sneer. "I believe he's in the dining room. When are you getting married, anyway?"

"We don't have the wedding date written in stone quite yet," Mamie replied.

"Oh, that's a shame," Annie said. "I'm to marry my husband-to-be Patrick in the summer, when we settle into our new house. It was my brother-in-law's house, but his family grew too large for it."

"Ah, I see," Mamie said. "What a blessing, Annie."

Peter appeared in the hallway, dragging their luggage by the length of his thin arms.

"You can help with your own luggage, yeah?" Peter said to Mamie. "You're built sturdy enough for it."

Mamie felt the excruciating sting of humiliation when those words escaped Peter's mouth. She knew what he meant. Mamie had never been obese, as few Irish people were. But she wasn't thin, either—a trait complete strangers felt privileged to remark upon. And now, Peter.

What a shame it was to be a fat Irish girl, Mamie thought to herself, feeling the first sting of a tear.

But she snapped out of it, taking a piece of luggage off Peter's hands.

"Good luck to you and your family, Annie," she said.

"Of course," Annie replied. "I'll be seeing you at our new church."

Eight

A throng of relatives awaited the steamboat, and Mamie could feel the nervousness of the crowd as the passengers began to disembark. During the famine years, many of the people scheduled to arrive aboard these boats never made it. They died during the journey, and the relatives went home with empty arms and broken hearts.

But those days were over. A flurry of hugs and laughter ensued as relatives recognized each other. Brothers greeted brothers; husbands reunited with their wives and children. As the last of the passengers departed the steamboat, the Chambers siblings stood around, looking lost, and waiting for the uncles they had never met.

"Those lads could be them," Tom said at last, pointing to two people standing near the docks. They were far from lads—both men appeared to be in their late forties and had the weathered appearances of men who did hard manual labor all their lives. Mamie removed her shawl so they could see her crown of auburn hair, which she'd secured in a chignon for the steamboat journey.

As they approached, the men clearly recognized them.

"Mamie Chambers, you look just like your Ma said you would," the younger of the two men said. They looked rough, but their smiles were warm as they greeted their nephews and niece for the first time.

"And you—you look like my sister," Uncle Dominick said to Johnnie.

"I do?" Johnnie said, frowning in response. "I was hoping to hear I look like my da."

"You have his build. He was like a workhorse," Uncle Joseph said, and Johnnie's face lit up.

"Your da is a legend 'round here, you know," Dominick said.

Mamie wondered if it was just good-natured joking. Her father had left Cleveland to return to County Mayo more than two decades ago, and she doubted anyone even recalled his name. Her parents did say there were many Chamberses in Cleveland—probably dozens of them in this neighborhood alone.

But Uncle Joseph shushed Dominick.

"Don't even start with that in front of the boy," Uncle Joseph said, and Uncle Dominick complied.

Just then, a hard airborne object struck Mamie in the back. She watched a piece of golden-red fruit roll at her feet as another one struck her brother.

"Go home, foreigners!" a man standing some distance away shouted. "Go home, papists! You catlicks aren't welcome here!"

Uncle Dominick picked up one of the fruits and hurled it square at the man's face. There was a group of them, Mamie realized. When it dawned on them that the Irish men were fighting back, they scattered.

"Ah, get out of here, ye feckin' derelicts," Joseph said. "Get a real job for once in yer life, you pigs."

"Catlicks?" Tom said, looking confused. "Why are they calling us catlicks?"

"Catholics," Joseph said. "Those men call themselves nationalists. They like to come here some mornings and harass the new arrivals. They call us 'papists' because they think we take marching orders from the Pope."

Mamie couldn't even name the current Pope. She said her prayers and she believed in angels, but in her heart, she cared little about answering to the hierarchy of the Catholic Church. There was still much bitterness in Ireland that the Vatican hadn't come to the aid of its flock during the famine. It baffled Mamie that these men, who gathered at the port hurling fruit at newcomers, thought she answered to some distant bishop in Rome.

"These are nice apples," Dominick said, plucking them off the ground and shining them with his shirt. "I'll take these home to me wife. She might use them to bake a pie for my little grandchildren. And my nieces and nephews, of course."

"I've never seen an apple," Mamie said, picking the unfamiliar fruit off the ground. She had heard of them, especially in that Bible story about Eve. Now, she was curious what they tasted like. She used her shawl to gather them.

"They're abundant here in Ohio," Dominick said. "The best part of America? The food. And you'll have plenty of it. Your aunt has been cooking all morning at Joseph's house."

"We'll take you to my house first," Uncle Joseph said. "We'll have you a welcoming party. Your cousins and neighbors want to meet you."

Tom was going to live with Uncle Joseph until he started working and could afford a place of his own. Mamie, Peter and Johnnie were going to live at a boarding house nearby. Mamie hadn't seen it yet, but Uncle Joseph said he would bring them to the boarding house that night.

Mamie looked around and hoped her new home was a bit cheerier than the drab old homes in this neighborhood.

Uncle Joseph's house didn't look like much, but Mamie's spirits lifted as they stepped inside. It was clean and roomy and smelled of fresh-baked bread. A woman was stirring an open kettle on the stove. She dropped her wooden spoon as soon as she saw the door opening.

"Welcome to America!" she cried, gathering Mamie in her arms. "I'm your Aunt Mary, Dominick's wife."

"I'm Mary as well," Mamie replied. "But my family calls me Mamie."

A visitor to Ireland would be hard-pressed to find a family that *didn't* have a daughter named Mary. It was another quirk of the Irish. Aunt Mary put her hands on her hips.

"Well, you are my family," she said. "So I'll call you Mamie."

Another man came in the back door, dressed in a stiff blue jacket with two rows of buttons down the front.

"Ah, there's Officer Michael," she said. "Mamie, this is your uncle."

Uncle Michael nodded. "I was on duty," he said, removing his hat. "I'm sorry I missed your arrival. I'm a policeman—"

"We know," Aunt Mary interrupted, putting her hand up. "It's all you talk about these days."

A thought dawned on Mamie as they ate a hearty breakfast. "My ma has a niece in Cleveland named Agnes," she said. "She cared for her when she was just a babe. Will I meet her?"

Her new family went quiet, exchanging glances. Mamie wondered if something had happened to Agnes. Maybe the woman, who could only be in her mid-twenties, had already died.

"Yes, Agnes is a wonderful lass," Aunt Mary said. "We don't see much of her these days. She's been...distracted."

"She went to the nunnery," Dominick said. "But they threw her out."

Aunt Mary kicked Dominick under the table.

"Dominick!" she scolded. "Are you serious?"

"What? It's the truth."

Mamie decided to drop the subject. Instead she told the family about her younger siblings, whom they had never met. There were the boys—Willie and Frankie and little Georgie, who just turned three. The girls—Katie, Bridie, and Bessie. Also Norah, the new baby.

After breakfast, Mamie helped her aunt with the dishes. Johnnie sat in the living room surrounded by giggling girls. Some were his cousins, some merely neighbors. Peter and Mamie sat at the kitchen table, listening to him regale them with stories about his journey.

"You came without your ma and da? Weren't you scared?"

"Scared? Me? Never," Johnnie replied. "I don't scare easy. I want to become a Dead Rabbit."

The Dead Rabbits were a notorious Irish street gang. They'd formed in New York after the Hunger and spread to other cities, including this one. For all Mamie knew, it was defunct. But if any Dead Rabbits remained in Cleveland, Johnnie would be sure to find them. Mamie cringed.

"He must have given your father fits," Aunt Mary said with a laugh.

Peter didn't look so amused.

"Ah, yes, joining up with the Irishman's most vicious gang," Peter said. "That's a smart bit of conversation to have around your new uncle, who's an officer of the law."

Mamie looked over at Uncle Michael, who seemed more interested in his pint of ale than anything Johnnie had to say. Still, Mamie's face burned.

"Peter. Let it go," she said.

Aunt Mary overheard them bickering and stepped into the room. "Mamie, are you tired from the journey?" she asked. "There's a bed upstairs, if you want to rest before we take you to the boarding house."

Mamie fell asleep, dreaming about apple trees and nationalists. There were all sorts of exciting things to dream about in this brand-new country, so full of adventure—and danger.

Nine

Around dusk, Uncle Joseph walked Mamie, Peter, and Johnnie to their boarding house. The owner ran a saloon on the first floor, he told them.

"This is the Viaduct," Uncle Joseph said as they stood at the bottom of a hill west of the city. "Do you see that village there, across the river? That's Whiskey Island."

They all paused to look at the sad village of small wooden structures. Mamie's heart sank into her stomach, and she gathered her shawl around her nostrils to block out the stench. The Cuyahoga River was filthy, jammed with floating refuse. Whiskey Island looked like a depressing little peninsula full of grimy hovels.

"It's no Clew Bay," Peter said, leaning into Mamie's back.

"No," she said, her eyes sweeping the Lake Erie shoreline. "It's not." Her chest felt crushed as she thought of windswept, desolate Clew Bay in County Mayo, with its pristine green cliffs and brilliant blue sky...

"You can thank Standard Oil for the filth," Joseph said, kicking at the trash with his boot. "They blame it on us, of course. And they wonder why we call them the Filthy Rich. They've turned the Cuyahoga into a cesspool."

"But don't fret," he added, studying Mamie's face. "Your boarding house is uphill from the river, right around the corner from St. Malachi."

It was getting dark, and Mamie's feet ached in her worn-out boots. She wanted to weep with relief when Uncle Joseph announced they'd reached their destination.

Mamie looked up and saw her new home was constructed of brick, not the rotting wood of Whiskey Island. Her moment of peace was shattered when she realized a man was urinating inches from her boots.

"Ah, sorry, m'dear," he said. "The ol' bair got me again."

He had a different regional accent—from Wexford, maybe—and he was slurring his words so badly that it took Mamie a second to realize *bair* meant *beer*.

The door flew open, letting out a rush of humid air into the frigid December night. Mamie expected a man to be at the helm of this establishment. Instead a woman, who appeared no older than twenty-five, came out to chase the drunkard away.

"Git!" she said, smacking him with a broom. "Shoo, you tosspot! My doorstep ain't a public privy, you hear?"

In one swift move, she set aside the broom and smiled at Mamie, ushering them all inside.

"I'm sorry," she said. "It happens sometimes, especially in late evening when everyone's had too much to drink. I call it the witching hour."

She shut the door behind them. The saloon was loud with merry sounds, a stark contrast from the squalor outside its doors.

"I'm Catherine Masterson," the saloon maiden said. "But you can call me Kate. I run this place; the owner died about six weeks ago. As you can see, I'm a bit harried."

Peter leaned in to Mamie and Uncle Joseph. "We were told a man ran this place."

"You heard the girl. He's dead," Uncle Joseph snapped. "What do you want her to do about it?"

That shut Peter up, and if Kate Masterson had overheard him, she ignored it.

"Allow me to show you around," Kate said. "This is your new home, after all. Wait right here."

Kate walked over to a little girl who sat at the saloon's piano next to an older man.

"Molly," Kate said, "Can you pour the ale?"

"Yes," the girl said. She looked the same age as Mamie's sister Bessie. She was a beautiful child, with long golden-brown curls, tamer than Kate's head of wild frizz and corkscrews.

Kate looked awfully young to have a child that age, Mamie thought. She also hadn't noticed a ring on Kate's finger. But Mamie brushed aside the thought. For all she knew, Kate was a widow.

"Follow me," Kate said, leading Peter, Mamie and Johnnie behind the bar.

"This is our kitchen," she said. There were bushels of gorgeous root vegetables hanging above the stove. The fragrant smells of stew and bread permeated the air.

"Back here," Kate said, pushing open the door to another room, "This was the owner's bedroom before he passed. My brother sleeps here now, when he's in town." The room was small and nondescript, but clean. It reminded Mamie of a room at an inn, the type of place you might pay to lay your head at night while traveling.

"Since you're to be living here, I'll let you in on a secret," Kate said, opening a makeshift curtain. "We have a water closet."

Mamie had heard of water closets, those new-fangled toilets that rich people owned. But she had never seen one. She'd grown up in County Mayo, where they used old-fashioned outdoor privies. Mamie couldn't even fathom such an invention.

"Surely you jest," Peter said, and Kate beamed with pride.

"I don't," Kate said. "But don't credit me; my brother built it. We keep it a secret 'cause we're not sure it's legal. I have the patrons use the outhouse in the back. But as long as you live here, you're welcome to use it."

Kate closed the curtain. "It's more hygienic, that much is sure. Cleanliness is next to Godliness, that's what my ma always said."

"My ma says that as well," Mamie said, and Kate grinned.

"Follow me upstairs," Kate beckoned them, and Mamie and Johnnie followed. Peter trailed behind, looking bored.

Kate grabbed a lantern to lead them up a steep staircase to the second floor.

"Watch your step; it's dark in here," Kate warned them as the light from the lantern swept across the room. "The men, when we have any, sleep on this side, near the door..."

The wan light of the lantern revealed a few ragged bed sheets strung across the room, dividing it in half. Mamie felt another searing sting of disappointment. She looked behind her and saw Peter's face twisted in disgust.

"...And the women sleep on the other side, where it's warmer. Mr. Sweeny and Mr. Chambers, you can take that empty bed there, under the window."

Peter crossed his arms over his chest. "No way will I share a bed with that boy," he growled.

Kate snapped to attention, capturing Peter with a sharp glare. "You can make do with the floor," she said matter-of-factly.

"Mamie, do you want to see your bed?"

Kate guided her to an overstuffed bed with a few worn quilts tossed across it. It looked warm and inviting, yet it had obviously been slept in recently.

"Who will I share a bed with?" Mamie asked.

Kate looked up at her with smiling eyes. "Me," she said.

"I know it's nothing fancy," Kate added as Mamie set her modest luggage down. "But you shared a bed with a sister or three in Ireland, aye?"

Mamie smiled. This fellow Irishwoman understood. "My favorite sister's name was Catherine, or Katie for short."

"I hope you don't mind that Molly sleeps on the floor beside me, on the trundle bed," Kate said, forcing Mamie to redirect her thoughts to the present.

"We have a bath tub on the women's side, which you're free to use," Kate said. She trained her light on a marvelous white bathtub that looked brand-new and quite expensive. "Me, I bathe myself and Molly in it regularly. You'll have to boil water first, though."

"Kate, where did you get this bath tub?" Mamie asked, reaching out to touch it as if it were a precious gemstone.

"A rich person on Millionaire's Row discarded it as soon as something a wee bit fancier came to market," Kate said. "My brother found it in a junkyard, the same place we got the piano downstairs. We go treasure-hunting in the rich people's trash." She winked. "It's great sport in a city like this, with so many millionaires."

Kate reached under the bed and pulled out a chamber pot, scrubbed and sparkling white.

"At night, when it's dark, you'll not want to fuss with the water closet. Use this," Kate said, handing the chamber pot to Mamie.

"You now have a pot to piss in," Kate said with a flourish. "Welcome to America."

Mamie started to laugh. Peter wrinkled his nose.

"Are you hungry? We have plenty of vegetable stew downstairs," Kate said. "Plenty of beer, too, if that's to your liking."

"I'll take some beer," Johnnie said, making a dash for the staircase. Mamie frowned.

"Not too much beer," she admonished.

"I'll wait for you downstairs," Kate said.

Mamie reached out for Peter, who was scowling and looking about the room with obvious disgust. He had grown up Lace Curtain Irish. He had never once lived in a shanty like this place, with its rags where walls should be.

"I know it's not much," Mamie said as they entered the loud saloon. It was hard to hear over the men's voices and the clattering piano. "But we won't live in this boarding house forever. Come spring, we could have our own house."

"No one told me some vulgar woman owned this place," Peter retorted.

"Peter, she's not vulgar," Mamie said. "She's done everything thinkable to be a gracious host. Why don't you humor her a bit?"

"Must you argue about everything?" Peter asked.

In the saloon, Uncle Joseph was telling Tom and Johnnie about the repairs he'd done on his house, since he knew Tom Chambers would be living there a while.

"How do you go about getting a house around here?" Peter asked.

Uncle Joseph's chin jerked up, and he looked a bit insulted by the question. "You buy some lumber," he said, "and you build it, slat by slat, with your own hands." He paused, staring at Peter. "And that's after you get a job on the docks and save your money."

Peter scoffed. "There must be jobs in this wretched city besides unloading ore ships," he said. "I'm the son of a lawyer. I ain't fit to be shoveling shit on the Cleveland docks."

"You could go West with us and pan for gold."

Mamie's head turned in the direction of the unfamiliar voice. She hadn't realized the two men at the next table had been listening to their conversation. The man's American accent caught Mamie off guard.

Everyone in this saloon was Irish. In fact, many looked like they were fresh from the farm and the boat, soothing their homesickness with alcohol.

What was he doing here?

"That's a myth," Peter spat, narrowing his eyes and sipping his beer. "You know us Irishmen don't believe your shite about your streets being paved with gold, do ya? The ones who came before us even wrote a song about it."

Mamie laughed a little, knowing her husband-to-be was right. "I got a letter from a relation..." she sang.

Both she and Peter knew the rest of the lyrics:

Alas, when I landed
I made for the city without delay;
But I never saw gold on the street corners—
Alas, I was a poor aimless person cast adrift.

"It's not a myth out West," the American man said. He was leaning over a map of the Continental United States.

Mamie had always thought America resembled a calf. New England was the head and ears, and the southeast peninsula was the front hooves. She couldn't remember the name of the peninsula, only that the name made her think of fresh spring buds.

"Floral," she whispered. "Flor...Flor-ida."

The man's fingers wandered to the hindquarters and ribs of the calf. "This territory is full of gold and silver and jewels, with nary a man to mine it," he explained to Peter. "It's there for the taking."

Peter's eyes filled with the longing Mamie had hoped to see during the voyage to America.

"Have you met Marie St. Jean?" the American asked. He pointed to a woman across the room, holding court with an audience of enraptured men. Mamie stared at her, admiring her lacy dress and perfect ringlets. Then she caught Peter staring, too.

"Marie St. Jean is a saloon singer on steamboats along the Mississippi River," the American said. "But now she wants to be a cabaret girl out West. She'll be traveling with us."

The man snapped his fingers to get Marie St. Jean's attention. "Marie, can you sing us a song?"

"Of course, monsieur," she said with a foreign accent, not American and definitely not Irish. Mamie didn't like her smile or her accent, and something about both was chilling. But as Marie St. Jean launched into an aria, a spell seemed to settle over the saloon.

Peter stared at her, mesmerized. "Do you think she's French?" he asked Mamie, without removing his eyes from her.

"Don't know," Mamie replied. She would take the wail of an Irish ballad over the sound of Marie St. Jean's voice any day. She looked over at Peter, alarmed by the lust in his eyes.

"Peter," she said, nudging him. "Stop it."

The American man rose from his seat. "We're stepping outside to have a cigar," he said to Peter. "Care to join us? Smoke 'em if you got 'em, I always say."

Cigars? Cigars were another luxury that Irishmen could not afford. In Ireland, only the British landlords could afford to fritter away money on such items. Mamie looked at the American with scorn.

"Och, but of course, my man," Peter said, and brushed past Mamie without another word to her.

Mamie stared into her food, feeling humiliated. Her thoughts were interrupted by the sound of Molly scampering across the room.

"Uncle Patrick is here!" Molly cried, hugging Kate's skirts behind the bar. "I saw him through the window!"

43

A group of men in boots and sailor's uniforms barreled into the saloon. Mamie's eyes settled on the one who was impossibly stocky—wide as the doorway, she thought. He had hugely muscular arms, and a heavy beard and black eyebrows that were so thick, they seemed to curl up toward his forehead. When he removed his cap, she saw he had a bunch of dark, curly hair, like Kate's. He had gone a while without a haircut.

"I've been waiting for ya, Patrick," Kate said. "We have new boarders. They come from Roskeen, in Burrishoole Parish. This girl is Mamie Chambers."

The stocky man grabbed Mamie's hand and kissed it. He had the strong scent of alcohol on him.

"I'm Patrick Masterson, Kate's brother," he said. He ran his fingers over his wild hair. "But everyone calls me Curly."

"Burrishoole Parish, eh?" Patrick Masterson asked before Mamie could say anything. "I tried to find a wife there once. It's a pity I didn't stumble upon the likes of you."

"A wife? You?" another sailor joked.

Patrick grabbed a bushel of mistletoe hanging above the door and held it over his backside. The sailors laughed.

"You're not the marrying kind, so it's hard to imagine you hunting for a wife," the other sailor said.

"Ah, but it's true," Patrick said. "On a dark night, at a dance in Castlebar. That was the night a ghost chased me home."

"Uncle Patrick, will you tell us the story?" Molly asked, wide-eyed. "Please?"

"Oh, sure, my darling," he said, "but only if your ma allows it."

"Here we go again," Kate said with a twinkle in her eye.

"Alright, then," Patrick Masterson said. "Like I was saying, when I was about eighteen years old, I went to a dance in Castlebar to find me a wife. Castlebar is in the West of Ireland near the sea, where the nights are so dark you can't see your own hand before your face…"

He held his palm a few inches from his face to show how close it was, and still invisible in the blackness of the night. "Ooh," Molly whispered.

"I was walking by meself on the road to my home in Mulrany. I was due west of Stoney Castle." Patrick's eyes met Mamie's. "Do you know it, Stoney Castle?"

"I know it," Mamie said, feeling a deep longing for home.

"Stoney Castle isn't much of a castle anymore," Patrick explained to the children. "It was abandoned long ago in the days of the devil himself, Oliver Cromwell. When some folks from the county ventured there in the modern day, they found bones strewn about."

Molly's eyes were as big as saucers.

"I was due west of Stoney Castle when I heard a blood-curdling scream. It was coming from a thorn bush," Patrick said, his shrieks filling the saloon. "EEEEEEEOW EEEEOW EEEOW. 'Tis how it sounded. I ran! I ran like the hounds of hell were after me."

"And then what?"

"When I stopped to catch my breath I heard it again. EEEOOW! I ran once more. When I finally thought the ghost was gone, I heard a voice. 'That was some good running, Patrick, but I'm still with you.' I ran again! I brushed past something I took for a rabbit. I told him, 'Out me way, and let the one that knows how to run, run.' And I outran the ghost all the way to my home in Mulrany…after the dance in Castlebar."

"And that's why Uncle Patrick is such a swift runner," Kate added.

"And a handball champion, at home in Mayo," Patrick reminded her.

"And a good boxer," one of the other sailors chimed in.

"A boxer?" Johnnie said in awe. "I want to learn to box."

Mamie laughed. Then she heard Peter's voice behind her.

"What's this?"

Mamie whirled around. "He was telling a story," she explained, feeling defensive.

"Is that why you're making eyes at him?"

"What?" Mamie stuttered.

"You're blushing like a lovesick schoolgirl," Peter said. Mamie balled her fists.

"I'm off to bed," Peter said. "I expect you to join me soon."

"Ah, she ain't your wife yet, me man," Patrick Masterson joked, but Peter returned him no smiles or pleasantries.

Mamie felt a chill run up her spine—and it wasn't the winter winds seeping through the doors.

Ten

Kate Masterson didn't fall asleep long after she shooed the last drunken loiterers from the bar. She lay in bed next to Mamie Chambers, with Molly on the trundle beside them. Both slept hard.

When an hour had passed without a sound from the street below, Kate tiptoed to the staircase. Then she slipped out to a dark house on the river, on the west bank of the wicked Cuyahoga.

The lamps were out; this house always appeared to be empty. But it never really was. The man who owned this house had too many secrets stashed inside to leave it unoccupied. So when he couldn't be there himself, he had his henchmen stationed in the dank parlor room. Other times, his mistress of many years, Oonagh, answered the door. She would peer through the little peephole before sliding the lock. Black Willie didn't appreciate people knocking on his door out of nowhere; instead, he summoned them.

Black Willie was the leader of the Angle Mob. Every immigrant neighborhood in Cleveland seemed to have a group like this. The Italians called theirs "the mafia." To Kate, "mob" was a good enough word, for they had only the power of group intimidation to give them legitimacy.

She rapped three times on the door. As she expected, Oonagh's raspy voice, weathered by cigars, called out, "Who is it?"

"Kate."

"There're a lot of Kate's 'round here."

Annoyed, Kate twisted the doorknob and pushed her shoulder into the door. It was unlocked all along.

When she got inside, she heard Oonagh's voice. Kate barged into the parlor room—if one deigned to call such a dirty and cluttered room a parlor—where Oonagh was sitting with a crystal ball and a hypnotized client.

"Jesus, Mary, and Joseph," Kate said, blatantly disrupting the session. "For the last time, Oonagh, you're not a prophet."

Kate looked at Oonagh's client. "You know she's a con, don't ya?"

Oonagh rose from the sofa where she was perched with her crystal ball. "I'm a clairvoyant, you *eejit*, and I've seen your future," she said. "It's at the bottom of the Cuyahoga River."

Kate didn't flinch. "Very well, at least I won't die penniless. The saloon is mine now, as Dan Dyra would want it." She put her hands on her hips. "Where's Willie?"

"Upstairs," Oonagh replied. "And don't take too long. I'll be joining him in bed shortly. So run along, unless you're inclined to stay and amuse the both of us, you shanty tart."

"I'd rather throw myself into the Cuyahoga," Kate replied.

They called the Angle Mob boss Black Willie because of his long black beard. These days, it was speckled with gray.

"You wanted to see me?" Kate asked, taking a few steps toward him in one of two upstairs rooms.

Black Willie didn't bother to stand up when she entered the room. He sat behind an old writing desk, and the light of his lamp flickered on his black beard. It was only when she stepped closer that Kate noticed he was displaying a pistol on the desk.

"Yes," Black Willie said, smoking the same brand of cigar that Oonagh favored. "When are you vacating the saloon now that the owner is six feet under?"

"The saloon is not for sale," Kate replied. "And I won't be going anywhere."

"It's not yours," Black Willie reminded her.

She'd already guessed this was why he summoned her. Black Willie wanted to own every business in the Angle, and the saloon was no exception.

"Ah, but it's not yours either, now is it?" Kate asked. She reached into her cloak and pulled out a copy of the late owner's will.

"Dan Dyra left the saloon to my brother Patrick. But, as you know, my brother is a sailor, so I will operate it in his stead," Kate said.

She didn't tell Black Willie that the document was fake. She'd done it in desperation. He had no way of knowing it was fraudulent, and anyway, Black Willie didn't care much about legal documentation.

The fake will was a ploy to keep Black Willie at bay. In the moment, it seemed to be working. Black Willie scoffed and tossed the document back at her.

"What if I make an offer you can't refuse?" Black Willie said.

"We'll see," Kate said. "I took on a new boarder, Mary Chambers, as well as two men who arrived with her. So I'll have to consult them before making any decisions."

"Chambers, aye?" Black Willie repeated. "My full name is William Chambers."

"I'm aware. You are of no relation, sir," Kate said, turning to leave. Black Willie stared at her.

"How old is Miss Mary Chambers?" he asked.

Kate shrugged. "Exactly how old? I don't know. About twenty."

"Many years ago, I had a bitter rivalry with another man with my same name—William Chambers," Black

Willie said. "It was about twenty years ago, in fact. He was the man who pushed me off Whiskey Island, and I always wondered what became of him."

Willie laid out his hand on the desk, showing off the big, ugly scar on the top of his hand.

"He left me with this," he said.

Kate rolled her eyes. She knew about Willie's scar, his slightly disfigured hand, and there were all sorts of rumors about where he got it. But it didn't seem to matter. That old injury to his hand hadn't stopped him from ascending the ranks of the Angle Mob and intimidating every business owner in the neighborhood into obeying him.

Well, *almost* every business owner.

"This conversation is mentally stimulating, to be sure," Kate said sarcastically. "But are we done yet? It's near on midnight."

"You don't find me stimulating, Kate?" Black Willie said, leaning back in his chair.

"Don't delude yourself, Willie. You're a bit old for me," Kate said.

As she turned to leave, his dark eyes looked hot, like burning charcoal. There was nothing Black Willie hated more than hearing he was too old.

"The saloon is not for sale," she repeated one more time.

Kate could see St. Malachi rising like a fortress on the corner of Pearl Street. On the Viaduct, she could see the lights from the hotel across the street from the saloon. Kate's dear old friend, Seán Fada, owned that hotel, and it was the one business that stayed open around the clock. People arrived at all hours of the night, and the drunks in the neighborhood favored the hotel's lounge as a late-night drinking spot.

As she turned right onto the Viaduct, Kate saw Mad Annie Kilbane, the red-haired girl who wandered the streets at night. Kate reached into her pocket and grasped about for a coin.

"A penny to keep quiet about seeing me out tonight," Kate said. The madwoman grabbed her shoulders, forcing Kate to look her in the eye.

"The newcomer," she said. "He is in grave danger. Lured away by a pretty stranger, you see?" She grabbed Kate's chin and guided her face westward, toward the river.

"He just left the hotel," Annie said. "With a woman and two men."

Kate shook her head and brushed her away. "I don't know who you're talking about. Goodnight, Annie," she said, loosening the madwoman's grip.

As she approached the saloon in the utter darkness, Kate thought she heard laughter, the sound of two illicit lovers stealing away in the night. She squinted into the darkness to see who it might be.

"Who would be out at this hour?" she asked, remembering what Mad Annie had told her.

Someone in grave danger...

But as the laughter rose and faded again, it sure didn't sound like danger. Kate shrugged and re-entered the saloon as quietly as possible. She watched two dark figures in the distance disappear in the direction of the lake. Then she closed the curtains and climbed the stairs to the sleeping quarters.

Not more than an hour later, as she was still willing herself to sleep, Kate thought she heard a distant cry in the night.

"What the..." she said, instinctively touching her foot to the ground.

But when a second cry never came, Kate settled back into bed. She had learned it was better to close her eyes than to become witness to something she'd rather not see.

Eleven

Mamie woke up early in the morning to the sound of a door rattling every time the wind blew. Someone had left it unlocked the night before, long after the last boarder had gone to sleep. She got up and tiptoed across the cold floor to the bed where Peter Sweeny was supposed to be sleeping.

Supposed.

She had thought she heard the door shut with a decisive slam last night. She figured she had been dreaming. But now, hearing the door rattle in the wind, she was certain someone had left in the dead of night.

"Peter?" she called.

Her face drained of blood when she saw that his coat and shoes were gone. He had tossed some money on top of the bureau on the men's side of the attic. It was a small condolence to the future wife he was abandoning.

He had taken the rest of Will Chambers' money and left.

"Peter!" she screamed.

She ran down the stairs and into the street. From upstairs, she heard voices, awakened by her cries: "What's going on down there?"

Mamie sank down to her knees in the street and began to weep. She heard a whoosh of air behind her, realizing someone had followed her outside.

It was her brother Johnnie and Patrick Masterson.

"What happened?" Johnnie demanded.

Patrick grabbed Mamie's arm as she struggled to break free. "Don't you run after him," he said to her. "I heard him leave last night. He ran off with that saloon singer, that *hoor*."

Mamie turned around, her face twisted with anguish. "You knew?"

"Oh, yes," Patrick replied. "Good riddance."

She bit back the urge to scream. "You heard him go and you didn't stop him?!"

Then she turned her rage on her brother, who, for once in his short life, was speechless.

"This is your fault!" she shouted, grabbing at his collar. "You chased him off, did you?"

"Mamie," he said, trying to grab her hands. "I didn't do this."

In the clamor, none had heard Kate Masterson approaching. She wrapped her arms around Mamie's shoulders, brushing the men away.

"Hush, you two," she said, hugging Mamie against the cold. "Let her cry her tears."

Twelve

Johnnie Chambers had always wondered what it would be like to run away, and now he had a chance, and a reason.

When Mamie woke up to find Peter Sweeny gone from his bed, Johnnie felt crushed by guilt. He knew he had picked fights with Peter Sweeny throughout the journey from County Mayo. He knew Peter hated him, and he relished it. He couldn't stand Mamie's fiancé and his high-falutin', Lace Curtain ways...

Still, it had been his sister's choice to marry him. Johnnie had no right to run him off. But he did, and now Mamie hated him for it.

The night after Peter disappeared, Johnnie decided it was his turn. He would make himself disappear for Mamie's sake.

As the last patrons lingered around the saloon that night, Johnnie told Kate Masterson he was going to use the outhouse.

"You may use the water closet, if you wish," she said.

"Nah, I shan't fuss with that," he said, unsure of how to use the new-fangled invention, anyhow. "I'll leave the water closet pristine for you ladies." He flashed Kate a grin, and she gave him an appreciative smile in return.

As he headed toward Whiskey Island, he wondered how long it would take Kate and Mamie to realize he wasn't coming back.

First things first, he wanted to visit a saloon. He had been to pubs in his life. In fact, his da towed him to the village pub in Roskeen on occasion, beginning when he was a toddler. But that wasn't the same—everyone knew everyone at the pub in Roskeen, and they patted Johnnie on the head, knowing him as William Chambers' little boy. But Johnnie was almost sixteen years old now, and he thought that was plenty old enough to go to an American saloon by himself.

He found a saloon on Whiskey Island that looked inviting enough. There was only one drunkard passed out in a rocking chair on the porch, his breath creating a cloud in the December air. Johnnie pushed open the door. It was dark and smoky inside, and small clusters of men sat at tables playing blackjack.

"What do we have here?" a ghostly-looking woman said. She had wiry hair and colorless skin, which made the half-moons under her eyes look as if they'd been drawn with charcoal. "A youngin'?" She grabbed his face and gave him a boozy kiss, leaving a stamp of greasy lipstick on his face. "He smells…virginal."

The men laughed.

"You're kinda cute considering you ain't had a bath lately," the woman said, ruffling his wavy hair.

"Let him be, Oonagh," the barkeeper said. "He looks young enough to suckle at his ma's breast."

"He looks like he was weared on the hind tit," the blackjack dealer said, and the men chuckled.

Johnnie's back stiffened. He walked to the bar and put a few American coins down. "I want a pint," he said evenly. He would not look scared. Not even in front of these people, who were more terrifying than any he'd encountered in fifteen years in County Mayo.

The barkeeper served him, and he leaned on the bar, taking large sips. It was bad ale, very stale, but he drank it anyway.

As soon as the ale was gone and the men turned attention to the blackjack dealer, Johnnie slipped out. He made haste for Uncle Joseph's house, the only place he might be welcome for the night.

He recognized Joseph McGlynn's house because it was bigger than most houses along the Cuyahoga River. It was built of wood that had begun to rot in some spots. When it got wet outside, Joseph placed seldom-used cooking pots throughout the house to catch the rain. But overall, the bachelor Joseph had kept it in decent condition.

Joseph wouldn't answer a knock at the door at this hour, so Johnnie had to jack a window open and climb through it. Johnnie found his uncle and a neighbor asleep in chairs near the fireplace, having drunk too much beer together after work. It was a funny sight to behold, these two grown men snoring with their heads tilted back. Johnnie shook Joseph awake.

"Boy, what you want?" Joseph said, snapping to alertness.

"I need a place to stay," Johnnie said. "Mamie doesn't want to even see me face now. I can sleep on the floor beside Tom. I don't take up much room…"

"I don't give a rat's rosy red behind where you flop for the night," Joseph said. "But you ain't about to lay up here with no job. I'll charge you rent, like your brother. So find some work and apply yourself."

"Consider it done," Johnnie said.

Joseph's neighbor roused himself as well, reaching for another bottle of beer. "How old are you, Johnnie?"

"I'll be sixteen in April."

He thought it made him sound a little older.

Joseph's neighbor grinned. "Boy, do I got a job for you."

The next evening, Joseph's neighbor led Johnnie to the drawbridge over the Cuyahoga River. On the other side was a train traveling the Michigan and South Shore Railroad, loaded to the brim with coal.

"You've never felt a cold quite like the cold sweeping off the frozen lake in the winter," Joseph's neighbor said. Johnnie knew he was right—it didn't snow in County Mayo, and the lakes didn't freeze. It was a different climate in Ireland. But now that it was almost Christmas, Johnnie could feel the relentless, icy chill settling over Cleveland. He'd heard they got snow here—lots of it.

Winter was here, and the people of the Angle neighborhood would need coal to stay warm. The only problem was that they couldn't afford it. So Johnnie, able to avoid suspicion on account of his age, was going to steal it.

The men who had devised the scheme would pay him a small fee for his troubles. Johnnie agreed to help distribute coal to their secret list of recipients.

"The train has to stop while the tender raises the bridge," Joseph's neighbor explained. "Don't fret—the tender knows what we're doing. He's a member of St. Malachi."

He waved to the bridge tender, and the tender winked at them. As the train slowed to a complete halt, Johnnie braced himself for what was to come.

"Ready?" Joseph's neighbor asked. Johnnie nodded.

As the train waited for the bridge to return to its normal place, Johnnie wriggled under a boxcar. With all his might, Johnnie punched out the steel pins underneath the car. Then they hid on the riverbank until the train began to move.

As the train inched forward, the entire haul of coal in the boxcar spilled onto the tracks. Johnnie laughed with delight.

"We did it, boys!" he hollered to his co-conspirators. "We feckin' did it!" Johnnie and a few other young teenagers grabbed their burlap sacks and stuffed them full of coal as the train took off.

"And only days before Christmas," Joseph's neighbor said. "Johnnie Chambers, you're a regular Robin Hood."

"Don't insult me like that!" Johnnie said. "Robin Hood was an Englishman."

The next morning, several families in the Angle woke to find sacks of coal that had been left for them overnight. Some were expecting the clandestine delivery; others weren't. One who did not expect to find a large sack of coal at her back doorstep was Kate Masterson. She knelt down and picked up the mysterious package.

"Heavy as rocks," she said to her brother Patrick, who took the load from her. He inspected the bag.

"It's coal."

This time of year, the children of the wealthy dreaded finding lumps of coal in their stockings. But for poor families in the Angle, there was no greater gift. Whoever had delivered the coal to the saloon had wanted the residents to stay warm at Christmastime.

Kate debated whether to tell Mamie Chambers about the gift, having few doubts about who had left it and why.

Thirteen

The winter equinox, the shortest day of the year, was on the horizon. Mamie couldn't distinguish day from night. She often sat on her bed and refused to speak, hugging the wool sweater that she couldn't bear to part with.

Kate Masterson checked on Mamie from time to time while tending the bar. She tried to talk to Mamie, but it was no use. There was no consolation for abandonment in a foreign country by a would-be husband.

Finally, on a Friday, there was a knock at the door. The regular visitors never knocked. Kate rushed to the door, intuiting that it must be official business.

"Who goes there?" she called to the other side, wary of anyone who felt obligated to knock.

"It's Michael McGlynn," the man outside replied. "Open up."

Michael McGlynn, Mamie's uncle, was a policeman. He was one of the few Irish men lucky enough to secure a position on the Cleveland Police Force. The Americans were wary of the Irish and their intentions; there were rumors that they intended to only enforce the Pope's law, not the law of the United States. Kate knew it was preposterous, and that many Irish-born, including herself, didn't give two hoots about the Pope and his edicts. But the Americans believed it.

"Kate," Michael said in a hushed tone, "This is urgent. We found a body on the bank of the Cuyahoga

River this morning. It washed up sometime last night. My niece's husband-to-be went missing from this place some time ago, and we suspect it's him."

"He didn't go missing," Kate said. "The bastard left in the dead of night and abandoned your niece here. Patrick saw him go."

Tom Chambers turned toward them. He happened to be drinking at the saloon that night, exhausted from a long day of searching for work.

"What does he look like?" Tom asked.

Michael cringed, his face looking haunted. "It's hard to know," he replied. "The body is in bad shape."

"Where is it?" Tom replied. "I'd know Peter Sweeny by the sight o' him, dead or alive."

Michael nodded. "Come to the morgue with me, will you?"

"Wait while I inform my sister."

Tom crept upstairs, where Mamie was still perched on the edge of the bed, dark hair spilling around her face.

"Mamie," he said, "Come downstairs, please. They've found a body on the riverbank."

Mamie crossed her arms over her chest. "What's it to me?"

"Don't you want to know if it's Peter's?"

She finally rose to her feet, staring out the lone window in the attic with her back turned to her brother.

"No, it's not Peter," she said. "Don't try to soothe my spirits by telling me Peter is dead. We know he left me."

Tom didn't respond, knowing she was probably right. Still, he couldn't stop himself from wanting to know for sure. Mamie deserved to know if Peter was dead. Maybe knowing the foul Cuyahoga had swallowed him up and spit him back out would give her closure.

"I'll be back later tonight," Tom said, as he returned downstairs, where Michael was waiting for him.

"I'll lead you to the mortuary," Michael said. "But I have to warn you. It's not a pretty sight to behold. If it is Mr. Sweeny, I didn't want to scar Mamie with the sight o' him."

The mortuary stank like death, to the point it took Tom's breath away. He had encountered plenty of death in his nineteen years. The Irish were known for their short lives and their vociferous mourning; their wild wakes. But nothing could prepare him for the stench of a big-city mortuary. The fact that it was housed in a stony basement, crawling with mold, made it even worse.

"Ready?" Michael asked, as they approached a long, motionless mass covered by a white sheet.

"Ready as I'll ever be," Tom replied. Michael yanked back the sheet.

"Christ almighty!" Tom gasped, taking in the grotesque sight before him: the yellowish, bloated limbs, the tattered remains of clothing. The battered, misshapen gourd that used to be a human head.

"What's that?" Tom said, pointing to the remains of the man's arm. "A gold watch?"

"Yessir," Michael replied. "If it's Peter Sweeny's, feel free to take it. Doesn't look like he'll need it anytime soon."

"Where's the rest of his head?"

"Blown off by a bullet," Michael said, eager to throw the sheet back over the body. "That's the strangest part, you know."

"Which part?" Tom asked.

"That whoever killed this man had a gun," Michael said. "Nobody in the Angle has a gun. When we investigate murders, we see they're carried out with crude weapons: kitchen knives, hammers, household tools used as bludgeons. The policemen don't even carry guns on normal occasions."

"Who does, then?"

Michael shrugged. "The rich," he replied. "The servants of the millionaires on Euclid Avenue will sometimes carry a pistol because they have something to protect. In this neighborhood, nobody does. The only thing they have to protect is their pride, and in that case, fists will do just fine."

"I wager whoever shot him is an outsider to this community, an outlaw. Whoever this corpse belongs to...maybe he wasn't one of us."

Tom nodded. "Good to know," he said, although there was little he could do with the information. And it still didn't answer the question of whether Peter Sweeny was dead—and if he wasn't, where exactly he'd gone.

"So what's the verdict?" Uncle Michael asked when they reached the street.

"It's not him," he said at last. "Peter couldn't afford gold."

Michael McGlynn shrugged, looking resigned.

"Another unknown corpse in the Cuyahoga," he said. "The Lake Erie monsters got him, it seems."

Fourteen

The temperature fell after the winter solstice. In the late afternoon on Christmas Eve, Kate finally enticed Mamie to come downstairs and eat.

"The crowd is merry tonight, Mamie," Kate promised her. "They're singing Christmas songs."

And she was right. Snow was falling outside, but the hearth kept the saloon warm, and the ale kept spirits even warmer.

Mamie sat at the end of the bar, still not cheerful enough to sing. But she had to admit the Christmas carols gave her a faint stirring of joy.

"Good girl, Mary Chambers," Kate said as she watched Mamie eat. "After Molly is asleep, why don't we watch the sled race on Millionaire's Row tonight?"

"What's Millionaire's Row?" Mamie asked.

"Euclid Avenue," Kate replied. "The richest men in the world live there. I don't usually enjoy gawking at the greedy and gluttonous, but they're a sight to see at Christmas. It will brighten the spirits."

Kate poured Mamie a pint of ale, which Mamie allowed herself to drink, just this one. "Should I invite your brother, Tom?" Kate asked.

"Aye," Mamie replied, finally taking some joy in her food and drink.

"Good," Kate said. "And we'll bundle up; it's cold out there."

As they walked outside, Mamie's eyes were downcast.

"Peter and I should be celebrating our first Christmas in America together," she said. Snowflakes caught in her eyelashes, and the glow of the streetlights made her auburn hair look red.

"Don't think of him," Tom commanded with unusual force. "With all the joy around you tonight, the last thing you need is to be lamenting the likes of Peter Sweeny."

Mamie said nothing. Kate, feeling the tension in the air, spoke up instead. "Let's have a hot drink at Seán Fada's," she said. "An Irish coffee sounds delightful, does it not? Or perhaps just some tea?"

"Who's Seán Fada?" Mamie asked.

"He owns the inn across the street," Kate said. "He's an old man, but he's a dear friend of mine. He looks out for me when I need it. Anyway, drinks are always on the house. Follow me."

Seán Fada's inn was across the Viaduct from the saloon. Mamie had observed this inn through the window, although she hadn't been sure what type of establishment it was. It looked like a rowdy place for rough men. As they stepped inside, Seán Fada appeared to be the roughest of them all.

It was clear why they called him Seán Fada, or "Long John" in Gaelic. He was well over six feet tall, with long, skinny limbs. He had a white ponytail and a stiff, wiry white mustache, which extended beyond the edges of his face.

"Kate, me girl," he said, bowing to kiss her hand. "Who is this lovely stranger you brought tonight?"

It took Mamie a long second to realize he was talking about her. She blushed.

"We're here for warm drinks, before we gawk at the rich people," Kate said. "What do you have for us?"

Seán Fada brought Irish coffees for Tom and Kate and black tea for Mamie.

"If you need advice about life in the Angle, you can always stop in here," he told Tom and Mamie. "You'll learn quickly who your friends are, and who they aren't. Do good for your friends, but don't take no shite, either. This is a tough neighborhood."

Seán Fada wagged a finger in their direction. "But stay tougher than the Angle Mob."

"Shhh, Seán Fada," Kate hissed. "Don't scare them with that talk."

When Seán Fada cleared their mugs, the three of them trekked up the Viaduct toward Pearl Street. Pearl Street was a major thoroughfare that was sometimes called West 25th Street. It was clogged with horse buggies. Scores of people were returning from the Pearl Street Market, where they did their shopping for Christmas dinner.

"Do you see that mansion behind us?" Kate asked. Tom and Mamie looked over their shoulders at the towering estate looming over Pearl Street, just south of St. Malachi. "That's the Hanna mansion," Kate said.

Mamie looked up at the snow-topped mansion, admiring its beauty.

"Mark Hanna is one of the rich men," Kate continued. "Not the richest, but he controls the politics of the other rich men. He was a lawyer, and an oilman, and now—well, now, I'm not sure what he does. But definitely politics. He used to own this horrid newspaper, the *Cleveland Leader*. It slandered the Irish community day in and day out. It was known as the most Catholic-hating rag in the whole country! But auld Hanna sold it to an equally horrid newspaper, the *Cleveland Herald*. Read it sometime, if you can stomach their rawmaish. You know how to read, don't you?"

"We do," Tom replied.

"Well, make sure you're not sour of stomach when you pick up the *Leader*," Kate said.

A sweet smell permeated the air as they trudged in the snow toward Euclid Avenue, a smell like brown sugar melted in butter. It was so sweet it made Mamie's mouth water.

"It's the Germans," Kate explained. "Their bakeries are heavenly."

She fished in her coat pocket for a few spare coins. "On our way home, we'll buy some pastries for our Christmas Eve celebration. We deserve it," she said, her eyes searching Mamie's, seeking confirmation that she agreed.

"We do," Mamie said, pushing aside any guilt she had about spending the money.

They ducked into the bakery. A German baker watched them as they stood in line, his face warmed by the sight of them.

When they reached the counter, he slid a few over-browned pastries toward them.

"God bless you," Kate said to the baker as she tucked the box of pastries under her cloak.

"You must eat one," Kate told Mamie. "You're looking much thinner now than when you arrived, what with your lack of appetite."

"'Tis just as well," Mamie said. She thought of the comments she had endured her whole life about her plumpness.

As they approached downtown, Kate and Tom started blinking as their eyes adjusted to an intense light they'd never experienced before. The street lamps seemed to glow with an ethereal brightness; like the light from a thousand candles.

"Ah, you've never seen electric lights," Kate observed. "We were the first city with electric streetlights!

Mr. Edison brought them to Cleveland about fifteen years back, when we were all living our little lives in Mayo."

As Kate, Mamie and Tom passed Public Square, a group of carolers walked down the center of Euclid Avenue. Their voices filled the quiet and snowy atmosphere, sounding like angels from heaven. Mamie again felt tempted to weep, but from joy.

Euclid Avenue was a succession of stunning mansions, sprawling estates so large Mamie had never imagined such homes existed. They were bigger than the biggest manor houses in Ireland, where the hated landlords ruled over their tenants. Their gates were decorated with Christmas wreaths.

"I didn't know they built houses so big," Mamie said, peering through the gates of a mansion shrouded with trees. Through the miniature forest in the front lawn, Mamie could see a house that resembled a Roman palace. Inside the palatial window was a glittering Christmas tree.

"They build them on our backs," Kate replied. "Six dollars a week they pay the Irish men who work on their docks. They call the Irish workers 'terriers.' They work them like dogs for a pittance."

"At least there's work to do," Tom said with a shrug. "For most folks in Ireland, the best job you can hope for is to work a piece of farmland owned by somebody else." He scuffed his boots on the frozen road. "I could have become a tailor, maybe, like my da, if only Roskeen needed more than one tailor…"

"Look!" Mamie exclaimed as a horse-drawn sleigh whooshed past. It was the most beautifully painted sleigh she could possibly imagine, made of expensive and sturdy wood.

"Och, that's Andrew Carnegie, of Carnegie Steel," Kate said, wrapping her arms around Mamie's shoulder. "He's one of the richest men in the world. And he's a Scotsman, Mamie. He was born there."

"Are you serious?" Mamie said, her eyes transfixed on his sleigh.

"Yes. Anyone can become rich in America, you know," Kate replied.

When they returned to the saloon that night, Kate pulled out an old Bible, one that had survived her trip from Ireland.

"Let's have our Christmas observance here, tonight," she said.

"We have to go to church in the morning," Mamie protested, and Kate looked up at her.

"Says who?"

So they took turns reading the Christmas story— Kate and Mamie, as well as the other guests who knew how to read. The ones who didn't listened quietly. Molly lit a candle in the window to welcome the Holy Family into the saloon. Then they sang the Christmas hymns from the old country.

As the snow came down harder, Mamie looked out the window at the poor homeless people gathered on the Viaduct. She noticed a woman huddled against the brick building next door with her two children, dressed in near-rags.

"We have to invite them in," Mamie said to Kate. "It's Christmas."

Kate nodded. "Yes, Mamie," she said with a smile.

Mamie opened the door, bracing herself for a whoosh of snow and cold air. "Come in," she called to the woman huddled with her children. "I'll give you a warm bowl of food and a place to sleep tonight."

A half-dozen homeless came in to eat supper, and slept on the empty bed in the attic and with blankets on the saloon floor. The homeless woman thanked Mamie in Gaelic, and Mamie responded in their native language.

"I'll make you oatmeal in the morning," Mamie promised.

They went to bed that night listening to the beatific songs of carolers outside. Kate hugged Mamie in bed.

"Merry Christmas, Mamie Chambers," she said. "We'll make a life here, I promise."

Fifteen

Kate Masterson and Mamie Chambers didn't know they were being watched as they walked home on Christmas Eve. In fact, the man who followed them made a job of it: The Angle Mob called him The Watcher.

The Watcher visited Black Willie at his old, ramshackle house on the river later that night. From the looks of Black Willie's abode, it would be easy to assume he was a poor man. But Black Willie, in fact, got a cut of the profits from most of the businesses in the Angle. He was one of the neighborhood's richest men, but he chose to spend the money on women, booze, and opium. Black Willie loved opium almost as much as he loved power.

"So, what did you see?" Black Willie asked when The Watcher sat down in his living room.

"I see no sign that Kate Masterson is going to abandon Dan Dyra's saloon," The Watcher said. "She's got that brother o' hers hanging around, working the door. He's posing a real problem for us."

Kate's brother was a wide, imposing man with a dark beard, thicker than Willie's in his younger years. Patrick Masterson was an intimidating fellow known to run his mouth, with and without the help of liquor. Black Willie and The Watcher were loath to admit they were getting older and were no longer primed for street fighting. That was why The Watcher carried a knife wherever he went.

"Patrick Masterson won't be around much longer," Black Willie replied. "He works for a shipping company based in Michigan, and he'll be laid up there for winter. That's when we'll get the saloon. Time is of the essence, for he'll return in the spring."

The Watcher leaned back in his chair, wishing Black Willie would give up on the idea of acquiring the saloon and turning it into a high-profit brothel.

"Did you know Kate Masterson has a new boarder?" he said. "I inquired around the neighborhood. Her name is Mary Chambers."

"I know, I know. You don't have to say it. I'm a Chambers," Black Willie said. "I assure you she is no relation of mine."

The Watcher stared at him, forcing contact with Willie's coal-black eyes. "True," he said. "I just wonder if she's related to that *other* William Chambers."

Black Willie's long-ago nemesis was the other William Chambers, also known as Tylor Mor. *Mor* meant "big" in Gaelic, and *Tylor* was a mark of respect. Back in the late 1860s, the people of this neighborhood had referred to the other William Chambers exclusively as Tylor Mor, which loosely translated from Gaelic as "the Big Man."

Black Willie could still see Tylor Mor in his mind: a large man with dark, coppery hair and a formidable demeanor. He was the reason Black Willie had a stake in so many Angle businesses, but none on Whiskey Island. Tylor Mor and his gang had forced Black Willie off that grimy peninsula years ago.

"Are you suggesting Tylor Mor returned to Cleveland?" Black Willie asked, finding the notion absurd.

"I'm suggesting his daughter did," The Watcher said. "I must tell you, sir, I see both their faces in hers. Tylor Mor's and that woman o' his."

Black Willie stroked his beard. The thought of acquiring the saloon excited him more now.

"She's Tylor Mor's daughter, you say?" Black Willie said. "I wonder if she knows about me."

71

Sixteen

On Christmas morning, Mamie slept late. It was her first sound night of sleep since Peter disappeared. She awoke to Patrick Masterson standing over her, his hand on her shoulder, shaking her awake.

"What are you doing here?" she asked, surprised at his boldness in crossing to the women's side of the attic. She crossed her arms over her chest, feeling overexposed in her nightgown.

"I'm leaving in the morning," he said to her. "I'll be drinkin' the night away with my crew, then tomorrow, I'll get back on my ship. The snow will be heavy this year, and the Lake will freeze over soon. I won't be back 'til the ice melts in the spring."

Mamie looked at him, still pegging him as the man who could have stopped Peter from leaving, but didn't. "You smell like whiskey and it's not yet noon," she said. "What're you doing at my bedside, anyway?"

"I don't want to part on bad terms," he said. She sat upright on the bed, tilting her face toward his. "You know why I thought it best to let him leave, don't you?"

"I don't," she said defiantly.

"You might hate me guts for it now, but one day, you'll understand," he said.

Then he covered her hand with his, a move that surprised her with its intimacy.

"I'll be seeing you in the spring, Mary Chambers," he said.

Mamie looked away, feeling too much bitterness in her heart to offer a proper goodbye.

Kate cooked a big Christmas dinner at the saloon, which was closed to patrons for the night. Mamie invited her new family—Uncle Joseph and Uncle Dominick and Aunt Mary, and the police officer Michael and his wife and children. Kate's other brother, Darby Masterson, visited with his family as well. Everyone was there except Johnnie. Mamie hadn't seen him since the night after Peter's disappearance.

"You know who left this coal, Mamie?" Kate said as she lit a coal fire.

"No, I do not," Mamie said.

"This Christmas Day, you should mull the principle of forgiveness," Kate said. "You might not be thanking him now, but one day, you will."

When Mamie shot her a doubtful glance, Kate repeated herself. "You *will*."

Mamie wasn't sure what Kate meant. Would she thank Johnnie one day for the coal? Or for running off Peter Sweeny?

"Both," Kate said with a twinkle in her eye when Mamie asked. "The Lord knows, both."

On New Year's Eve, there was a party at the LaSalle Club. The LaSalle Club was the St. Malachi club for men only, but for holiday parties, women could attend as well, provided a man invited them.

"Are you ready to meet the matrons of St. Malachi?" Kate asked as she helped Mamie get dressed.

"I'd rather not, Kate," Mamie said. "In fact, I'd rather not go to this party at all."

The label "matron" had a negative connotation among the Irish. They used it to describe women who were

73

overbearing, nosy; in everybody's business. And that was the last thing Mamie wanted tonight.

Kate had insisted they should go, even though Mamie had yet to attend mass at St. Malachi. She was too humiliated by her situation to show her face at a new church. How would she explain that she had arrived in America with a husband-to-be, but that he had abandoned her?

"You're going," Kate said. "You have as much right to be there as any woman of this parish, and I'll be damned if I let you hole up in this place any longer."

They donned their cloaks and headed up the hill to the LaSalle Club with Molly in tow. On the way, Kate passed Mamie a flask full of Irish whiskey.

"I can't, Kate," Mamie said, handing the flask back to her.

"You've earned it, Mamie," Kate said. "For your hard work last night, and for all you've endured here."

Mamie felt it useless to argue with her, and took a few sips as they walked. She had learned growing up in the Catholic Church that drunkenness was a sin, at least for women; that a good woman did not drink. A good woman did, however, tolerate a drunken husband—even one who beat her. Behind closed doors, even Mamie's parents scoffed at the blatant hypocrisy of the Church.

To Mamie, it felt good to break one of the little unwritten rules, even if it meant taking a few sips of whiskey from a flask.

It turned out she needed it. When Mamie entered the LaSalle Club with Kate, she overheard a woman's voice sneering at them.

"There's the bar maid," someone said as they walked by. "She can make it to a party but she can't come to mass?"

"Hello there, Maggie Carney," Kate said, turning sharply. Mamie looked at the table Kate was addressing and saw four women. One of them was Annie Joyce, her snooty neighbor from Roskeen.

"Merry Christmas," Kate said.

Maggie didn't return the blessing. "Kate, why didn't we see you at church on Christmas?" Maggie said. "In fact, you've barely attended all year."

Kate stared at her. "Did the Good Father himself tell you to address it with me, Maggie?"

"Well, no," Maggie admitted, crossing her arms. "We just found it unusual that a young widow, with such struggles, would miss Christmas mass."

"We observed Christmas on our own at the saloon," Kate replied. "If the Good Father is concerned about my absence, he'll pay me a visit himself."

Maggie glared at her.

"Come on, let's go," Maggie said, motioning for Annie and the other women to rise to their feet. "Kate, I'll ask Father Molony to visit you."

"Please do."

"What was that all about?" Mamie asked. "Annie Joyce has been in Cleveland less than a month, and she's the matron of St. Malachi?"

"She's one of Maggie's handmaidens now," Kate replied. "Remember, Father Molony is the head of St. Malachi, not Margaret Carney or Annie Joyce. Now let's go find my brother, Darby."

Darby Masterson brought a flask to the LaSalle Club, too. Kate stepped into a dark corner as she took another drink from it. The Masterson siblings laughed, reveling in their power to rankle people by not giving a rip about their rules. Mamie could feel Maggie Carney's hateful eyes on her from somewhere else in the room.

"Who is that girl with Kate Masterson?" Maggie asked Annie Joyce.

"Her name's Mary Chambers," Annie replied. "Her family owns a tailoring shop in Roskeen. I've known them all my life. Her da is a most vulgar person; very mouthy, very rude. Her ma's a little red-haired woman with a big herd of children. Mamie's little brothers…they were the terror of Roskeen."

Annie rolled her eyes. "Only her oldest brother, Tommy, is presentable. I'm just wondering what happened to Peter Sweeny. He's a polite and handsome lad. No one has seen him since the day they arrived. I'd wager her brothers ran him off, and it's a shame for her. She could never do better."

"She fits in well with the Mastersons," Maggie said.

Maggie's other friend, Bridget Kelly, was watching Kate and Darby Masterson from across the room.

"Kate is lucky she's so pretty," she said. "Otherwise, she'd be a gutter whore."

"She's by no means pretty," Maggie shot back. "And what makes you so sure she's not a whore? She's living alone in Dan Dyra's saloon now, and she's somehow paying her own way for the cost of ale and food. God knows she doesn't make enough pouring pints to afford that."

The four women at the table looked at each other, raising their eyebrows.

"We should take it up with Father Molony," Maggie said. "Kate operating that saloon is such a hideous example to her poor, poor child. And it's a threat to the morality of this neighborhood."

The other women nodded in agreement. They watched Kate Masterson and Mamie Chambers sip whiskey from a flask, laughing like scandalous women.

Seventeen

Snow didn't fall on the west coast of Ireland, even on the coldest days of winter. But the last week of the year brought rain—sheets of it, drowning Roskeen. It caused the roof of Will and Bridget Chambers' cottage to leak. So when Bridget heard a sound like rolling thunder in the distance, she didn't think much of it.

After Bridget nursed baby Norah and put her down to sleep, she sat in her rocking chair and began composing a letter to her children. She addressed it to Mamie, who would be the most diligent about reading and responding to mail.

"My dear daughter," she began, speaking aloud as she wrote. Although she had learned to read and write as an adult, she still did both slowly, and had to check her lettering several times. "I hope you have arrived safely in…"

She wasn't sure how to spell the city's name. Was it C-L-E-V-E-L-A-N-D? Or C-L-E-A-V-E-L-A-N-D?

Her mind began to wander. She wondered what she would have wanted to hear from her own mother when she first arrived in that strange city over twenty years ago.

A series of sharp knocks on the door punctuated the din of the rain.

Bridget knew the sound of that knock. Will knew, too.

It was a frantic neighbor. "Come quickly!" he said. "They're taking down the Mulchrone's cottage."

Old Sully Mulchrone and his wife had lived in that cottage all their lives. And now—because they had fallen behind on the rent by a few months—the British landlord was destroying it. The sound Bridget had heard wasn't thunder. It was the bailiffs blowing off the Mulchrone's roof.

"Mind the babe," Bridget said to her children, whoever was listening. She didn't care which one of them did it. She had seven children remaining at home, five of whom were old enough to watch Norah. She and Will ran down the well-worn path to the Mulchrone's.

"Sully," Will said to Mr. Mulchrone when they arrived, "Why didn't you come to us for help with the rent?"

Mr. Mulchrone turned to the Chambers with tears in his eyes, his face red and splotchy. "You just sent three children to America."

He said it too loudly, and one of the bailiffs for their British landlord overheard. Johnnie was supposed to stand trial when the landlord returned. The landlord, Lord Browne, had Johnnie arrested for vandalizing his precious carriage.

Will Chambers didn't give one whit that his son had damaged Lord Browne's property. Browne owned most of the land in Burrishoole Parish, the parish that encompassed Roskeen. But he didn't own Will Chambers. And he couldn't force Will Chambers to apologize for what his son had done. When Johnnie saw Browne's carriage coming toward the manor house, Johnnie Chambers drew a pocket knife and made a large scratch along the side.

To Will, it was child's play, a harmless prank on the landlord they all hated. Besides, Lord Browne could afford to buff out his carriage. Considering the English had let the Irish starve two generations ago, it was a small price to pay.

But the next day, the Royal Irish Constabulary had arrested Johnnie. Knowing he could be exiled anyway, Will

Chambers had put his son—and his two older children—on a ship to America instead.

Will embraced Mr. Mulchrone, man to man. "Roskeen will pool resources and pay your rent," Will promised him. "We'll build you a new roof. The English won't get away with their wickedness, not this time."

But a few hours later, Bridget and Will Chambers heard another rap on their cottage door.

"Stay back," Will said to Bridget, as she picked up the baby, instinctively cradling her. As they expected, a constable from the Royal Irish Constabulary was at the door.

"What do you want?" Will asked as the constable stepped inside.

"Mr. Chambers, where is your son?" the constable asked, challenging Will with a steady glare.

"Which one?"

"Don't ask me which one, Will. You know which one. We're looking for a John Chambers. He's facing trial soon. Surely you didn't forget?"

"He left of his own accord. He went to live with his uncles," Will replied, truthfully, crossing his arms over his wide chest. William Chambers was the biggest man in Roskeen, and no weasel sent by the RIC could intimidate him.

A look of rage overcame the constable's face. "Of course he did," he replied. "But we suspect your younger sons were involved as well."

"Again, which one?" Will Chambers spat. "The schoolboy? Or perhaps the baby?"

He looked over his shoulder. Eight-year-old Frankie and three-year-old Georgie stood inside the cottage, looking frightened.

"Don't get flippant with me, Will Chambers. No one has ever accused you of being stupid," the constable replied. "You have another son, on the verge of manhood. Just like John."

He meant the younger William, or Willie, who was thirteen years old.

"What's your evidence?" Will asked. "If you think I'll hand over my son, you're a fool."

It was obvious, then, that the RIC officer had no evidence. Willie hadn't been there, and they knew it.

Instead, the RIC officer set his sights on Bessie, Will's little daughter.

"She's a pretty one, isn't she?" the officer said out of the blue.

"She's seven," Will said.

"Is she? By golly, she looks like she's on the verge of womanhood." He reached out and stroked one of Bessie's chestnut-brown braids.

At that moment, Will knew what he was threatening.

"Off with you," he said to the RIC officer, shooing him out the door. "Come back when you have something of value to discuss."

Will slammed the door, commending himself for not wringing the man's neck.

"Bridget, I need you to start over with your letter," he said. "We're sending Bessie to live with Peter and Mamie."

"What?" Bridget gasped, as Bessie wrapped her arms around her mother's legs.

"Yes," Will replied. "My children will not be crushed under the tyrant's heel."

Bridget Chambers didn't talk to her husband for a full day after he made the proclamation. When he entered the room, she turned her face from him, busying herself with the cooking or the children. Finally, in bed the next night, Will reached over and pulled her closer.

"What's bothering you, *acushla*?" Will asked, calling her by an old Gaelic term of affection. It was short for *cuisle mo chroí*, "the pulse of my heart."

And she was. This woman, after all, had borne him ten children.

She turned and looked at him in the dark. "You want to send our babies to America, do you?" she challenged him, looking cold. "Do you remember what it was like?"

"I remember."

"I think you forget," Bridget said, recalling her own journey to America all those years ago.

Bridget and her siblings grew up in County Mayo with a drunken father and a hapless mother who could do nothing to stop Tom McGlynn as he ran roughshod over his two families: the one he sired with his first wife, and the children by his second wife, Maggie Hoban. The older McGlynn siblings remained in the cottage they'd lived in before their mother died, and their father Tom McGlynn went back and forth between his two homes, causing a rift that never healed.

"You dirty-faced brats warn't even his," the older McGlynns called out when they saw the new McGlynn children on the road. "You belong to your hoor mother and God-knows-who."

But then Bridget came out with red hair, like a ripe apple. And then Tommy McGlynn, the only man with such hair in the whole parish, was forced to admit he really was her Da.

Then the second wave of a smaller, but just as devastating, potato famine hit, and the petty feud meant nothing now.

"We have to leave," Joseph, the oldest, told his brother Dominick. "We know our father ain't gonna do shite to find work, besides maybe use the last of the potatoes to make housemade liquor. We'll die if we stay here."

"What about our brothers and sisters by the other woman?" Dominick asked. "We can't just leave them here."

The other McGlynns were young—too young, barely teenagers.

Joseph grimaced. "We'll take the girls," he said. "We can't pay for the whole family's fare, and the boys still have their mother."

So they went to their teenage sister Bridget and told her they were leaving, to only bring what she could carry to Galway. Their slightly older sister, Mary, refused to leave her husband—but she handed over her girl baby to Bridget.

"Care for Agnes," she told her. "I will keep my boys so they can care for me shall we all need it." She was using the veil she wore to church to block out the smell of rotting potatoes all across the county. They knew that wicked smell and they knew what was coming. If a devil had a smell on him, that would be it.

And they knew what came next: all across the bailiwick, the bailiffs would go to the homes where the rent was overdue and turn the tenants out on the road. With no food and no place to turn, they would starve.

"God help us," Mary said as she watched Bridget walk away with her baby.

As they passed Tom McGlynn's second cottage for his new family, they saw the youngest boy, Michael, sitting on the stoop, his head in his hands, having nothing to eat for several days. He looked pale and weak. Even his red hair looked dull.

Joseph and Dominick looked at each other. "We must have the money for one more child," Dominick said.

"He's eleven," Joseph said. "That's old enough to work."

Dominick turned around and looked back at him.

82

"No, it isn't," he said, and turned back to grab him off the stoop.

When Tommy McGlynn saw them trying to take his son, he ran after them, trying to snatch Michael away.

"My boys aren't leavin,'" he said. He ignored his daughter Bridget.

"What of us?" Joseph replied. "I forgot you found a new family." He shoved him away.

"You better get back here, boy!" Tom McGlynn shouted after Michael. They all realized he was too drunk and in too poor of health to chase them. Michael kept walking, obeying Joseph's orders to stop looking over his shoulder.

It was right that he didn't return home. A few days later, Tom died in his small plot of land, face-down with a flask of whiskey in hand.

"Would you look at me father?" Mary asked her other sister, watching the scene from the cottage window as they tried to salvage the last edible potatoes. She still had bruises on her face and neck from where he'd cuffed her the other day. "Exactly where he belongs, face down with his dick in the dirt."

"At least we can finally be rid of the smell o' him," her sister said, closing the curtains. They'd drag him out of the yard later to find out if he was really dead ·or just passed-out drunk.

But he never woke up, and that was the last anyone heard of old Tommy McGlynn. By the time the rest of the siblings made it to Cleveland after a months-long journey, many of the other McGlynns were dead, too.

The journey to America was barely survivable, aboard a crowded and leaky sailing ship that moved incredibly slow. When they made it to New York, they had just enough money to travel by slow boat along the canals that snaked through the Great Lakes states. They had to cook their own food on the open deck or go without.

"These canals were built by Irishmen," Joseph assured them. "It's a good luck sign; they built them just for us to arrive at a better place."

But it wasn't much better for Bridget. She quickly accepted a job as a maid in the household of Daniel Rhodes, a lawyer with a mansion on Franklin Avenue, across the Cuyahoga River from downtown Cleveland. Bridget lived in the servant's quarters with the rest of the staff, and she was thrilled to have a clean bed and clothes. They let her bring baby Agnes to work frequently, and return her at night to her brother Dominick's house to be cared for by his new wife, Mary Gannon. The work she did wasn't heavy and Daniel Rhodes liked her enough to let her eat dinner with them some nights.

Her life on Franklin Avenue was comfortable and predictable, of course, until Daniel Rhodes' son-in-law and his wife moved in. The son-in-law was a young businessman named Mark Hanna. Although he wasn't the man of the house, it was clear Mark expected Bridget to serve him…in more ways than one…

Bridget shook her head in disgust and snapped back to reality, shooting her husband a piercing look.

"Yes, I am haunted by it," she told him. "I'm lucky I had you to rescue me. Mamie, she has Peter Sweeny. Our other children might not be so lucky, you know. Especially if we send them too young."

The words hung over both of them like a storm cloud. But in the end, both of them knew William Chambers' mind was made up.

Eighteen

One evening in the first week of January, Kate took Mamie to meet Father Molony, the priest of St. Malachi. She left Molly to prepare dinner before the saloon opened for supper. Molly was a skilled cook, having apprenticed in Kate's kitchen for years.

"We'll be back at supper time. If you have the chance, peel a few turnips for stew tonight, will ya?" Kate asked her, and Molly, ever the obedient child, nodded.

"How do I explain myself to the Father?" Mamie asked as they walked up the hill from the saloon. St. Malachi sat like a castle at the top of the hill, guarding the neighborhood that sloped below it.

"What do you mean?" Kate asked. "Are you referring to Peter Sweeny running off on you? Oh, you carry so much shame. It's time to shed it, my dear."

On their way to the Church, they passed a man in a black top hat and a prim woman standing in the snow, clattering a bell on a metal bucket.

"A penny for the children!" the woman called in a hallowed voice. Mamie read the inscription on the bucket: CHILDREN'S AID SOCIETY.

She reached into her pocket, fishing for a penny. Kate grabbed her arm.

"Do not give them money," she said sharply. "Not one red cent."

"Why?"

"The Children's Aid Society kidnaps Irish children accused of crimes and puts them in a children's prison," Kate said. "They call it the Industrial School. Ha! They get their child workers from the American courts, and they take our Catholic boys and shove Protestant rawmaish down their throats."

Mamie put the penny back in her pocket, feeling foolish.

"Don't worry," Kate said. "You'll learn who to trust in this neighborhood as time goes on. You'll also know how to spot a con."

St. Malachi was built from stone, which made it feel drafty and even colder than the wintry air outside. It wasn't yet supper time, but it was dark enough outside that the oil lamps shone brightly.

"Catherine Masterson, is that you?" Father Molony asked.

Father Molony had led St. Malachi since it opened twenty years ago, right after the War Between the States ended. He was the spiritual leader in and outside the church. He often ventured to Whiskey Island after dark, breaking up saloon fights and imploring the men to go home to their wives. He leaned on an old staff that had made the journey from Ireland with him.

"It is, Father," Kate replied, bowing her head for a moment. "I have a new friend, as well. Her name is Mary Chambers, but we call her Mamie."

"What town did you come from?" Father Molony asked her.

"Roskeen, in Burrishoole Parish. County…"

"Mayo," Father Molony finished for her. The Irish in Cleveland were mostly from Mayo, especially Achill Island in the Clew Bay.

"Mamie's husband-to-be abandoned her the night they arrived," Kate said. Mamie flinched. "Father, could you offer her words of comfort? But first, I would like to speak with you."

"Yes, Catherine," he said, and Mamie knelt in the first pew as Kate entered Father Molony's chambers.

"What is it?" he asked her when they found some privacy.

"First, I have to thank you again for forgiving my absence at Christmas mass," Kate said. She met his eyes to let him know she was sincere. "Many priests wouldn't."

"Many priests value man's opinion over God's," Father Molony replied.

"But now, I must seek your counsel for another reason," Kate said. "My friend Mamie, who's waiting out there? She doesn't know about my past, and I can see she's wondering."

"So tell her," Father Molony replied. "You say her betrothed abandoned her. A man abandoned you, too, Catherine. You just happened to have a child when he left."

"And I was too young to be married," Kate replied. Much too young.

She was sixteen and pregnant with a child when she married, the child who grew into her dear Mary Margaret, or Molly for short. Kate's mother in Ireland was born Sarah Farry, and Kate gave her daughter her mother's maiden name. For many years, she had told strangers that Mary Margaret Farry was her baby cousin.

It was a lie, of course, one that she didn't keep well-hidden. Over time, Kate stopped caring so much what the strangers of St. Malachi thought of her. This wasn't Mulrany, the town where she was born in Ireland. It was a big city with a lot of people, and the only people she cared about knew the truth anyway.

"Don't be afraid of the truth," Father Molony said. "You say she's your friend. If she is your friend, make your confession. If she judges you, she's assumed God's role...and mine."

Kate smiled and bowed her head. "Thank you, Father. Mamie is a good woman. On Christmas Eve, when she saw the people in the streets, poor and hungry, she invited them in and fed them. When she sees poor children outside the saloon in the mornings, she invites them in for oatmeal."

"And she should continue to do so," Father Molony said.

Mamie entered the priest's chambers next, weeping quietly to herself. As she knelt before him, the story tumbled out. How she had planned to start a new life with Peter Sweeny in Cleveland. But instead, he had run away, throwing some money on the table as consolation.

"Do you know whether he's dead or alive?" Father Molony inquired. He had performed burial rights on unidentified corpses many times. They turned up on the shores of Lake Erie or behind the saloons on Whiskey Island. It happened less often now than when the Irish first settled in this area, but that was the reality. So many funerals to attend. So many deaths.

"I believe Peter is alive," Mamie said. "He was alive and well when he left me, anyway, and he disappeared of his own accord."

Father Molony grasped her hands, which she clasped in prayer. "And if he reappears," Father Molony said, "You must not return to him."

Mamie looked surprised. "I mustn't?"

"No," Father Molony replied. "At least not until he comes to me and confesses, and maybe not even then."

"For now, you've been called to serve this neighborhood," he replied. "Make your oatmeal in the morning. Serve it to the poor children who come to you. In the meantime, you'll find your husband, even if he's not Peter Sweeny."

Father Molony had never seen a woman look so relieved by his advice. "Thank you, Father Molony."

✝

Nineteen

Mamie found her grief lessened when she helped the poor who congregated outside the saloon. She asked Kate's permission to serve them oatmeal some mornings, as long as she rose early to cook it herself. She was still suffering from Peter's disappearance, but others suffered so much more.

Word spread around the Angle that a new boarder at Kate's saloon made oatmeal. She served it to the poor women and children in the neighborhood for free. Before the sun rose, she had a crowd of cold, hungry people streaming into the saloon, looking grateful and slightly ashamed as they took their bowls. Sometimes, they'd offer her a penny. She told them to keep it.

As Mamie cleaned up after breakfast one morning, Kate looked worried. Her furrowed brows cut deep creases in her forehead.

"What's wrong?" Mamie asked.

"Nothing," Kate said, never one to bother others with her troubles. "We just need more money, that's all."

Mamie, lacking the information to form a response, said nothing.

Kate shrugged. "We always find a way," she said. "But getting into financial straits makes us vulnerable to the Angle Mob."

Mamie's heart sank, and she felt flooded with guilt. "I can move to my aunt and uncle's house," she said.

"No, no," Kate replied. "Don't even speak of it. I want you here. I need your help." Mamie knew from her friend's voice that she meant it. "We just need to make more money at night."

A few days later, Kate came home with a few bolts of fabric in different jewel colors: ruby, sapphire, emerald. There were a few faint water stains around the edges, but the colors still dazzled Mamie.

"Kate, where did you find it?" Mamie asked, running her hands over the red fabric.

"My ma taught me to sew," Kate replied. "This is throw-away fabric the rich ladies rejected because of the water stains. I'll sew us some new dresses."

Kate held the bolt of fabric below Mamie's chin, comparing it to her dark hair and light eyes. "Which color do you want? Red suits you. As does green," Kate said. Then she took Mamie's hand.

"This is how we're going to make extra money," she said, as if it were a secret between them. "We're going to be the two loveliest saloon maidens in Cleveland. Just you wait."

Mamie was so excited she wanted to jump up and down. "Oh, thank you, Kate!" she cried.

Kate worked fast. The first spring-like ray of sunshine peeked through the clouds as she sewed the last buttons. It was the day before Ash Wednesday, which happened to be the same day this year as St. Valentine's Day. The Irish called this day Shrove Tuesday. The Louisiana French, known for their rowdy debauchery on this day, called it Mardi Gras. Americans called it "Fat Tuesday."

It was a day of feast before the Lenten sacrificial season began. Whatever people wanted to call it, Kate warned Mamie that the saloon would be packed to the brim that night. It was the perfect night to wear their new dresses.

The morning of Shrove Tuesday, Mamie stood before the lone, dusty mirror in the attic. She examined herself in her new scarlet dress.

"It fits like a glove," Kate said, admiring her own handiwork. "Peter Sweeny would be put to shame."

They rarely spoke Peter's name anymore, but Mamie blushed. The dress hugged the contours of her body in a daring way. Although no scandalous inches of skin were showing, Mamie felt immodest.

"You have the perfect proportions, Mamie," Kate continued. "The rich women wear girdles and corsets to achieve a figure like yours."

"I can't wear this, Kate," Mamie said.

"You can, and you will," Kate said. Then she took the pins out of Mamie's bun and let her auburn hair fall around her shoulders in long waves. "We'll use what God gave us to keep this saloon afloat."

Mamie's brother Tom stopped by the saloon with Uncle Dominick after a long day of work. As he escorted her to St. Malachi for mass a few weeks ago, Tom told Mamie he'd found work at the mortuary.

"The mortuary?" Mamie replied. "You found work at the mortuary?"

"After I went to see the body they thought was Peter's, Uncle Michael told me I 'do death well,'" Tom replied. "With all the tuberculosis and malaria among the poor, and all the violence, there's plenty of work."

Mamie knew from his face he must detest the work; that it wore on his soul.

"But it's far better than working on the docks with all the other Irish men," Tom added. "'Tis better pay, and the work won't kill me."

Tom was drinking more now, Mamie noticed. But she wouldn't dare scold him over it.

As Kate had predicted, the patrons were shoulder-to-shoulder in the saloon that night. And as Kate also predicted, the men couldn't keep their eyes off either of them in their new dresses. Their hair had been washed with Castille soap and tied up in lace ribbons. Many of the men lingered at the bar long after Mamie had filled their glasses, making excuses to talk to her.

"Can you mind Molly tonight while I take care of some personal business?" Kate asked her, avoiding eye contact.

"Kate," Mamie said, alarmed, "what personal business do you have late at night?"

Kate didn't answer.

"These streets aren't safe for a woman," Mamie added.

"I'll manage," Kate replied. "Don't question me, Mamie."

And Mamie didn't, suspecting that she didn't want to know what Kate was really doing. Instead, she focused on putting a smile on her face and making as much money as possible tonight. Kate was doing her an enormous favor by allowing her to live here. Mamie would do whatever she could to contribute.

Halfway through the night, she looked up to find a well-groomed man peering at her from the other side of the bar.

"May I help you?" Mamie asked.

The man studied her, as if he was inspecting fruit at a market. He appeared to be her age, and he was cleaner and better-dressed than the other men in this saloon. Mamie took this to mean he earned a decent amount of money, and not the six dollars a week paid to lowly dock workers toiling on ore ships.

"You'll want to get that stain out your dress," the man said. Mamie looked down at the length of her scarlet red gown, which brushed the tops of her feet.

"Not there," the man said, and touched his fingers to the bustline of her dress. There was a small liquid stain on Mamie's breast, one she wouldn't have noticed without his overbearing eye. He let his hand linger a bit too long.

"It's only spilt ale," she said.

"You'll want to scrub that out," he said with a smirk. "You don't want to smell o' beer, like a cheap brothel madame."

He tossed a coin on the bar. "Bring me ale," he demanded. "I'm sitting at that blackjack table over there."

"We don't allow…"

Mamie was going to tell him they didn't allow gambling in this saloon. But by the time she finished her sentence, she was gone.

Kate appeared at her side. "Did he make an excuse to touch your bosom?" she asked.

"He said I had a stain on my dress."

Kate turned to Mamie, a steely look in her eyes. "That's Maggie Carney's husband," she said. "She refuses to believe he drinks here all the time. She thinks he visits his brother after she's gone to bed, resting well for church in the morning." She looked disgusted. "Some women will believe anything a man wants them to believe, it seems."

"Do I have to serve him?" Mamie asked.

"No. Let him get up and fetch his own ale. You're not his parlor maid," Kate said.

A pounding on the saloon door interrupted her.

Mamie opened it a crack and saw Mad Annie Kilbane—the woman with scarlet hair and paper-white skin. She would be pretty if she didn't have the gritty appearance of a madwoman who wandered the streets. Mamie let her in.

"I'm hungry," Mad Annie said as she entered. "Too much hunger makes the babe restless."

"You have a baby?" Mamie asked her.

Mad Annie patted her belly, which to Mamie's eyes looked slim and flat, although it was hard to tell under her skirts.

93

"The baby is inside me," Mad Annie said.

"I see, my dear," Mamie said, refusing to be anything but kind. "I'll get you stew." Knowing that Mad Annie was homeless, she wouldn't charge her.

"I didn't know Annie was pregnant," Mamie murmured to Kate when they were both in the kitchen, ladling stew.

Kate harrumphed, puffing a loose curl out of her eyes with her breath. "She's not," she replied. "Annie always thinks she's pregnant. By my estimation, she's been with child four years now."

Kate handed Mamie a bowl of stew. "Let's feed her anyway," she said. "The poor woman; I've offered to let her sleep here. She only takes me up on it when the cold gets her. In the past, the other boarders have been annoyed by her constant pacing and howling at night."

Mamie delivered Annie a bowl of stew and some bread. Her appetite was ferocious, and she gobbled it like she hadn't eaten in days. Mamie cringed, hoping that wasn't the case.

"Thank you, my good woman," Annie said, handing the bowl back to her. Mamie went back to the kitchen to fill it again.

When she came out, Austin Carney had Mad Annie perched on his knee. He was grazing his lips along her neck; smelling her wild red hair. But when he spotted Mamie, Austin shoved Mad Annie off his lap.

"Your hair smells like a hog enclosure," he said, pushing her away in disgust. "Off with ya, you slattern!" The other men laughed.

Mamie ducked into the kitchen. "Kate," she said urgently, "We have to get rid of these men."

Kate emerged from the kitchen, hands on her hips, looking irate. But when she looked at Austin's table, she gasped and ducked behind the bar.

"Kate," Mamie hissed. "What are you doing?"

Kate crouched on her heels, refusing to stand up. "I'll explain later," she said.

"But what are you hiding from?"

"My husband is out there!" Kate hissed.

Mamie felt as if the world stopped spinning and sent her reeling, unprepared, into reality. "Your *what?*"

"My husband," Kate repeated. "Well, he's not my husband, because I annulled the marriage long ago, in Mulrany. But perhaps we're still married, legally. I don't know. I knew he ran off somewhere, but I didn't know it was here."

Mamie would have been angrier, if Kate didn't look as if she might pass out on the floor.

"Why didn't you tell me?" Mamie asked. "...After all that happened with Peter?"

"I meant to tell you. I told you, I'll explain later," Kate said. "I have to go somewhere tonight. If it weren't important, I wouldn't be going."

✝

Twenty

Kate slipped out to see Seán Fada, her friend and the owner of the hotel across the street. This wasn't a grand hotel, the kind of place a millionaire from Euclid Avenue might favor. It was an old, run-down inn with peeling paint and faded green wallpaper. Still, the interior was warm and comforting, and the hotel bar reminded Kate of a pub in Ireland. She loved it so, and she loved Seán Fada too. Although he was a man in his seventies, he always watched out for Kate. When there was trouble at the saloon, she counted on him for help.

And now she needed his help with a more pressing issue.

"I'm glad I found you," Kate said when she saw Seán Fada sitting at the check-in desk. "The ale distributor is jacking up my rates by *fifty* percent."

Seán Fada reached under the check-in desk and produced a letter he'd received the day before. "You're in company," he said.

There were only two ale distributors in the Irish community in Cleveland. Both were under the thumb of the Mob. They delivered ale to the taverns, hotels, and saloons in Irishtown Bend and the Angle. And if any place that served alcohol was cut off from ale, staying in business would be near-impossible.

"I have to commend Black Willie for his cleverness," Kate said, her voice flat. "I never imagined they would go after our ale supply."

She slapped the letter down on Seán Fada's check-in desk, next to his identical letter. "What should we do?"

Seán Fada shrugged. "The Irish aren't the only people in the booze business," he reminded her. "We can go to the German breweries. They're making money hand over fist. The newspapers are calling them 'The Beer Barons.'"

Kate narrowed her eyes, considering the idea. She had never thought of going outside her own neighborhood to get alcohol to sell at the saloon. It would cut the Angle Mob out of the process.

"Do you think our patrons would drink German ale?" Kate asked.

"It's not ale, it's lager," Seán Fada corrected her. "And let's not pretend they wouldn't drink taplash from the bottom of the barrel and hardly notice the difference. If German lager is edible, and it tastes enough like beer, they'll drink it." He leaned in to her across his desk.

"Give Carl Gehring a visit," he said. The Gehring Brewery was a short walk up Pearl Street, right near the Pearl Street Market. Kate had never met Carl Gehring, but he was a German immigrant, and a self-made Beer Baron.

"I'll consider it," Kate said. "I'm tempted to confront Black Willie first."

"Don't do that," Seán Fada replied. But he knew how stubborn Kate was. If she wanted to go, no one was stopping her.

As she tromped through the snow to the saloon, Kate heard a moan that chilled her to her core. It sounded like the moans of the dying her grandmother had described after surviving the Great Hunger in Ireland: low, agonizing, and hopeless. The moon reflecting off Lake Erie provided just enough light for her to make out Mad Annie, splayed in the alley with her skirts flipped up and her ratty pantalettes torn at the seams.

"Annie!" Kate shouted, rushing to her. She turned Annie onto her side, fearing she was dead, until she heard the noise coming from her again.

"Annie," she said, examining her torn undergarments, "who did this to you?"

But she already knew. It had been one of her patrons. And here Annie was, lying on the side of the saloon—freezing, face-down, and violated.

"Don't worry, Katie," Annie said, hobbling to her feet. "It's happened before."

"That doesn't make it right!" Kate said, putting her arm around her waist to help her walk to the saloon door. "Who did it? Was it Austin Carney?"

Mad Annie's expression became flat and emotionless. "No," she said. "But he saw it. The older man pushed me against the wall and threw up my skirts. He was halfway finished when Austin and his friends walked by, laughing at me. 'Who knew Mad Annie Kilbane was a Three-Penny Upright?' That's what Austin said."

A Three-Penny Upright was an ugly term for a prostitute who dispensed her services while leaning against a wall. They tended to be the poorest and most desperate of prostitutes. They were the ones who merely hiked up their skirts for clients because they had no bed in which to work.

"He held my hands against the wall so I couldn't escape."

Annie looked into Kate's eyes, showing the first signs of lucidity Kate had seen in a long time. "I don't care anymore, Kate," Mad Annie said. "They do it to me all the time. Sometimes, they'll toss a coin at me after. I'm not even a Three-Penny Upright to them. I'm worth only one penny."

Kate put her hand over her mouth, wanting to scream with disgust.

"I'm afraid they'll harm the babe is all."

"Annie, you're not pregnant," Kate said, although she didn't want to argue the point. "Come inside. Come on."

Twenty-One

Kate coaxed Annie inside the bedroom that once belonged to Dan Dyra, the saloon owner who had died. She coerced her to go to sleep. She pushed a table against the door so she couldn't escape.

"I'll take it up with Seán Fada in the morn," she said to herself, mumbling as she went upstairs. Seán Fada had let Annie sleep in his hotel many nights—whenever she wanted to, really. But she tended to wander off before morning, even in the freezing cold.

When Kate reached the attic, she could see Mamie Chambers' silhouette in the darkness. She was sitting up in bed, her arms folded across her breasts.

"You never told me you were married," she said.

"I am not married."

"Well, unless that man you saw was a ghost, you're no widow, either," Mamie replied, sounding more perplexed than angry. "What is the truth, Kate?"

"Sit down. I'll tell you."

They sat beside each other in the semi-darkness, the room shrouded in a sheer light from Kate's small lamp. Kate scuffed her feet on the floor.

"When I was sixteen, I got married," Kate said. "Four or five months later, I delivered Molly."

Mamie did the math.

"My husband was a boy from my town, from Mulrany," Kate said with a sigh. "We were so young, teenagers. Like your brother Johnnie. I was sixteen, but he

100

was a little older. He wanted me and the babe at first—until his kin got into his head. 'If she lay down with you before the vows, there's no telling what other wicked acts she committed.' They told him that. As if *I* seduced *him*."

She scoffed at the absurdity—the rawmaish, as the Irish called it.

"Then he denied lying with me before the wedding! That would mean Molly wasn't his. He knew it was a lie, but they had him—what's the word? He was poisoned against me. He disappeared, with his ma and da claiming no knowledge of where he'd gone," Kate said. "I knew they were lying. So did my ma and da, Darby and Patrick and my other brothers and sisters. Even the priest in Mulrany knew they were lying. He granted me an annulment, although it means nothing, legally. We've always known the Morans sent their saintly, blameless Patrick away somewhere. But we didn't know it was here."

Kate flopped back on the bed, sighing again. "I've never come across him before," Kate said. "He must have been living somewhere else before making his way to Cleveland. It makes sense, doesn't it?"

Mamie nodded.

"Smart of him to come here," Kate said bitterly. "Marriages presided over by a priest in County Mayo mean nothing to American courts. For the most part it doesn't matter, because Irish men and women don't want to divorce each other. But if they do, a man who's brought his wife here can simply leave if he wishes. No court recognizes them as married. In America, Patrick Moran is a legal bachelor."

"Father Molony wouldn't call him a bachelor," Mamie replied.

"Which is why we're not going to tell him," Kate said, popping back up and looking into Mamie's eyes.

"We're not?"

"No, we're not," Kate said. "Father Molony is a good man. But his idea of justice comes from the Good Book. I do believe in God's justice…but I happen to believe a bit o' Angle justice might do Patrick Moran some good." In the darkness, she winked.

Mamie smiled—until she heard Mad Annie howling downstairs, pounding on the door of the dead Dan Dyra's bedroom.

"Angle justice for Annie, also," Kate said. She told Mamie how she had found Annie tonight, and why she was here.

"We'll say a prayer to Saint Rita of Cascia," Kate said, grabbing Mamie's hand. "She's my favorite of the saints."

Rita, the patron saint of lost causes and impossible cases.

"And abused women," Mamie murmured, thinking of Annie.

Saint Rita sat in the Communion of Saints now. But in the not-so-distant past, she had been a lowly Italian widow, forced into an abusive marriage when she was just a girl.

Twenty-Two

On Ash Wednesday, Mamie went to St. Malachi for mass, despite barely sleeping the night before. Her brother Tom met her at the saloon, and they walked together.

"You look weary," Tom remarked.

Mamie harrumphed. "You could say that."

They knelt beside each other on the cold stone floor toward the back of the church. Mamie spotted Maggie and Austin Carney huddled together up front, looking well-groomed and pious.

They must have arrived early. The people who wanted to look best to Father Molony always came early, so they could sit in front. They wanted everyone to see them.

"He must have a wicked hangover," Mamie grumbled when she saw Austin.

Tom looked over at her. "What?"

"Nothing," Mamie said, bowing her head and hoping the Carneys wouldn't see her. "A hypocrite worse than the Sweenys, that's all."

On the walk home, Tom pulled a small square of newspaper from his pocket.

"What's that?"

"I found a newspaper advertisement for a domestic position," he said. "A household on Franklin Avenue is looking for a cook. You're a wonderful cook, Mamie, just like Ma. And I worry that you shouldn't be keeping bar in the wee hours. The witching hours."

Mamie took the ad and gave it a cursory look-over. "I promised Kate I'd help her," she said.

"I know. But sometimes, your desire to help goes too far," Tom said.

Mamie looked up at him, forcing their eyes to meet. "Are you ashamed I'm tending bar, Tommy?"

He didn't deny it.

Mamie stuffed the advertisement in her pocket. "I'll consider it," she said, slamming the door to the saloon behind her.

The next week, a brutal snowstorm pounded Cleveland. The snowdrifts reached halfway up the saloon's front windows. The usual number of patrons halved during the blizzard.

But one group of human beings was ever-present in the midst of the season's worst snowstorm: the poor and hungry, women and children and men and families. Many were booted from their homes for falling short on the rent during the winter months, when the ore shipments on the Great Lakes stopped and men were out of work.

"We have to help them," Kate said to Mamie, touching her arm as they looked out the window. "I have stew in the kettle. We have hot tea and plenty of blankets."

Mamie knew what Kate was asking of her. Bracing herself for an icy blast, she pushed open the saloon door. She tried not to let in too much snow as she trudged down the Viaduct.

She found a few men crowded in the alleys, trying to stay out of the cold. Standing a short distance away was a lone woman. At first Mamie thought she was holding a large quilt against her body to keep warm. But when she looked closely, she saw the woman was holding a toddler, his face so raw from the wind it looked scorched.

"Oh my sweet Jesus," Mamie exclaimed. "Come with me." She whipped around in the snow, her black skirt billowing around her. It was already coated with white.

"Whoever needs a place to stay tonight, follow me," she said.

Then she repeated, *"Tar liom!"* in Gaelic, in case they were Shanty Irish from the country and didn't speak English. Upon hearing Gaelic, the woman holding the toddler, comatose from the cold, finally raised her chin. She followed Mamie.

As they waded through the snow to the saloon, a deliveryman seized Mamie's arm. "Miss, you don't understand," he said. "If you let them in, they'll come begging every night!"

Mamie pulled her arm away, giving him a fierce look. "And if I don't, they'll be too dead to beg, won't they?"

He tipped his hat to her. "God bless you, miss."

As soon as they were inside, the toddler awakened from a semi-conscious, frozen state. He began to scream.

"Oh my, oh my," Kate said, snatching the child from the woman's arms to examine him. "Molly, could you go outside and gather snow to boil for the bath? They need to warm up immediately. This babe might have the frostbite."

Kate preferred clean snow, boiled and cooled, to provide water for baths and drinking. It was the cleanest water they could come by in Cleveland, and they were never in short supply.

Annie emerged from Dan Dyra's bedroom, holding the extra quilts. They looked faded and smelled a bit musty, but they were clean and warm.

"She needs to get out of those wet clothes immediately," Annie said. She motioned for the woman to follow her to the bedroom. There, she could stay out of the men's sight as she undressed. "The child, too. *Tar liom.*"

Mamie watched the poor homeless woman follow Mad Annie into the bedroom. They emerged redressed in odd clothing. But the color had returned to their skin, no longer bearing the grayish color of impending death.

Maybe Mad Annie wasn't so mad after all, Mamie thought to herself. She went to fill bowls of stew for the homeless who'd sleep in the saloon tonight.

In the morning, the snow had halted long enough that business in the Angle resumed as usual. The milkman came and went; a mysterious delivery of coal appeared at the back door.

"Your brother came last night," Kate said, showing the sack of coal to Mamie. "A regular Saint Nicholas, ain't he?"

"What makes you think it's my brother?" Mamie said, stirring her oatmeal.

"I have my ways of knowing these things."

"Well, I hope it wasn't him," Mamie said. "I'm no fool. If he's coming by that much coal, he's stealing it."

"And some would say that by feeding the poor and sick last night, we're enabling their idleness," Kate retorted.

"That's nonsense," Mamie huffed. "That would mean—"

Kate held up her hand. "See?" she said. "What is lawful does not always dictate what is right."

They heard a knock at the saloon door.

"Can I answer it?!" Molly cried, and Kate nodded.

But her smile faded when she saw Father Molony standing there, looking as if he felt a bit foolish. He was dusted with snow. Behind him were three women, the foremost of whom was Maggie Carney.

"Kate," Father Molony said, trying not to stammer. "Do you know anything about prostitution taking place here?"

"About *what?*" Kate cried.

"People have come to me with complaints…"

"First, Father, I mean no disrespect, but this is my home as well as my business. I know everything that happens under this roof, and that ain't one of them." She put her hands on her hips. "Second, who's *people?*"

Maggie Carney pushed forward into the saloon, as if she'd be able to find something Father Molony hadn't.

"Don't lie," she said to Kate. "The good people of this neighborhood see women—single women—coming and going from this place every night. They come after dark and leave in the morning, looking a wee bit perkier than the evening before." She glared at Kate. "There was a girl here last night. Where is she?"

"I am happy you asked," Kate said, pushing the door to the bedroom open. After some muffled confusion, the homeless woman emerged with her toddler in her arms. She greeted Father Molony, making it clear she was a parishioner. Father Molony looked relieved to see her here, safe and warm, and talked with her and the toddler in Gaelic.

"She's no stranger to me, Margaret," Father Molony said. "I've tried to help her find work and shelter…"

"We took her in for the night," Mamie explained. "I was afraid she, and the little lad, might freeze to death. There were men here as well. We fed them and let them stay warm for the night."

Father Molony looked back and forth between Maggie and Kate, who were glaring at each other. "This is all a misunderstanding," said said.

"No, it's no misunderstanding, Father," Kate replied. "But I'm curious. How does Maggie Carney know who visits this place at night?"

"My husband saw it," Maggie said. Then she immediately moved her hand to her mouth, realizing she let a secret slip she hadn't wanted to reveal in front of Molony.

"Ah, I see," Kate said. "And how would he see it unless he was drinking at Seán Fada's place across the street? Lord knows he's banned from this place."

"She's a liar," Maggie said.

"Is Seán Fada a liar?" Kate challenged her. "Because he told me this morning he had to remove your drunken husband last night."

Maggie rolled her eyes, dismissing Kate. "Father Molony," she said with an air of confidence, "are you going to take the word of a bar maid over the word of my own husband? A married man who is never disloyal to our parish?"

"Annie," Kate called to the bedroom, "Come here, please."

Annie stepped out of the bedroom. Her right eye was still bruised. Kate lifted up her hair, revealing the bite marks on her shoulder, the ring of bruises where she'd been choked.

"You can see someone attacked her," Kate said. "Annie, who else was there that night, when I found you on the ground?"

"Austin Carney."

"And what did he call you?"

"A three-penny upright," Mad Annie said, her eyes downcast.

Kate looked up at Father Molony. "If anyone seems to know a thing or two about prostitution 'round here, it's Mr. Carney."

"I won't listen to her ridiculous slanders," Maggie harrumphed. "Father Molony, I'm sorry I involved you in Kate's blather, her endless lies. I shouldn't have expected much different from such a scandalous woman."

Father Molony turned to Kate, placing a hand on her shoulder before he left. "I'm sorry, Catherine."

"Tá brón orm," he said. It was Gaelic. Americans might translate it as "I'm sorry," but it meant, literally, *the sorrow is on me.*

"Thank you, Father," Kate said. But as Father Molony left to walk back to St. Malachi, Maggie Carney stepped back inside.

"One more thing," she said to Kate. "I hear you're not cooperating with the neighborhood council."

Kate burst into laughter. "The *neighborhood council?*" she repeated incredulously. "You do mean the Mob, I presume?"

"Willie Chambers keeps this neighborhood well-run and livable, unlike Whiskey Island," Maggie replied. "Do you want to live like the people on Whiskey Island? Whiskey Island is filthy."

"Whiskey Island is free," Kate said. "They don't answer to the Angle Mob."

"This neighborhood would shrivel up and die without the Council," Maggie said. "We'd be forced to compete with foreigners. You want this saloon to be bought out by the German 'beer barons'?"

"I'm thinking of buying from them, actually," Kate said. "Maggie, just because your husband's family benefits from the Angle Mob and their finagling, doesn't mean we all do."

Austin Carney came from a banking family that gave out loans to small businessmen in the area and foreclosed on their properties when they couldn't make the payments. The Carneys were in full cahoots with the Angle Mob—which Maggie insisted on calling the "neighborhood council."

Maggie crossed her arms and stared at her. "You're a nervy woman, that's for sure," Maggie replied. "But you'll not keep this place in business if your own neighborhood turns against you. Know that."

109

Kate locked the door after she left, almost as if she expected Maggie Carney to come back again, uninvited.

✝

Twenty-Three

One morning after the snowstorm, Mamie got up early to dress herself in her best wool dress. She put her wool sweater from Ireland over it, looking herself over in the dusty mirror in the attic.

In her pocket was the advertisement for a job as a cook, the one her brother Tom gave her on Ash Wednesday. In light of the troubles at the saloon, Mamie had decided to at least go and meet the man of the house.

She had learned a thing or two when Peter Sweeny ran off on her. She learned, in the cruelest possible way, that her world could be upended at any moment. She'd best be prepared with some money in her pocket.

Tom had done some sleuthing and learned the owner of the house was a man named Mark Hanna. He was the one Kate had told them about on Christmas Eve.

But she hadn't worked up the courage to tell Kate what she was doing.

"You look lovely today, Miss Mamie," Molly said when she appeared downstairs.

Kate looked up from the kettle of oatmeal she was stirring. She raised her eyebrow. "Aye, she does," she agreed. "Mark Hanna is known for his fondness of lovely and naive Catholic girls."

Mamie went slack-jawed. "How did you know I'm to meet with Mark Hanna today?" she asked.

"I saw the newspaper clipping you left on the nightstand," Kate said. "As you may have guessed, I'm against it. You have employment here."

Mamie looked at the floor as she played with the buttons on her sweater. "I see you counting every last coin and despairing over it, Kate."

Kate didn't argue with that, knowing it was true.

"If I couldn't afford to put you up here, I would tell you," she said.

"I'm going to make some extra money," Mamie said. "For both of us. When I've finished cooking for the day, I'll return here to keep the bar at night."

As Mamie headed out the door, Kate followed her, shutting the saloon door behind her so Molly couldn't hear.

"Keep your hackles up around auld Mr. Hanna," Kate said. "I know girls who have worked for him. He's kind to his staff, of course. Too kind."

Mamie looked down at her drab dress. Her dark hair was secured in a chignon. She felt as plain as can be.

"What would Mark Hanna want with me?" she asked.

Kate slapped her on the back. "You're far too humble," she said with a slight grin, and Mamie went on her way.

Mamie wondered why Mark Hanna chose to build his mansion so near the Angle. His mansion was practically across the street from St. Malachi. Most of the rich men in Cleveland secluded themselves on the other side of the river, along Euclid Avenue in gated estates.

She rapped the door knocker, taking a deep breath as she waited.

The door creaked open, and a man with large ears and combed-back hair stood over her. His face bore an expression that wasn't quite a smile.

"Can I help you?" he asked.

"I'm here to see Mr. Hanna," she replied, feeling her heart start to pick up speed.

"I am Mark Hanna," he said, extending his hand.

She stalled for a moment before she realized she was expected to shake it. The Irish didn't do this hand-shaking business. She extended hers anyway, her small, pale hand trembling.

"You answer your own door?" she blurted, surprised. Mark Hanna laughed.

"Yes, I answer the door from time to time," he said. "Come in. Sit down. You're inquiring about the domestic position, yes?"

Mamie didn't know what "inquiring" meant, but she understood the word "domestic." She followed Mark Hanna to a sitting room, where he positioned himself in a chair across from her.

"You're Irish," he said.

"I am."

"How long have you been in America?"

"A few months, sir."

"How old are you? Are you married?"

It was an odd question, she thought, folding her hands in her lap. "I'm twenty. And no, sir, I am not."

"What experience do you have with domestic work?" he asked, leaning back and grinning at her seriousness. He could tell she was nervous, and it seemed to amuse him.

"I live at a boarding house on the Viaduct," she replied. She wasn't sure whether he was familiar with the neighborhood he lived so nearby. "It's down the hill from St. Malachi. I help run the saloon there…"

She paused, ashamed to reveal she worked as a bar maid at night. "I cook, and I help to keep it clean."

"Very good," Mark Hanna said. He examined her clothes and hair with his piercing eyes. "You appear to take care of yourself. You're bathed. Your clothes are clean."

113

She nodded.

"I need a new cook immediately. My old cook caused quite the ruckus around here, showing up drunk to work on the daily," Mark said. Mamie gasped, which made Mark laugh again. "She was Irish, too. But I thought I might try my luck again with a younger woman who has more to lose."

"Why don't you come back next Monday?" he asked. "I only have a few rules. First, be on time every morning. I don't like to wait."

"Yes, sir."

"And I require clean clothes and baths at least twice a week," he said. "I don't want to smell you." He leaned in, sticking his nose uncomfortably close to her neck. "Not that I can."

"I bathe," Mamie said. She didn't bother to elaborate.

"Good, good," Mark replied. Then he added, as if it were an afterthought, "What is your name, young lady?"

"Mary Chambers, Mr. Hanna," she said as he led her to the door.

He shook her hand again, squeezing it a little too hard. "Mary Chambers, you may call me Mark."

✝

Twenty-Four

On her first day of work, Mamie rose early to fix her hair and pick the lint from her black dress. She studied herself in the dusty mirror Kate had acquired from the rich people's trash, checking for any glaring stains or other markers of bad hygiene. Mark Hanna's words echoed in her head: *I don't want to smell you.*

Mamie took offense to his assumption that the Irish were dirty, but she refused to dwell on it. Mark Hanna's low opinion of her people had nothing on what the British thought of them. She reminded herself that was one reason she was lucky to live in America now: she had escaped from under the tyrant's heel. The heel of the hated English. And she had the opportunity to make her own money now—an opportunity she would hold tight.

Mr. Hanna opened the door before Mamie could knock.

"Hello, Miss Chambers," he said, ushering her inside.

He led her to an attractive but stiff-looking woman in the parlor room. "This is my wife, Charlotte," Mr. Hanna said. "I might count your cash, but she's the woman of the house. You will answer to her."

Mamie wasn't sure how to greet the woman, so she offered a little bow. "You have a lovely home," she said.

"Thank you," Mrs. Hanna replied. "And you Irish girls are the best at cleaning them."

Mamie realized she was trying to make a joke. She smiled a little.

"I'll give you the tour," Mark said. "Then you can get on with your day."

Mamie followed him up the staircase to the second floor. He showed her the guest bedrooms and the rooms that had once belonged to his children—a son and a daughter who were now grown.

"My son Dan comes by often," Mark said. "He just got married, against his mother's wishes. He was a legal minor at the time. We tried to stop him, but his heart was set on wooing a sophisticated older lady." He grinned at her. "My son takes after me, of course."

Mark took her to the third floor, which was an open room with several beds and nightstands. "If you choose to live with us, you will stay here," he said. "The maid's quarters."

"How lovely," Mamie said, meaning it. The room was far more spacious and less drab and dusty than the attic in the saloon.

"You look overwhelmed," he said. "I'll tell you ahead of time, if you do a good job and meet my expectations, I'll give you your own room." He paused to make sure she was listening. "My favorite servant always gets her own room."

"Och, no, sir," Mamie replied. "I appreciate the offer. But I live in a boarding house now. My friend Kate needs my help there."

"All you Irish girls are Mary or Katie, aren't you?" he said. "Or maybe Bridget."

"Bridget is my ma's name," Mamie replied immediately.

Mark Hanna's eyes twinkled. "Ma?"

Mamie shook her head, forgetting to set aside her Irish dialect and speak more formally in this house. "My mother, sir."

116

He nodded. "I had a maid named Bridget," he said, "But it was before you were born, and before we moved into this house. You wouldn't know her."

Later that afternoon, Mark Hanna met with his high school classmate and fellow millionaire, John Rockefeller. Mark had convinced Rockefeller to donate hundreds of thousands of dollars to the Republican Party. They were only three months away from the Republican convention. As a major player in the Republican Party, Mark had an insurmountable task to present to the Republicans' rich benefactors.

"We need the Irish vote," Mark said.

It was a presidential election year. The Republicans needed to overthrow Grover Cleveland, the Democratic darling. Grover Cleveland was the scourge of the Robber Barons, whose mansions lined Cleveland's most exclusive streets. In 1884, the Republicans had nearly toppled Cleveland by unveiling his deepest, darkest secret: he had an illegitimate son with a scandalous woman. Throughout the 1884 campaign, Cleveland was taunted by chants of "Ma, Ma, where's my Pa?"

But in November of 1884, the Democrats jeered back, "Gone to the White House, ha ha ha!" Cleveland had won.

Now, Mark Hanna was determined to put Ohio Senator John Sherman in the White House. His distant second choice was Benjamin Harrison, the former Senator from Indiana—but Mark had his heart set on Sherman winning the nomination.

John Rockefeller's face was stony. "The Irish of this city will never vote Republican."

In other years, he would have been right. The Republican Party was run by and for men who were rich—very rich—and intended to stay that way. The Irish immigrants who had flocked to this city during the potato famine had produced a new American-born

117

generation. They worked on the Cleveland docks, unloading iron ore ships owned and operated by Robber Barons. For this dirty and often deadly work, they earned six dollars a week. Mark Hanna imagined that most Irishmen would rather pitch themselves off the docks than cast a vote for a Republican.

But 1888 was going to be different.

"This election is all about the tariff issue," Mark replied. "As you know, Grover Cleveland's free-trade policy is favored by the British, and the Englishman is the Irishman's blood enemy."

He looked through the glass doors of the parlor at his new cook, hard at work in the kitchen.

John Rockefeller stared at Mamie Chambers, too. "Do you trust this woman?"

"I do," Mark replied. "Their Catholic consciences make them good employees, and their desperation for money helps as well. If they can be persuaded that Grover Cleveland will create a problem for the Irish back in the motherland, we can get their vote. Women can persuade their brothers and husbands to vote against Grover Cleveland."

"Mark," John said, "Don't you have another 'Irish problem' to worry about?"

Mark Hanna looked away. "I see no chance of that issue resurfacing."

Still, he went to bed that night thinking of the maid who'd lived in the Hanna mansion decades ago—the woman who'd been haunting his imagination since the day she disappeared.

Twenty-Five

Mamie came home from her first day of cooking at the Hanna mansion rosy-cheeked and sweaty. It had been hot in that kitchen, even though winter forged on outside. But Mamie was proud of the luncheon and dinner she cooked, and Mark told her she was free to eat of her own creations—provided there was enough left over.

"You'll have to go to the Pearl Street market to replenish your stock," Mark told her. "I will give you money to shop at the market, of course."

He counted out some paper bills and handed it to her.

"I can see that you're trustworthy," he said.

"Thank you, Mr. Hanna," she said, beaming with genuine gratitude as she accepted the money. She couldn't wait to show Kate what she had earned.

"You're back!" Kate said as she walked in the front door of the saloon. A few patrons were already at the bar, drinking ale and whiskey. "Is Mr. Hanna friendly?"

"He is."

"Not too friendly, I hope," Kate replied.

Mamie crossed her arms, wondering why Kate kept alluding to something nefarious about Mark Hanna.

"What are you getting at, Kate?" Mamie said. "If you know something about Mr. Hanna that I don't, you should say so."

Kate shrugged. "I can't offer specificities," she said. "Seán Fada knows more than I. He's old, so he knows

119

stories about Mark Hanna going back years. I've heard that he gets handsy with his 'help.' Always has. He keeps getting older, but the age of his maids and cooks remains the same. I hear he favors unmarried Irish girls. Virgins, I should say."

"Unmarried" and "virgin" tended to go hand-in-hand for Irish girls. Heaven knew they did for Mamie. But as Kate proved through Molly's untimely birth, there were occasional exceptions.

"He thinks our accents are sweet and our rigid Catholic rules about virginity are an exciting challenge."

Mamie cringed. "He kept his hands off me," she said.

"Good," Kate replied, winking at Mamie. "Because if he lays a hand on you, I'll ruin him; make him poor as me."

Mamie smiled, feeling a bit of relief because she knew it was true.

Mamie fell asleep early that night. She was in the midst of a dream when she awoke to the most terrible scream. It was so ear-piercing she thought only a *bean sidhe* could be responsible.

"Mama!" Molly shouted as they all woke up. In an instant, Mamie and Kate were on their feet, Kate scooping Molly up to comfort her.

"Shhh," Kate said. "It's Annie. She does this from time to time."

Kate held onto Molly as she and Mamie went downstairs to see what the commotion was about. Nothing on the first floor seemed amiss.

"Annie," Kate said. "What in God's name is the *damn* screaming about?"

Annie opened the door to Dan Dyra's old bedroom, where she was still sleeping every night. "A man was right outside my window," she said. Even in the scant lighting, her face appeared whiter than ever, like a piece of bone bleached in the sun. She was shaking.

"He was watching me," she said. "I saw him through the window. It was him...The Watcher."

Kate threw aside the curtains and looked out the window. "There's no man there, Annie."

"It was The Watcher!" Annie insisted. "Or perhaps it was the friend of the woman—the one who led Mamie's lover astray. He knows I saw them that night; that I got a good look at him. 'Twas the last night anyone saw Peter Sweeny alive."

"Annie, there is no 'Watcher,'" Kate snapped, putting her hands on her hips. "Nor was it Peter Sweeny or any of his cohorts. This is absurd. It was probably our Good Samaritan, delivering coal."

"I saw—"

"Hush, Annie, hush," Kate said. "I'll hear no more of it. Now come to the attic and sleep with us."

But when they awoke the next morning, Kate noticed there was no coal at the back door. In the slushy, melting remains of snow was a man's shoe print, right outside the window.

✝

Twenty-Six

The Feast of St. Patrick was a solemn day for the Irish in Cleveland. This year, 1888, it fell on a Saturday, which meant the Irish would spend two mornings in a row at St. Malachi, bowing their heads in prayer.

Father Molony led them in prayer, as they petitioned God to protect them in the upcoming summer months. Summer was the most dreaded season for poor people in the Angle, because with warm weather came mosquitoes—and malaria. Outbreaks of deadly waterborne illnesses, like cholera, were sure to follow. They were less of a threat these days, now that people had learned to boil their water and burn herbs to keep the mosquitoes at bay. But dozens of people perished each summer no matter what precautions the people took.

They prayed, too, for the sick and suffering of this city, and for protection from criminals. The beggars became more visible as winter melted into spring—as did the pickpockets and muggers. They bowed their heads.

St. Patrick's Day was a solemn day, indeed—until evening fell. Then it was time to celebrate.

"I hope you're ready," Kate said. "'Twill be the longest night of the year at the saloon."

Mamie frowned. "I have to cook for the Hannas," she said. "But when I return, I will be ready to help you."

"Do remember to change into your red dress," Kate said.

When Mamie came back from the Hanna mansion after dinner, she could hear the saloon before she could see it. An Irish band was playing music—the music of their people. She could hear the lilt of the fiddle, the stomping of feet. The sounds pulled her like a magnet, because it sounded like home.

For the first time, she used the rickety back stairs to enter the second floor. Kate had advised against using these stairs, because they were icy in winter, a prime condition for accidents. But Mamie didn't want to go through the front door because of the crowd.

She slipped into her scarlet saloon dress and came downstairs, where it was so crowded she had to rub shoulders with several men on her way to the kitchen. The patrons turned to look at her in her red dress. She felt their eyes on her, and it made her cheeks feel warm—although that could have been from the smoke and body heat, too.

"You can't say I didn't warn ya," Kate said when she saw Mamie, handing her a glass of whiskey. Although Mamie once balked at drinking alcohol, especially in public, she downed it. In this moment, at this American saloon on St. Patrick's Day, all the rigid old rules about women's modesty and proper decorum seemed not to matter.

"Help me behind the bar, please," Kate said, and Mamie got to work.

Molly was underfoot, stirring the kettle of stew and slicing soda bread. "Why don't you take a rest outside?" Kate suggested to her daughter. "This smoke must be hard on your lungs."

"Yes, mama," Molly said. "Then, can I go upstairs?"

"Aye," Kate replied. "Although I doubt we'll do much sleepin' tonight." They could barely hear their own voices over the music.

Molly stepped outside, sitting on the stoop outside the saloon where the air was free of smoke. The days were getting longer now. Daylight lingered until well past suppertime.

Molly walked a small loop around the saloon's back yard, twirling in her simple dress and apron as if she were a ballerina. She had never seen a ballet, but she'd seen drawings of ballerinas in the advertisements for the theater.

"Work hard, save your pennies, and maybe one day we'll afford to go to the ballet," Molly's mother had told her.

As she twirled, a man's voice called to her from the side of the building. "Hey, little girl."

Molly looked up, caught off guard. "Hello, mister," she said.

The man had a mustache and big white teeth; his incisors sharp as razors. He looked well-groomed and clean in his tweed jacket and matching hat. Still, he was a stranger, and Molly began to back away.

"It must be a long night for you, little girl," the man said. "What do you say we get a pastry at the German bakery?"

"I must ask my ma 'bout that," Molly replied shyly.

"Oh, I already asked her, dear," he said with a broad smile. "Your ma is a dear friend of mine."

Molly hesitated for a moment. The man offered his hand, beckoning her to come toward him. Very slowly, Molly reached out until they were clasping hands.

"All right," she said, and they took off down the Viaduct together.

✝

Twenty-Seven

From the shadows of Pearl Street, Johnnie Chambers saw Molly and The Watcher walking together. Johnnie was with his friends, who had also been his co-conspirators in stealing coal. Now that there was less demand for coal as the weather warmed, they were bored.

"That's Kate Masterson's girl," Johnnie said aloud. He found it odd to see a young child walking with that smarmy-looking man. He had to be at least the age of Johnnie's father, maybe a little older.

"Kate Masterson," his friend repeated, "You mean the saloon madame?"

"Aye, that's the one," Johnnie said. "And there goes her child with an auld chap." Johnnie thought of calling out the girl's name, but he couldn't remember it.

"Maybe he's Kate's brother, Patrick, the boxer," Johnnie's friend said. "She will be safe with him. Don't no one mess with Patrick Masterson!"

Johnnie narrowed his eyes as Molly and The Watcher moved further into the distance.

"That's *not* Patrick Masterson."

He told his friends he'd return later, and they shrugged. Without another word, Johnnie got up and began to follow Molly and the strange older man at a distance.

It was getting dark by the time Johnnie tracked them to a restaurant in Lincoln Heights. Lincoln Heights was the neighborhood south of the Angle. It was a long distance to walk with a little girl, and Johnnie grew more suspicious by the minute. He loitered across the street as he watched Molly through the window.

She and the man sat in the front window of the restaurant. At least Johnnie thought it was a restaurant, judging from the smells emanating from the place. A foreigner owned it—a Ukrainian, he thought, or perhaps a Pole. There were a lot of them in Lincoln Heights. Supposedly, this neighborhood was an encampment for Union soldiers after the War Between the States, but now it was full of recently arrived Europeans. Johnnie never heard a lick of English in this neighborhood, which was why he liked it here. He liked to peruse the storefronts and look at items he couldn't afford. Sometimes, if he had a few pennies left over, he would buy a cookie from one of the German bakeries. Trying to communicate with people who spoke no English made Johnnie feel less foreign himself. The Irish were lucky to speak English.

They were not lucky, however, to be so distracted by their work that they let their children run wild. Even the newspapers complained about the way Irish children roamed the streets unsupervised. Father Molony of St. Malachi had tried to intervene by walking the streets at night. He beseeched the children to go home when darkness fell. Kate was too busy to notice her child was missing from the saloon.

"I ain't gonna do nothin'," Johnnie muttered to himself. He watched the smarmy man drink coffee and nibble at a pastry. "I'm just gonna watch, and see to it that *he* doesn't do nothin'." For all he knew, he could be a friend of Kate's.

But Molly looked nervous, clacking her shoes against the back legs of her chair. Whatever the man put in front of her, she didn't eat. She picked at little bits of the food, and nodded in agreement with whatever he said. Occasionally, she appeared to be answering a question. But the longer she sat with the man, the more Molly shrank against her chair, looking scared.

When they left the restaurant, the man led Molly on a different route than the way they'd come. At that moment, Johnnie knew.

He knew this man wasn't taking Molly home.

He was bringing her somewhere else. Somewhere Kate wouldn't find her.

And Johnnie was going to follow them.

Twenty-Eight

"It's dark," Molly said to the man who had taken her to Lincoln Heights. "I have to go home now."

Like the evening sky, the man's demeanor had become darker as they walked home. He spoke less, and gave her gruff orders to stay at his side and not stop to peer in storefronts.

"You will go home when I say you will," he said. "Now sit in that chair."

Molly was inside an empty house that smelled dank, like mold. It also had the smell of dogs. A black dog was lying near the fireplace, nursing a litter of puppies. Molly wanted to pet them, if just to distract herself. But the man wouldn't let her.

"Has your ma taught you to wring a chicken's neck?" the man asked. He had stepped outside for a minute. When he returned, he was holding one of the chickens that had been clucking in the yard when they arrived.

"We've no chickens," Molly replied.

"It's easy, once you learn to do it in one swift move," the man said. Molly heard a loud crack as he twisted the chicken's head in a full circle. A hard, loud, sickening crack.

Molly froze. She felt tears springing to her eyes.

"Oonagh, the woman who lives here, will boil this chicken tomorrow," the man said. "You'll eat of it, and you'll like it. We've none of that vegetable slop your ma makes, with the stringy green beans."

Molly jumped up for the chair and began to run. She didn't know where she was going, because her captor was blocking the front door. So she ran toward the back of the house. If she couldn't escape, she would hide.

Then she felt the punch to the back of her head. The man corralled her like a calf, cupping a hand over her mouth and dragging her by her apron strings.

"I said sit in that chair!"

Molly heard a sound like ice crunching underfoot in winter. Sprinkles of broken glass littered the floor, and she saw a dark shadow climbing in through the window.

"Who goes there?" the man cried, releasing Molly from his grip. The man who broke the window shouted to Molly, "Run home!"

Molly ran out the door. She turned her head enough to see the stranger who had climbed through the window beating her kidnapper, pounding him into semi-consciousness.

As Molly stood in the middle of the street, wondering where she was, she heard footsteps behind her.

"Come on," the person who had broken the window said. As Molly looked up at him, she realized he wasn't a man, but a teenage boy—and that she'd seen him before.

At the same time the last tear trickled down her cheek, Molly smiled when she saw Johnnie Chambers had stolen one of the puppies from Black Willie's house.

✝

Twenty-Nine

Johnnie and Molly heard Kate's frantic voice before they saw her. She was going in and out of each ally; behind every building. She'd never dreamed that Molly would end up in Lincoln Heights with a member of the Angle Mob.

"I've got her!" Johnnie shouted, holding Molly's hand with one of his own, the puppy in the other. "I'm coming! No need to panic, Kate."

Kate ran to them when she saw them beneath the street light. She looked as if her knees would buckle when she saw Molly. *"Where were you?"*

"You don't want to know," Johnnie said. "But she's unharmed. That I can tell you, because I followed her the whole time."

He looked up and saw his sister, Mamie, whom he hadn't seen in three months. She'd followed behind Kate as they searched for Molly.

"John Chambers, what in God's good name are you doing here?"

Johnnie looked over his shoulder. He was afraid The Watcher or one of his minions had followed him. They were dangerous men; that much wasn't in doubt.

"Let's have this conversation indoors," he suggested.

Kate took Molly upstairs to bed, then joined Johnnie and Mamie in the now-empty saloon. Johnnie was telling Mamie what had transpired and how he'd smashed the window at Black Willie's house.

"I don't believe you," Mamie said, putting her hand on her hip. "You were out stealing again, I bet, and convinced Molly to come with you for cover."

"The only thing I stole," Johnnie said, "was this." He reached into his coat pocket and pulled out the tiny, wrinkled puppy.

"He's right," Kate said behind Mamie. "Molly told me the same version of events. And the truth is worse than I thought. I thought she merely wandered off. But she told me she was led away by a strange man who claimed to be my friend. They tried to kidnap her."

She looked over at Mamie for a hard pause. "And if Johnnie hadn't had the right mind to follow them, God knows what they'd have done to her," she said. "Mamie, your brother's a hero."

Mamie said nothing, rubbing the back of her neck and looking out the window. She still had nothing she wanted to say to Johnnie.

"I can see I'm not welcome here," Johnnie said. "I'll be going now."

"No, you won't," Mamie said. "These streets are unsafe for a child, and you're not as mature as you think."

Johnnie parted his lips to argue with her, but she interrupted.

"The bed on the men's side of the attic is still empty," she said. "You can stay, at least until you've had a bath. I can smell you from over here."

They both laughed a bit, cutting through the tension in the empty saloon. Johnnie knew a small part of his sister had forgiven him—even if it was just a little.

Thirty

Over breakfast the next morning, Mamie saw Kate shed a tear for the first time ever. It didn't come easy, and Kate bowed her head in shame as she let a teardrop slip from her chin into the black tea before her.

"They...stole my baby," she said to Mamie. "My Mary Margaret. That's what they'll do to chase me out of this saloon. They know saving this saloon is my hill to die on, but not if it means losing Molly."

Mamie put her hand over Kate's. She didn't know what to say. "Are you going to sell the saloon?"

Kate stared into her tea a bit longer. Then she snapped to attention, staring into Mamie's eyes.

"No. Never," she said. "But I have to send Molly somewhere safe. Somewhere that isn't this place. I've thought of putting her on a ship to Michigan with my brother Patrick. He knows people there."

She gazed out the window now, sipping the tea. "But I'd scarcely see her again, if at all," Kate added.

"Don't be rash," Mamie said. "I know a woman who can help us."

She stopped to correct herself. "Ah, I haven't *met* her yet, but I know her."

Kate laughed wryly. "Are we all losing our heads?" she asked, shaking hers.

"No," Mamie replied. "Just give me a day to find her."

Instead of taking the direct route to the Hanna mansion, Mamie left early and went to see her Aunt Mary. Mary was outside her modest home, gathering the wild green onions and asparagus that sprouted in the spring. When she saw Mamie approaching, she set down her basket and ran to greet her.

"Mamie!" she shouted. "I've scant seen you since you began work for auld Mark Hanna."

"I meant to visit," Mamie said. "Aunt Mary, I have a cousin in Cleveland who's a wee older than I am. Do you know her?"

"You have many cousins," Aunt Mary replied.

"Aye. But this one—she was born in Mayo. My mother cared for her as a babe."

"Ah, yes, your cousin Agnes," Mary replied. "I am afraid she's a bit…estranged."

"Why?" Mamie said. "Because she left the convent? That doesn't prejudice me against her."

Mary nodded, going back to plucking vegetables.

"Do you know where she lives?"

"She lives in a home on Jay Avenue, in Lincoln Heights," Mary said. "She rents it from a German. Father Molony gave her employment as a laundress and cook at the rectory after she was cast out."

"What does the house look like?"

Mary did her best to describe it. "It's a German Christian home. You know where the Germans live by their houses. There's a round arch over the door to represent an angel's halo, and another pointed arch—that one symbolizes the blessings raining down from Heaven."

Mary shrugged. "That's what I've been told, anyhow," she said. "True to her Irish nature, Agnes did put lace curtains in the window."

Mamie committed the details to memory. Jay Avenue was outside The Angle, but it wasn't far. As soon

133

as the opportunity arose, Mamie would go there to seek out the cousin she'd never met.

✝

Thirty-One

"Mamie, my dear, as long as you're going to Jay Avenue, I have something important to ask of you," Kate said.

"Of course, Kate. What is it?"

"Go see Carl Gehring at his brewery," Kate said. "He's the German gentleman." Kate's Irish accent made *German* sound like *Jorman*.

"They say he sells seventy thousand barrels of lager a year," Kate said. "He'll be happy to sell us a few more. And I'll bet German lager tastes far better than the shitty ale we serve. Seán Fada wanted to buy from Carl Gehring years ago."

Seán Fada's hotel served whiskey and ale from Mob-approved distributors. But German lagers were all the rage in Cleveland. Several German immigrants had fashioned themselves into so-called "Beer Barons." The Irish saloon owners continued to stick with ales and whiskey out of ethnic loyalty and pure habit. But after the Angle Mob had convinced their ale distributor to cut Kate off, that was about to change.

The Gehring family's brewery was on Pearl Street, just past the Hanna mansion and the Pearl Street Market. Mamie didn't know what to expect as she entered the Gehring Brewery, which sat on a lot on the east side of Pearl Street. The Gehring Brewery looked like a military fort. It had a malt house, two ice houses, and a new brew

135

house built a few years back. Mamie entered the main building, unsure where to find Carl Gehring.

No one here spoke English.

As Mamie wandered through the brewery, inhaling the warm, bready scent of German lager, a young man noticed her.

"Hallo," he said, before realizing she didn't speak German. "Can I help you?"

Mamie straightened up, wondering if he would take a sales pitch from a woman seriously. "I work at a saloon on the Viaduct," Mamie explained. "We want to sell your lager."

The man looked at her. "The Viaduct," he repeated, "In the Angle?"

"Yes."

"We have tried to sell lager in the Angle for years, to no avail," the man said. "They are set in their ways."

"We want to sell lager," Mamie said again, hoping he wouldn't ask too many questions. "And soon." The saloon's ale supply was dwindling fast.

"Very good," the German gentleman said. "I am Frederick Gehring, Carl's son. We would be happy to supply our lager to your saloon. Who is the owner?"

Mamie took a deep breath. She should have known these questions were inevitable.

"His name was Dan Dyra," she said, "But he died a few months ago. Our supply is running low and we need more barrels of beer, fast."

"Of course," Fred Gehring said. "We can deliver. You've seen our delivery carts, no?"

Mamie had, indeed, seen the Gehring's horse-drawn delivery carts on Pearl Street. But she hadn't thought much of them until today. She wondered if Gehring Brewery would have trouble delivering to the Viaduct; if the Angle Mob would harass the deliverymen. But she handed over the money Kate had given her anyway.

136

"We'll pay up front for the first delivery," Mamie said to Fred Gehring.

A stone's throw from the Gehring Brewery was Jay Avenue. Mamie repeated Aunt Mary's description of the house in her mind: *There's a round arch over the door to represent an angel's halo, and another pointed arch...she put lace curtains in the window.*

There was only one house on the small, modest avenue that fit the description. The door opened before Mamie had a chance to knock.

"Hello, can I help you?"

The woman standing before her had light hair with a hint of red, like the rest of the McGlynn family. She had big, expressive eyes that reminded Mamie of her mother's. Still, the woman looked wary, leery of anyone knocking on her door out of the blue.

"Agnes? I'm your cousin, Mary Chambers," Mamie said.

At once, Agnes' stiff poster dropped, and she broke into a smile as she embraced her. "I've been waiting my whole life to meet you!" she exclaimed, ushering Mamie into the main room of the house.

"What brings you here? How did you find me?" Agnes asked, as she went to pour Mamie a customary cup of tea. The house was clean—immaculate, really—and seemed large and cavernous for a single woman living alone.

Mamie told Agnes about her journey from Ireland and how Peter Sweeny had left her. Instead of looking scandalized, Agnes had the sympathetic look of a woman who knew.

She had clearly been through troubled times with a man, as well.

"I was a nun until very recently," Agnes said. "I figured I should tell you now, before you find out through

137

rumors and whispers. I was a nun, but I left the convent. I had an indiscretion with a priest."

Mamie said nothing.

"Sinful, I know," Agnes said. "But when we were discovered, I confessed my sins. He denied it. So I left."

"That's not fair," Mamie protested, and Agnes shrugged.

"Of course it's not fair," she replied. "But what recourse do I have? The man's word always takes precedence over the woman's in these matters. It's not the way it's supposed to be, but it is."

Mamie took a deep breath. "That's part of the reason I came," she said. "I have a friend who might need to send her daughter away, at least for the time being. She's divorced, or so she says—had a baby very young..."

"She had babies outside her marriage vows," Agnes filled in for her, and Mamie nodded reluctantly.

"Well, just one babe, mercifully," Mamie said.

"She's hardly the first poor Irish woman to do so," Agnes said. "In the early days of the Cleveland Irish, the famine years, many prostituted themselves in Public Square when their husbands died or abandoned them. Many children were born outside the marriage confines." Agnes sighed. "But go on."

"I believed you might know a place her daughter can go," Mamie said.

In Ireland, the nuns often helped so-called "fallen women" bear their babies in secret. They would arrange for the pregnant woman to live with another family, pretending she was a widowed cousin or sister-in-law. Some gave their babies up to a Catholic orphanage, to be raised by the nuns. Irish women learned quickly which nuns were kind-hearted—and which ones were wicked. The kind-hearted nuns were the ones they turned to when they fell pregnant and couldn't dare tell anyone the whole truth.

Agnes took a sip of her tea and gazed across the room at Mamie. "She can live with me," she replied.

Mamie was taken aback. "She can?"

"Yes, of course," Agnes said, looking around the big cavernous house with only one person to occupy it. "I love children, and I live alone. Because who's going to marry a disgraced nun…?"

She laughed wryly before regaining her composure. "It might be good for the both of us," she said.

Mamie put her head in her hands, wanting to shout with relief.

"I'm not sure Kate Masterson will take you up on it," Mamie said. "But if she does, I'll come back to you."

"Come back whenever you'd like," Agnes said. Mamie couldn't help hugging her as she departed.

When Mamie returned to the saloon one April evening, Kate was waiting for her with a parcel. It was tied with twine.

"You have a letter," Kate said, looking excited for Mamie. "It arrived today from Ireland. Your Uncle Joseph dropped it here for you."

"My ma!" Mamie cried, tearing into the package. "She promised she would write."

Then her heart sank, realizing this meant she'd have to write back. And what good news did she have to report? She had only sorrows to share: Peter had left her and the marriage never happened.

It would break her parents' hearts.

Mamie's heart fluttered as she got to Ma's last paragraph.

"Big news?" Kate asked.

"My ma and da are sending my younger sister to live in America."

Mamie's heart filled with joy that she would be a little less alone when Bessie, the little sister who loved her so, arrived.

Mamie frowned. "How am I going to tell them about…my…circumstances?"

Kate left the kitchen and re-emerged holding a paper and a worn-down pencil.

"You'll write and tell your ma and da everything," Kate said. "By the stories you tell, I know they love you very much. The sooner you write them, the sooner you can get it off your heart."

Mamie cringed. Part of her felt the ghost of Peter Sweeny would haunt her until the day she died—whether he was really dead or still alive out there, somewhere.

✝

Thirty-Two

Mamie's father, William Chambers, had spent the winter stashing away money to send his young daughter, Bessie, to America. He gave the savings to a neighbor who was planning to leave for Cleveland with his new wife in the spring. For a modest fee, the couple was willing to chaperone Bessie. Bessie had always loved Mamie dearly, and Will Chambers knew the opportunities for Bessie would be much brighter in America.

To the well-heeled, it sounded drastic—sending a small child to a new country. But Irish parents had done it for three generations now. To them, it was the most loving thing they could do in this oppressive, British-ruled society where opportunities were so scarce.

Especially for women. William hadn't wanted Mamie, or Bessie, or any of his daughters to follow the path of most Irish women. He wanted them to be more than dutiful broodmares for the Catholic church, bearing baby after baby.

Will had tried to give his own wife more freedom, treating her as his partner at the tailoring shop. Still, even she had ten babies in twenty years.

Maybe he was being hypocritical when he lectured Peter Sweeny on the issue.

"If she's in poor health, or struggles with her growing brood, stay off of her," Will had told Peter. Peter looked affronted by the advice. Oh, well.

Will hoped Mamie had found her own gainful employment in America, instead of simply relying on Peter to care for her. He had advised her about that, too.

Will didn't want to send only his daughters to America, though. He was planning to send his younger children, one by one, to Cleveland. The only one who would remain in Ireland with her parents was seventeen-year-old Katie, who had a sweetheart in Roskeen she planned to marry.

Now it was late March, and Bessie was leaving soon. Bridget had finally grown to accept the idea. Still, she cried at night, wondering how Bessie would fare without parents.

"Bessie adores Mamie," Will gently reminded Bridget one night as the children slept and Bridget was steeping tea. Then he proposed the unthinkable. "We could join them someday, a few years down the road."

"You want to return to America?" Bridget said.

"I've thought about it," Will replied honestly.

"We never did get a fair chance to make it there," Bridget said.

That night, in her dreams, Bridget returned to the home of Daniel P. Rhodes on Franklin Avenue in Cleveland, Ohio.

It was the spring of 1866.

That year, Marcus Alonso Hanna was a failing thirty-year-old businessman. He and his wife, Charlotte, lived with Charlotte's parents on Franklin Avenue. Charlotte was pregnant—but that didn't stop Mark from having eyes for the young Bridget McGlynn, who hadn't even completed her teen years yet.

One March day, Mark dropped a heavy stack of clothes into her arms. "You're going to take this suit to the best tailor in town," he told her. "He's one of your people."

"My people?" Bridget repeated.

"He's a young Irish thug they call Tylor Mor," Mark replied. "He has a talent for sewing. All my friends take their garments to him. His shop is down near the river, on the west bank. Take my suit there. I need it in two weeks."

"Yes, Mr. Hanna," Bridget said. Mark scowled at her before she left.

"Come back here immediately," he said. "The man's a gangster, apparently. It's not safe for you to be carousing with him."

Bridget would never forget that initial glimpse she got of Tylor Mor. He was sitting inside his ramshackle wood-framed shop, sewing away. It was an odd sight indeed, to see a man like this sewing.

He had dark copper-tinted hair, the color of a dirty penny, and an even darker beard. He was tall, with defined muscles under his shirt. He looked twice as big as Bridget, who was fine-boned and fair.

Tylor Mor rose to his feet when he heard her coming. "Who goes there?" he asked, until he saw that it was a woman.

He looked up and asked, 'Who are you?"

She stepped in and stood in front of his chair. "You have an accent. You're Irish," she said to him. And he nodded.

"They call me Tylor Mor."

Tylor Mor. "Mor" meant "big" in Gaelic, and "tylor" was a mark of respect. His nickname was "the big man." She could only imagine what he had done to earn such a nickname.

"I'm Bridget," she said, handing him Mark's clothing.

"Bridget? Ah, I must say, I've *never* heard that name before."

She realized he was teasing her. Almost every Irish family had a daughter named Bridget, or Mary, or Catherine.

She glanced at the ceiling above his head, where a giant straw-man mask loomed over his head. Mummering was a peasant tradition at home, in Ireland. Bands of poor Irish dressed up in elaborate costumes made from whatever material they could gather—straw, old sheets, and the like. The mummers went house to house on All Saint's Day and Christmas, demanding whiskey and gin and sweet treats. They then performed the story of Irish heroes, like Brian Boru and King Connor of Ulster.

Bridget could still hear the mummers singing as she watched them from a darkened room.

"Here we stand before your door,
As we stood the year before;
Give us whiskey, give us gin,
Open the door and let us in."

"Are you a mummer?" Bridget asked Tylor Mor, an unconscious smile touching her lips as she recalled one of the few happy memories from her childhood. Then she noticed the stuffed rabbit—a dead rabbit—dangling alongside it.

He looked up at her, seeming drawn in by her blue eyes, her pink lips, and the soft golden-apple color of her hair.

"You want me to be a mummer?" he asked, smiling back at her.

Tylor Mor's assistant piped up from across the shop. "Ah, man, are ya trying to pick her up?"

Bridget blushed bright red and snapped back into formality, unfolding Mark's jacket. She explained the work Mr. Hanna wanted; she threw down the money Mark had given her to pay him.

"I'll be back in a fortnight," Bridget said over her shoulder as she rushed out of the shop. She entered the wan sunlight as she heard Tylor Mor rise to his feet.

"Hey, girl, where are you going?" he called after her.

"Home," she said, looking at her shoes. "I live at the Hanna house."

Tylor Mor nodded, studying her demeanor, looking a bit confused by her timidity and eagerness to leave.

"It won't take a fortnight to sew that man's suit," he said. "Come back in five days, maybe six."

"Very well," she said, and turned, again, to leave. She turned around, and they looked at each other for a lingering moment.

She did return the next week—and again after that, whenever she could find an excuse. When she retrieved the laundry from the line, she looked for falling hems and loose buttons. She took them to Mark's wife, Charlotte, and asking if she could bring them to the tailor. She would nod and dismiss her. No one seemed to notice her frequent absences—except for Mark. By late May, he was sending his manservant to pick up the clothes.

Then, one night in June, while the Rhodeses and the Hannas were hosting a garden party in the yard, Bridget heard a commotion at the door.

> *"Here we stand before your door,*
> *As we stood the year before;*
> *Give us whiskey, give us gin,*
> *Open the door and let us in."*

"What's this?" Daniel Rhodes' voice boomed behind Bridget as she stood in the foyer.

"Did you hire them?" Mrs. Rhodes, entering the foyer with her daughter, Charlotte Rhodes Hanna, exclaimed. "Oh, Daniel, what a wonderful surprise!"

145

It was the middle of the party. The full cast of mummers—King Connor of Ulster, Brian Boru, and the dragon slayer—poured into the foyer. Bridget could see the outline of Tylor Mor behind his bulky costume and straw mask. Tylor Mor whisked her away to dance with him.

"How did you know I live here?" she asked, looking over her shoulder. As he whirled her around, she caught Mark Hanna glaring at them. She panicked a bit, wondering if he knew who this man was. Tylor Mor, the tailor. Bridget didn't even know his real name.

"The Hanna house, aye?" he replied. "You know I would never forget."

She held her breath because she knew something bad was about to happen.

"Alright, that's enough," Mark said, and Daniel Rhodes, his father-in-law, seemed to agree. "Thanks for the show...men. Er, gentlemen."

Tylor Mor squeezed Bridget's hand before he left. "Will," he whispered.

"What?"

"That's my name," he said, as Mr. Rhodes shooed them out the door. "Will Chambers."

After that, Bridget snuck out almost nightly, fully dressed as if it were day. She snuck down to Tylor Mor's apartment on Whiskey Island, where he rented a room in a crumbling shanty house. It was a tiny apartment, but they had privacy there, where they could talk about home. And kiss. Tylor Mor was the first man Bridget kissed willingly, and to her own surprise, she had to fight the urge to press him for more.

Hanna's other maids, as well as the manservant, covered for her—until that awful night she was caught.

This was the part when Bridget always woke up. She had to remind herself she had survived those last few days at the Rhodes mansion. She and Will had left without warning, leaving a letter at the newspaper exposing all of

Hanna's dirty deeds, and then gone home where he'd never find her.

She prayed none of her daughters would ever cross paths with Marcus Alonso Hanna.

✠

Thirty-Three

When Mamie got home from work a few days later, she saw a horse-drawn carriage in front of the saloon. Some sturdy German gentlemen were unloading huge barrels of beer from the carriage. Mamie wanted to leap with joy.

Gehring Brewery had come through with the lager.

"We got it!" she gasped. "Oh, we got our lager at last!"

Kate guided the German men into the saloon.

"We're placing a big new sign in the window," she said, pointing to a hand-painted wood sign the Gehrings provided.

Mamie frowned a bit. "I think that will antagonize the mob," she said.

Kate grinned a little.

"Why else would I put it there?" she asked.

Throughout the evening, Mamie saw people stop to read the peculiar sign in the saloon's window. German beer was outpacing traditional ales in all sectors of America. But the Irish barkeepers, out of stubbornness and fear of the Angle mob, were the last to catch on.

For the first few nights, only the saloon's regular patrons came in to drink, as they did nearly every night. They chatted about work and how summer was just around the corner. But each day, a few new faces appeared at the saloon, asking to try the Gehring lager.

"Word must be traveling fast," Kate said as she poured another glass of lager from the barrels.

When Mamie returned from a long Saturday at the Hanna mansion, a crowd was waiting outside the saloon.

Kate looked red-cheeked and frantic when Mamie found her in the kitchen. "I need your help!" she said. Then, as Mamie grabbed two empty glasses and went to fill them from the barrels, Kate caught her shoulders.

"God has answered my prayers," she said. "We're making money hand over fist. No one will be able to buy us out now."

All Mamie could do was hug her. "Thank God, Kate," she said, for the first time wanting to weep with joy at the sight of the enormous crowd.

Mamie's police officer uncle, Michael McGlynn, was patrolling the Viaduct this evening. He waved to Mamie from the window, and she stepped outside to talk to him.

"You are beautiful, Mary," he said, kissing her hand.

"Thank you, Uncle Michael," she said. "But can you promise me something?"

"What is it?"

"If Austin Carney comes around, please turn him away," Mamie said.

"Austin Carney? He's a respected man in this neighborhood. He—"

"Please, Uncle," Mamie said, shutting down his questioning.

Michael shrugged. "Alright, m'dear," he said, his eyes scanning the Viaduct.

The saloon was rowdy with games of blackjack and arm-wrestling. Most of the patrons were laughing and having fun, and Mamie's cheeks were bright from the heat. Mamie brushed past a table of German men who had sought out this place for its lager.

"I beg your pardon, *schöne Frau*," the man she bumped into said. The other men at the table started laughing.

Mamie frowned when she joined Kate behind the bar. "The German gentleman just called me *schöne Frau*," said. "What's it mean anyway? Some German insult, I suspect?"

Kate patted her arm. "Must you always assume every man you meet is Peter Sweeny?" she said light-heartedly. The sound of Peter's name made Mamie's heart sink. "It means *pretty lady.*"

Mamie broke into a smile.

"It does, doesn't it?" she said, feeling a surge of new energy to keep this saloon going all night long.

✝

Thirty-Four

Across the street, at Seán Fada's inn, Maggie Carney was eating dinner in the hotel lounge with her husband. Her new friend Annie Joyce and Annie's husband-to-be, Patrick Moran, had joined them.

The Carneys didn't have much money by Euclid Avenue standards, but by Angle standards, they lived well. The Carneys were probably the richest young couple at St. Malachi, a point of pride for both her and Austin. They even had the money to dine at a restaurant once a month. In the Angle, the only real restaurant was the lounge of Seán Fada's hotel. The Carneys had trouble enjoying their meal as they watched the scene at Kate Masterson's saloon across the street.

"What nerve she has," Maggie fumed.

Austin watched the people going in and out of the saloon. Many of the patrons were not even Irish.

"She's got gall," he said. "That much is not in doubt."

He thought of how he'd been kicked out of that saloon and how he'd urged his friends to boycott the place. It angered him to see Kate's saloon fuller than ever. He imagined the money passing through Kate's hands, profit made off German beer. She was being rewarded for her traitorous flip to the Gehrings and their lager.

Of course, it had been Austin's suggestion that the Irish ale distributors raise their rates for certain bar owners. He had suggested it at a Town Hall meeting at the LaSalle Club, under the guise of keeping the riffraff out of

151

the Angle and putting the seedy bars out of business. But everyone knew the seedy places were all on Whiskey Island. The Dead Rabbits had pushed the Angle Mob off Whiskey Island twenty years ago. The only places that served alcohol in the Angle cooperated with the Angle Mob. All except Seán Fada's hotel and Dan Dyra's saloon, which had been commandeered by the Mastersons.

They needed to go.

"Kate Masterson is bringing a bunch o' feckin' foreigners into this neighborhood," Austin said. He looked over at Patrick Moran. "Say, Patch, do you want to go over there? We could stir the pot a bit. It's always a jolly time seeing Kate Masterson with her hackles up."

Austin just hoped her brother wasn't there. He'd never deign to admit it, but Patrick Masterson intimidated him. That was why Austin avoided the saloon when Patrick was in town.

Patrick Moran stared into his ale. "I don't want to see the likes of Kate Masterson."

Annie Joyce turned to her fiancé. "You said you don't know her," she said.

"I'm acquainted with the family," Patrick corrected her, clearing his throat. "The Mastersons are from Mulrany."

Patrick had grown up in Mulrany, but when he was a teen, he came to live with an aunt and uncle on the Clew Bay, in the nearby parish of Burrishoole. That was where Annie met him. His relatives' homestead was a short distance from her hometown of Roskeen.

"That saloon oughta be burned to the ground," Austin said. "Smoke the rats out. What do you say, Patch?"

Maggie and Annie laughed, and the men exchanged a knowing look.

Thirty-Five

Patrick Masterson was too superstitious for his own good. He knew it, and his fellow sailors and friends on the Lake Erie ships knew it too. They teased him about it often.

"Curly, what's the weather forecast?" a fellow sailor called to him. They were departing Michigan for Cleveland.

Pat looked up at the expanse of heaven above.

"Red sky at night, sailor's delight. Red sky in morning, sailors take warning," he said, repeating the old adage. He turned back to his friend. "The sky's a bit pink this evenin'. We should make it there alright."

But they knew they had to leave now, while the weather was mild. The Great Lakes states got hit with sporadic snowstorms in the spring. In some years, blizzards had come through as late as mid-April.

Despite the good weather, Pat Masterson had that superstitious inkling again. Something bad was brewing in Cleveland.

Patrick would turn twenty-six this year, and he had called Cleveland home since he was a teenager. The Masterson siblings had left Mulrany after his sixteen-year-old sister, Kate, gave birth to a daughter named Mary Margaret. Kate was married to Molly's father, a young man from their village named Patrick Moran. But when the Morans discovered Kate had been pregnant before the wedding vows, Patrick Moran disappeared. His family said he ran away. The Mastersons knew they were lying.

Patrick Moran leaving Kate humiliated, with a fatherless child, was the force that sent the Mastersons to America. In America, no one had to know that Kate's child was illegitimate—or even that the child was hers at all. She often told nosy strangers that Mary Margaret was her niece or cousin. She called her Mary Margaret Farry, because Farry had been their mother's maiden name.

It hadn't been much of an issue until more people from tiny Mulrany began arriving in Cleveland. From there, rumors flew, and it pushed Kate into a life of isolation—until she found work at Dan Dyra's saloon. Dyra gave her a place to live and her own income. Things were going along fine until Dyra died and the Angle Mob started demanding Kate give them the saloon.

That was when Patrick and Kate drew up the fake will. Black Willie hadn't caught on to their ruse—but it hadn't stopped him from harassing Kate, either. That was the last Patrick knew. He had left days after Christmas.

As Patrick's ship reached Lake Erie, a harsh wind picked up, whipping the ship back and forth.

"Pat!" one of his fellow sailors bellowed over the wind, gripping the ship's steering wheel. "Come here and help me steer!"

As he tried to make his way to the front of the ship, Pat's boot caught on a wooden slat, and he was nearly washed overboard. His hands found the side of the ship and gripped it as hard as they could. But for a moment, he feared for his life. He felt certain he would disappear into the depths of rocky Lake Erie, where he'd be eaten by a Mishipeshu.

The giant underwater lynx. The Ojibwa Indians at their winter quarters in Michigan had told him about it—about the underwater panther who guarded the copper stores in Lake Erie.

He believed in the Mishipeshu—just like he believed in ghosts.

As his fellow sailors struggled to haul him back onto the ship, Patrick swore he saw another figure appear. White and translucent, a bony man with hollow cheeks. A near-skeleton.

In that moment, in his dangerous encounter with Lake Erie, Pat Masterson was certain he saw the ghost of Peter Sweeny.

"What's the matter with you, Masterson?" one of the sailors said with a laugh. "I'll slap the shit outta ya. You look like you saw a ghost."

"You don't even know, man," Patrick replied, trying to wring the water out of his socks.

"You know Curly believes in sea monsters," another sailor said. "Ever since that auld Ojibwa Indian told him about the Lake Erie monster, he's been scared of 'em."

"The Mishipeshu," Patrick corrected them. The Ojibwa insisted the Mishipeshu existed, and Patrick found no reason to doubt them and their millennia of experience on these fearsome lakes.

"Why am I not surprised?" his sailor friend laughed. "When we were at Camp in Detroit, he was on the lookout for the Nain Rouge."

The Nain Rouge was the legendary demon of Detroit. The Demon of the Strait. Patrick believed in him, too.

And now that he'd seen the ghost of Peter Sweeny, Patrick believed with all his soul something evil was brewing in Cleveland. He could feel it in his bones as Lake Erie tossed his ship side to side that night, forbidding even a moment's rest.

Thirty-Six

Mamie was hard at work cooking lunch in the Hanna's kitchen when Mark came up behind her. She startled when she heard his voice, which seemed to amuse him.

"Miss Chambers, I have a favor to ask of you," he said.

"Yes, Mr. Hanna. What is it?"

"I have tickets to see a comedy production at the Cleveland Theater next week," he said. "Charlotte has another social obligation. If you're so inclined, I'd like you to join me."

"Oh, thank you, Mr. Hanna," Mamie said, then thought of Kate, managing the crowd at the saloon alone. "But I couldn't possibly..." She looked down at her plain black skirts; the thick braid she wore to keep her hair out of the food. She didn't belong at the theater.

"I admire your humility, but you'll be joining me," Mark said. "You do have other clothes, I presume?"

"Not many," Mamie said.

Mark looked at her black dress and the apron she was wearing over it, holding his chin. "We'll see what Charlotte's tailor can do," he said. "I'll have him come by to take your measurements."

"I'm not sure any tailor could construct a dress within a week," Mamie replied quietly. She didn't want to sound defiant.

"Ours can," Mark said, sounding a bit insulted.

"Oh, I see. It's just that my father is a tailor, and…"

Mark cut her off. "Your father is a tailor?"

"Yes, sir."

Mamie tried to read the emotion on Mark's face, but she couldn't name it.

"We'll get you some new clothing," Mark said. "You're my favorite servant, Mary. You're punctual, you never perform half-heartedly, and most important of all, you respect me. I like that about you."

Mark delivered on his promises, and the day before the show at the Cleveland Theater, Mamie had a new dress. It was high-end and fashionable, yet modest—a more austere version of something Charlotte Hanna would wear, Mamie surmised.

"I told my dressmaker to tone it down," Charlotte said as she stood behind Mamie in the mirror. "I know you're not accustomed to all those frills. And besides, the etiquette guides say a servant is never to upstage her mistress." Charlotte smiled into the mirror.

Mamie was wise enough to know she should never back-talk her mistress, either, so she simply thanked her for her kindness.

The Cleveland Theater sat at the northwest corner of St. Clair Avenue and West 2nd Street. It was a short carriage ride southeast of the Hanna mansion and the Angle. Mark explained that it was a melodrama theater that also showed comedy productions. Mamie didn't tell him she didn't know what a melodrama was.

"This theater is the brainchild of H.R. Jacobs, the diamond baron," Mark said. The carriage prodded along through the city. "He's building cheap theaters all across the country."

Mamie had an inkling that this theater was considered seedy. Maybe it was a bit low-class for the likes of Mark Hanna and his friends. But as the carriage stopped,

Mamie noticed a deluge of well-dressed society people headed for the front doors.

If this was Mark Hanna's idea of low-class, people from the Angle didn't have a chance of meeting his exacting standards. Mark offered his hand to help Mamie from the carriage.

"Are you going to stay there all night?" Mark joked as she hesitated to take his hand. She finally did, taking an awkward step in her new, unfamiliar clothing.

Mark seemed to know everyone in the crowd. Mamie walked a few steps behind him, knowing it would be scandalous to stay at his side.

"Mark, who is this *morena*?" a man asked, grabbing Mamie's hand and kissing it. "I didn't know you'd developed a penchant for raven-haired ingenues."

"She's my servant," Mark said. "One of them, anyhow."

An usher whisked them away to the second floor, where the highest-paying customers enjoyed the box seats.

"We're meeting a friend of mine, Mr. Carnegie," Mark told her.

He said his name so casually. In the Angle, people spoke Andrew Carnegie's name in whispered tones of reverence. Everyone, even the poorest Irishman, knew Carnegie was the richest man in America.

A few minutes later, the ushers brought in an impossibly short gnome-looking man.

"Sit down," the gnome man said to Mamie when she stood up to greet him, as if she were his employees and not Mark's. "Have you ever discussed politics with a group of fellers before?"

"No," Mamie replied, and the men smirked at her seriousness as well as her Irish accent.

"I am Andrew Carnegie," the short man said as they took their seats. "You are from Ireland. I can hear it in your voice. Which county?"

What did this human gnome know about Ireland? "County Mayo," Mamie replied, keeping her voice even. "On the Clew Bay…"

"I was born in Scotland," Andrew Carnegie said, which caused her to break in a smile of relief. The Scots and the Irish had a special bond in their hatred of the British.

The lights on the stage came on, and the usher shut the heavy velvet curtain to Mark Hanna's box seat.

"An usher will wait outside until the performance is over," Mark explained to Mamie. "We don't take our chances these days, after President Lincoln got shot in a theater."

The lights inside the theater dimmed, and the curtain opened with a great whirl. Mamie didn't grasp much of the humor in the show. She laughed along with Mark and Mr. Carnegie at the appropriate moments.

At last, intermission came. The theater was hot and crowded, and the patrons enjoyed getting a glass of lemonade in the lobby. As always, Mamie lingered behind Mark and his associates.

Then she felt someone grip her shoulder from behind.

"Patrick Masterson!" she gasped, spinning around to meet his green eyes, his wide face. His beard had grown longer since he'd been away in Michigan.

"What the *hell* are you doing here?" she asked as she overcame the shock of seeing him.

"Kate told me where to find you," Patrick replied. "I had to make sure you were faring well with ol' Mark Hanna, he of the wandering eye…"

"Excuse me, who are you?"

Mamie and Patrick both looked at Mark, at a loss for words.

"Do you know him?" Mark asked Mamie.

Mamie panicked, wondering how to explain Patrick's presence here. He wasn't dressed for the occasion, and he stood out like a black sheep in the pasture.

"No," Mamie replied. "I mean, yes, I know him…"

"Do you have a ticket?" Mark asked Patrick.

Patrick looked up at the ornate ceiling. "Do you own this place?"

"If you do not have a ticket, you'll have to wait outside," Mark said. "They are quite serious about theater security since President Lincoln was assassinated in a theater." He looked sideways at Patrick. "Do you require someone to show you out?"

"I'll show myself out," Patrick replied. "But I will wait for the lady outside your house on Franklin Avenue to walk her home."

Mamie had enough time to overcome her mortification on the carriage ride home that night. As the horses clopped to the gates of the mansion, she saw Patrick waiting there, just as he had promised.

"I did not ask him to come here," Mamie said to Mark. "He's the brother of my friend, Kate."

"Should I permit him to escort you home?" Mark asked. He looked supremely annoyed by Patrick's presence outside his home.

"Yes, you may permit him," Mamie said, looking down at her hands.

"I don't want him loitering around my house," Mark said as they exited the carriage. "So tell him he shouldn't make a habit of it."

Mamie waited until Mark was inside to acknowledge Patrick.

"I can't believe you!" she cried, walking at his side. "Coming to the theater like that…"

"I thought it real strange auld Mark is paying for your new clothes, your shiny new boots," Patrick replied.

"And paying for theater tickets. I decided to drop by, in case he was expecting repayment later this evenin.'"

Mamie grit her teeth. "He would never."

"He would, and he has," Patrick replied. "Ask Seán Fada what Mr. Hanna expects from his maids. It ain't just a pressed shirt and a fancy meal."

As Patrick and Mamie approached the saloon, it was so crowded that the German and Polish men were waiting outside. A group of Austin Carney's minions walked by to insult them.

"Feckin' Polacks," they hissed. "Goddamn Krauts. Go back to your own neighborhood, will ya? And take yer smell with ya."

The men, most of whom spoke little English, paid them no mind. From the street, Austin's cronies could see the Polish men laughing and drinking and having a good time. It drove the hecklers crazy with rage.

Seán Fada, the old man who owned the hotel across the street, was sitting in a chair he'd parked outside the saloon.

"Don't worry, Patrick," he said, reaching behind him and pulling out a shotgun. "Kate asked me to stand guard, and I've got the place under control."

Mamie recoiled at the sight of a gun—and so did the men across the street. As long as old Seán Fada was sitting there, brandishing a shotgun, they could yell all they wanted—but they wouldn't dare try to enter the saloon.

The saloon was rowdy with games of arm-wrestling. Most of the patrons were laughing and having fun. But then Mamie noticed a mean-faced man at the end of the bar, with a cap pulled low over his brows, just like Austin Carney.

"This beer ain't that great," he spat at Mamie, throwing some coins down on the bar. "Get me some whiskey."

"Hey, that's no way to talk to a lady," Kate said to him.

"A lady? You fancy yourselves ladies, aye?" the man sneered. "This joint is run by a hoor with a bastard child and her saloon maiden. It's not even yours. It belonged to that old curmudgeon, Dan Dyra."

At that moment, Mamie knew this man had been sent by Austin Carney to bother them. By all indications, it was working. Every eye in the saloon was upon him.

"Hey, shut up, you," a familiar voice boomed behind the man. "No one invited you here."

It was Johnnie, Mamie's in-again, out-again brother who had been missing all week.

The mean-looking man turned his head. "Who the hell are you?"

"I'm the barmaid's brother," Johnnie said, "And I say get out."

"You wanna fight about it, boy?" the man asked, leaping to his feet.

"Ach, sure, I'll fight you," Johnnie said. Now the whole saloon watched.

"Johnnie, no," Mamie said, shaking her head frantically across the bar. But Johnnie ignored her.

"Who wants to put money down?" Johnnie challenged the crowd. "Me versus this cranky arsehole. Take your bets."

Slowly but surely, coins and dollar bills began to pile up on the small blackjack table at the center of the bar. Someone pushed it out of the way, and the older man swung at Johnnie. They tussled for a few minutes, with the men in the bar screaming encouragement and insults.

Mamie had to look away as Johnnie locked his big arm around the man's neck and wrestled him to the ground. The room erupted in cheers, and Austin's friend snatched some money off the table as he ran for the door.

"It was a lucky fluke," he said. "I'll be back. You better sleep with one eye open."

That night, Mamie awoke to the sound of shattering glass. Downstairs, Johnnie's dog barked frantically. She heard footsteps running into the night.

"Annie!" she shouted, jumping out of bed. Mamie surmised she was the one making a ruckus—until she saw the bright flame of Annie's red hair, peeking out from beneath her quilt.

Patrick and Kate jumped out of bed, too. The woody smell of smoke and hot ash wafted up the stairs.

In the darkened saloon, a small fire was burning below the shattered window. Patrick grabbed a pail of water and dumped it on the crackling flames.

"What happened?" Kate gasped. When the flames died, Patrick Masterson picked a charred rag off the floor.

"Looks like a piece of clothing soaked in kerosene," he said. "Someone tried to burn this place down with all us in it. Including a child."

"Good God," Kate said. "These people are hoping to kill us."

✝

Thirty-Seven

"Molly can't keep on livin' here, in this lawless pissant neighborhood," Patrick Masterson said.

Patrick Masterson didn't know Kate and Mamie had already discussed sending Molly away.

"The fumes from smoke kill the little ones first," Patrick continued. "That's why, in a fire, the man of the house often escapes, but the children…"

"I would run through the flames to retrieve Molly before I even thought of rescuing meself," Kate said.

"So would I," Patrick replied. "And that's why I think my niece should be sent away. Not forever, of course—just until that Black Willie finally croaks and Austin Carney gets his due."

In the morning, on her way to work at the Hanna mansion, Mamie spotted the Gehring Brewery delivery cart. Mamie recognized the driver as the delivery man who had brought barrels of beer to the saloon. She hailed him over, and he stopped the horses.

"Do you remember me? I'm from the saloon on the Viaduct," Mamie said.

"Of course, my lady," he said with his guttural German accent.

She produced a few paper bills from the waistband of her skirt—a cut of her own pay. "I need your help," Mamie said. She looked over her shoulder to ensure that nobody from the Angle neighborhood was in sight, watching her.

Leaning inside the carriage, Mamie told the German man their predicament, and their plan.

When she finished, he handed back her money. "Keep it," he said. "We'll meet again tonight."

After dark, Gehring Brewery's carriage pulled up in the narrow alley beside the saloon. The German man unloaded their usual order of lager. Kate manned the bar, serving customers as usual, so as not to throw up red flags.

As quietly as possible, Mamie slipped out the rarely-used back door of the saloon. Mamie held Molly's hand, and in her other hand Molly held her sack of belongings. Molly had finished crying and was ready to face what came next with bravery, as Kate had gently implored of her. When she was sure no one was watching, the German man helped Molly into the delivery carriage.

Patrick Masterson stood guard, helping hoist Mamie into the front seat of the carriage.

"I'll be watching for you at the top of the hill, in an hour or so," he said. His eyes lingered a little too long on hers. "Don't make me come looking for you."

The deliveryman yanked the reins, and the horses began clopping up the hill towards St. Malachi, beginning the bumpy fifteen-minute trip to Jay Avenue.

Mamie looked for the lace curtains and the distinct arches of a German Christian home. When she spotted the house, she motioned for the deliveryman to halt.

Mamie walked Molly to the front door. She knocked once, and Agnes opened it.

"Hello again, cousin!" she said, and she knelt down to greet Molly.

"Molly, this is my cousin Agnes, who will care for you," Mamie said, biting her lip. Mamie wasn't sure how Molly would receive it.

"But only for a little while," Molly said bravely. "Just until the Angle Mob is off our backs."

Agnes and Mamie smiled nervously.

165

"Molly, why don't you put your things in the loft?" Agnes suggested. Molly obeyed, bounding up the stairs to the loft jutting out over the kitchen.

"The child will be safe with me," Agnes said. "Jay Avenue is removed from the Angle. That's why I chose to live here. We're just out of reach of the Angle Mob, and the gossip mill. Kate can come here when she likes, but I advise her to be discreet."

"We owe you the world, Agnes," Mamie said.

"Think nothing of it," Agnes replied. "I'm grateful for the company."

As he'd promised, Patrick was waiting at the top of the hill near St. Malachi, where Pearl Street and the Viaduct met. As she drew closer to him, she noticed he was holding a small bunch of spring blooms.

"For you," he said, handing her the flowers with a dramatic flourish.

"Oh, thank you!" she cried, lifting the flowers to her nose. The sweet scent momentarily overcame the ever-present stink of horse manure and refuse on Pearl Street. "Where did you buy them?"

He winked at her. "I picked them from the garden outside the rectory," he said. She laughed, realizing she should have known better. "I thought you deserved a little something for being such a loyal friend to me sister."

"Kate deserves all my loyalty," Mamie said, lifting her chin. "She housed me when she wasn't obligated, and never asked for a dime of rent. She knew I didn't deserve what Peter Sweeny did to me."

"Kate has been in your shoes," Patrick said as they rounded the corner. He offered Mamie his arm again, as he did when he walked her home from the Hanna house.

But they had reached the corner at precisely the wrong time. The LaSalle Club was emptying at this hour, when it had just become solidly dark outside. A large group was walking directly toward Patrick and Mamie—and in

166

the thick of it, she spotted the Carneys and Patrick Moran, as well as Annie Joyce.

"Well, well, well. Would you look at this," Austin Carney said, knowing that Mamie could hear him. "Where do you suppose she's coming from? Cassie Chadwick's brothel?"

Cassie Chadwick was a notorious Cleveland brothel madame and con artist who had supposedly been jailed dozens of times. As the group got closer, Patrick sucked back a mouthful of saliva and spat on Austin's newly polished boots.

"You dog!" Maggie Carney shouted.

"Ah, shut up, you hag," Patrick shot back. "And keep that mouth closed. You got teeth on ya like a Donegal graveyard."

Mamie couldn't help breaking into nervous laughter.

"What are you laughing at?" she said. "Should you not be at home tending to Kate's bastard child while she keeps bar?"

"Annie Joyce oughta ask her husband who sired that bastard child, about twelve years ago in County Mayo," Patrick said, shrugging confidently as the two groups passed each other. This time Annie Joyce whipped around and began cursing at him.

"That's a lie!" she yelled after Patrick, who didn't turn around. "Don't you dare speak ill of my husband ever again, you filthy swine! You son of a..."

Patrick laughed. "Ah, that's when you know you've hit on a blinding truth," he said. Mamie glanced behind her. Annie had stopped walking and was now weeping as her husband-to-be stood beside her, coaxing her to keep walking.

"Tell me again it's a lie," Annie sniffled. "Please, Patch."

Patrick Moran watched Mamie and Patrick Masterson continue down Washington Avenue with a cold stare in his eyes, a stare that all but said he wished to kill them.

✝

Thirty-Eight

A few days later, Mamie's uncle, Cleveland police officer Michael McGlynn, was summoned to the saloon for the second time in just a few months. This time, his niece had pleaded with him to investigate the arson at the saloon.

His partners, also first-generation Irish men who had the good fortune to land jobs as police officers, didn't even want to go. Police officers born and raised in the Angle knew better than to look too deeply into crimes that implicated the Angle Mob. If they pursued the Angle Mob too doggedly, they became targets—and their position on the Cleveland Police force, with its reluctance to admit Irish men and other Catholic immigrants, was precarious enough.

"What do we care about a burning rag through a window?" Officer McGlynn's partner, Officer Whelan, asked. "Sounds like the nightly Angle mayhem. Who are these women, anyway?"

"One is my niece," Michael replied gruffly. "She's my sister's daughter."

"I didn't know you had a sister."

"Yes, I have—had—several. This one returned to Ireland many years ago," Michael said. "The police couldn't help her, either—not that she asked. She was a maid at Mark Hanna's house and he was all the time violatin' her…"

He stopped himself. And in the meantime, his partner changed the subject.

"I do suspect this was run o' the mill, drunken shenanigans at this establishment," Officer Whelan said as they approached the saloon.

Michael knew that would be the Cleveland Police force's conclusion in the end, but for now, he prepared to go to his niece's saloon and take a report.

When they arrived, Michael's partner refused to go inside. "I'm going to look around the property," he told Michael. "They said someone smashed the window, aye? I'll look around the back; see if I spot some footprints."

Officer Whelan paced around outside the saloon, walking the perimeter a time or two. He looked in the small yard behind the saloon, which was patchy and muddy this time of year. There were no footprints.

As Officer Whalen rounded the corner, he ran into a well-groomed woman and several male companions. He had seen this woman before, at St. Malachi and at the LaSalle club, always surrounded by a group of friends. But he had never spoken to her until now.

"Officer, what's going on in there?" the woman asked, looking wide-eyed with concern. Too concerned, really. Even Officer Whalen could tell she was just being nosy; digging him for information for the gossip mill.

"We're investigating an arson," he replied tersely, declining to elaborate.

"Oh," the woman said, rolling her eyes a bit. "Don't you think that madwoman Annie Kilbane started it? She's set fires before. Last winter, she set a pile of newsprint on fire in the alley for no good reason."

"I have no idea, miss." Officer Whalen glanced at the man next to her. "Missus. Whoever."

"And you know Kate Masterson loves to make a spectacle of herself," the woman continued. "Always the victim, she is. But don't you think it's odd that in all the incidents 'round here—Mamie's husband-to-be going missing, Mad Annie found bleeding on a pile of snow, the fire—Kate is the only common thread? She's the only witness."

"We're aware."

"And now something else has come up," the man said, with his best gravely-serious expression. "You know Kate's child? She's gone. No one who frequents this saloon has seen her all week; she's simply vanished."

"The child is missing?" Officer Whalen repeated, looking alarmed.

"Yes. And Kate didn't go looking for help," the woman said. "I tried to broach the issue with Father Molony months ago. I said Kate is a real scourge in this neighborhood. I tried to get him to talk some sense into her, for her own sake. But he wouldn't do anything about it. So perhaps you can."

The woman reached into a satchel she was carrying and produced a few dollar bills.

"Please do something about that menace to our good neighborhood," the woman said.

Officer Whalen stared at the bills for a minute, turning them over in his hands. Then, slowly, he nodded, and stuffed the bills in the pocket of his uniform.

✠

Thirty-Nine

Now that coal season was over, Johnnie Chambers was hurting for money.

Johnnie won fights regularly, on Saturday nights in Whiskey Island's roughest saloons. It covered his rent to Uncle Joseph, but it didn't cover everything. Johnnie, who had just turned sixteen, had yet to commit his first robbery.

His friends wanted him to rob the operator of the Lake Erie steamboat that ferried immigrants from Buffalo—the same steamboat Johnnie had arrived on months earlier.

"You want us to start a chapter of the Dead Rabbits, but you're scared to rob the steamboat fare collector?" his friend demanded as they sat on the bluffs above Whiskey Island. "You're too big for your britches sometimes, Johnnie Chambers."

"I ain't scared," Johnnie said. "I'll do it Friday, just you wait."

If there really was a hell, Johnnie wondered if he was going there. When he was alone on the upstairs floor of Uncle Joseph's house, he knelt and said a prayer, pre-emptively asking Jesus to forgive him.

He thought of the saints, too. St. Michael, who protected soldiers in battle. Johnnie wasn't one of those, but he felt like one sometimes. Who was the patron saint of thieves?

Last night, Johnnie and one of his friends had sat on the bluffs and watched the ferry come in, observing the immigrants with their pitiful sacks of belongings. They looked Eastern European, and they spoke a language Johnnie didn't recognize.

"I ain't gonna rob the penniless," Johnnie said. "What's the use? They have no money anway."

"Not them, you dolt," his companion said. "Rob the ferry operators. They have the money, and you know they like to gyp people, eh? Whenever they get immigrants who don't know any better, they charge them to unload their luggage. It's a bit o' cosmic justice."

Johnnie heaved a sigh, watching the ferry operators demand money from the Eastern Europeans disembarking the boat. They formed a human fence with their arms, preventing the immigrants from leaving until they paid the baggage fee—and if they didn't, they had to go on without their luggage, empty-handed in the New Country.

Johnnie was hungry. He had no money for food left. So he stood in the dense trees near the docks and watched the ferry chug into the port.

He had a pocketknife that he planned to brandish when the time was right. For now, he watched the immigrants paying their fare, and waited.

When the moment was right, he sprung.

"Your money or your life!" he was prepared to cry from behind the ferry operator's back, with the knife to his jugular vein.

But the second he went to pull his knife, he heard a familiar voice, a curious child's voice that sounded confused and frightened.

"Johnnie?"

The sound of his own name made his heart jump into his throat, and he thrust the knife back into his pocket. Then he locked eyes with his seven-year-old sister, Bessie.

"Johnnie?" Bessie repeated, looking astonished to see him here. "Is that really you?"

"Bessie!" Johnnie cried, rushing to embrace them. He felt shame wash over him when he noticed his sister—

and the adult couple chaperoning her—recoil from his disheveled and dirty appearance.

"Johnnie Chambers?" the man, his former neighbor from Roskeen, said, looking bewildered. "My God, it is you! Your hair hasn't been shorn in a while, eh? How did you know we were on our way?"

"I like to watch the ferry arrive," Johnnie replied. It wasn't a lie. "When I saw you were on it, I ran down the hill."

He nodded to the hill that rose above the sands of the Lake Erie shoreline.

He prayed that none of his fellow hoodlums were watching this, waiting for him to pony up the stolen fare. He stretched his hand out to Bessie, who still looked cautious. She took it.

"Come on, now, sister," he said. "I'll lead you home."

Forty

Mamie knew from reading her mother's letter that Bessie was arriving soon. She knew Ma expected Bessie to live with one of her brothers and their wives—Uncle Michael or Uncle Dominick. Tom, of course, was already living with her bachelor Uncle Joseph. Or, if it weren't too much imposition, could Bessie live with the married couple, Peter and Mamie Sweeny? Ma assumed they owned their own home by now.

Ma's letter had assumed so many things. She assumed that Mamie was happily married to Peter. She congratulated her on the wedding, giving her regrets that she and Da couldn't be there. She assumed Mamie was happy and adjusting well in America.

Mamie had wept as she read it a second time, in privacy, away from Kate and Mad Annie. She still didn't have the heart to respond. She knew she had to write back, to let Ma and Da know that her siblings had made it there safe.

Mamie made a habit of watching the street from the window, expecting that Bessie would appear any day now. But she wasn't prepared for the moment she actually saw her, her chestnut brown braids swinging with each step.

"Mamie!"

"Bessie!" she cried, dropping the ladle she held and rushing over to embrace her. To her relief, Bessie's cheeks looked full and healthy, and she wore clean clothes. The journey hadn't taken too great a toll on her.

Then she glanced at Johnnie, musty and streaked with dirt.

"John Chambers, where have you been?"

"Ach, I'm sorry, Mamie," he said, removing his dirty cap and holding it over his heart. "I forgot to knock."

"I'll deal with you later," she said, as Kate entered the saloon.

"Who is this darling lass?" Kate asked, kneeling down to Bessie's level.

"Kate, this is my sister Elizabeth," Mamie said. "But we call her Bessie."

"Well, I'm Catherine Masterson, but people call me Kate. I have a daughter a wee older than you, but she isn't here now. This is my saloon."

"Does Johnnie live here?" Bessie asked.

"Nah," Kate said. "Johnnie will tell you about his adventures here and what he's been doing since he got off the boat."

"Making my own way in the world, that's what," Johnnie replied. "Don't get used to seeing me here. I'll be leavin' again soon. I only wanted to lead me sister home."

Johnnie leaned in to Mamie. "I told Bessie about Peter Sweeny on the walk here," he whispered. "I don't think anyone is missing him."

Mamie nodded. "Let's take your belongings upstairs, Bessie." Bessie would have to sleep in the trundle bed that had belonged to Molly.

As Bessie bounded upstairs, Johnnie said to Kate, "What's this I heard about a fire?"

Kate peered at him. "Why do you ask?"

"I know some folks who might exact revenge."

Mamie overheard them talking as she came back downstairs. She raised her eyebrows. "You're in too deep, Johnnie," she said. "Why don't you take off your shoes and rest a while before you plot your revenge?"

"Fine. But I can't stay," Johnnie repeated. "It's dangerous. For me as well as you, Mamie."

He thought of his friends, who had been waiting for him to return with the ferry operator's money tonight. As his sister boiled bath water over the stove, Johnnie drew the curtains, just in case anyone was watching him through the window.

Forty-One

The 1888 Republican National Convention began on June nineteenth. Mark Hanna wasn't there. But as the Republicans gathered in Chicago to choose their nominee, Mark monitored the convention via the newspaper.

Mark's support—not to mention his influence and money—went to John Sherman, the Ohio Senator. Mark had helped put him in office, and he wanted to see an Ohioan win the presidency. It would bolster Mark's reputation as Kingmaker of the Republican Party.

Mark had grown up in a small Western Ohio town, working for his father's grocery store. He sometimes had to sit back and marvel at his own stupendous rise to the highest ranks of power and influence in Cleveland.

Mark's son, Dan Hanna, was the one to deliver the news: John Sherman had lost to a former Senator from Indiana, Benjamin Harrison.

"Even worse," Dan said, "Sherman is claiming Russell Alger paid the Southern delegates to switch their votes from Sherman to Harrison at the last minute. The entire convention was a horrible mess."

Russell Alger was a Michigan millionaire who had also run for the Republican nomination. He had finished in third place.

Mark allowed himself to fume for a few days, before he summoned Dan to discuss what they'd do next.

"There's no point in playing the sore loser," Mark told Dan. Daniel Hanna was only eighteen, but he was already grooming for life as a Renaissance man: a life of politics, business, law, journalism.

"We've got to get the Democrats out of power, one way or another. They're horrible for business interests," Mark said. "Besides, if Harrison can't pull it off, I have my nominee for 1892—William McKinley. Mark my words, I'll make him president one day."

Dan nodded as they lit cigars, sitting in the parlor room of Mark Hanna's mansion. Dan grew up in this house. They moved in when he was a toddler, after a brief stint living with Daniel Rhodes, Dan's grandfather and Mark's father-in-law. Dan didn't know much about the time his parents spent living with the Rhodeses, since he was too young to remember. All he had heard was that it was a dark blemish on Mark's otherwise charmed life. Those hadn't been good years—not for business, and not in his marriage...

"So what is the strategy against Grover Cleveland this time?" Dan asked. "Are we trotting out the bastard son again?"

"No," Mark replied, shaking his head. "We need to drop the issue of Cleveland's bastard son."

"Why?"

Mark moved his chair a little closer to Dan, drawing his son in, letting him know he was serious. Very serious.

"Dan, you're eighteen now, and newly married yourself," Mark said. "The time is right to tell you some things you don't know about me. I'm coming to you as a man."

Dan drew his fist to his mouth, as if he were about to chew his fingernails. "Go on," he said.

"Grover Cleveland is hardly the only politician with a sordid affair or an illegitimate child in his past," Mark said. "Some of my biggest donors in Cleveland have paid bribe money to mistresses. Or have had their former maids come pounding on their doors, demanding they acknowledge a child."

"What does this have to do with you?" Dan replied.

"Dan, years ago…before you were even born…I had an affair with a young Irish woman who worked at your grandfather's house," Mark said.

Dan's mouth settled into a straight line. He looked disappointed, but not surprised. "An affair?" he replied. "Was she…willing?"

"She never resisted me," Mark said. His back straightened a little, revealing his profound discomfort with that statement. "She wept a bit about it, because you know what a big to-do those Catholic girls make of their virginity." He rolled his eyes. Dan snorted a semi-laugh.

"Anyway—and don't you dare tell your mother or sister this—that woman disappeared without warning one day," Mark said. "I never saw her again. I think I know who she left me for, though. He was my tailor. And his name was Chambers. And that maid I hired a few months ago…Mary Chambers…"

Dan shook his head in disbelief. "Don't say what I think you're about to say," he interrupted.

But Mark proceeded anyway.

"When they left, they gave a letter to the newspaper accusing me of outrageous deeds. It was slander, really. They said I had attempted to take her against her will, that I was an adulterer and a liar. I had to bribe the paper to burn it. And then I bought the newspaper a few years later, just to make sure."

Dan said slowly, *"Did they burn it?"*

Forty-Two

Mamie decided to enroll her sister Bessie in school. She was just old enough to start attending the girl's school run by the Ursuline nuns, which was down the street from the saloon.

Mamie worried about how Bessie would fare at the Catholic girls' school. But the Mother who ran the place had a reputation as a kind and loving woman, even if many members of her order were not.

"You'll like school," Mamie reassured Bessie as they walked hand-in-hand down the Viaduct. They were careful to sidestep the muck and piles of horse manure. Summer was coming, and the increasing temperatures made the stench even worse than usual. "You enjoyed attending school at home in Roskeen, right, Bessie?"

Formal education in Ireland was barely organized. The British Penal Code had forbidden anyone to teach the Irish how to read and write until a generation ago. But during Mamie's childhood, a little parish schoolhouse sprung up next to their church. The children of Roskeen received religious instruction and learned to read and write. Mamie hoped St. Malachi's girls' school would be much the same.

"I do like school," Bessie said, scuffing her boots in the dust. "Mamie, why doesn't Kate's lass go to school?"

Mamie cringed. "Molly learned at home," she said. And it was true—in fact, Molly was a strong reader and could compose simple sentences on her own. But Kate, with good reason, didn't trust the nuns, and she still refused to attend mass at St. Malachi.

"But since I work, I can't teach you," Mamie said as they approached the school house. "The Good Mother and the nuns will teach you, and you'll make some friends as well."

School was in session as Mamie and Bessie entered the building. Based on the time, Mamie knew they were scheduled to break. When she saw the girls pile out of the building, she took Bessie's hand and led her inside the classroom.

The girls in the schoolyard stared at Bessie.

"Hello," Mamie said, giving a little curtsy of respect to the Ursuline nun in the doorway. The nun stared at her with cold, judging eyes.

"You're that saloon madame," she said.

"I'm not the madame," Mamie stuttered, taken aback. "But I help my friend with the operations."

"Catherine Masterson, yes," the nun replied. She looked down at Bessie. "Who is this?"

"This is Elizabeth Chambers," Mamie said. "I would like to enroll her in school."

The nun studied Bessie's features. The long, reddish-brown braids, the full rosy cheeks, the slight pudginess of her pre-womanhood body. "Is she yours?" the nun asked, her voice sharp.

Mamie's heart thudded. "Pardon me, sister?"

"Is. She. Yours?" the nun repeated.

Mamie would be twenty-one in mid-May, far too young to have a child who was school age. Most Irish women got married and had their first babies between age eighteen and twenty. Only the most desperately poor, rural Irish women married and gave birth in their mid-teens. Even that was becoming rare—unless they were in a situation like Kate's, where they fell pregnant before the marriage vows.

Mamie realized this nun assumed she had the same history as Kate, that she was the mother of an illegitimate child.

"She's my sister," Mamie said, pursing her lips to contain her anger. She touched Bessie's shoulder.

"Bessie, what's your ma's name?" Mamie asked.

"Bridget Chambers," Bessie said evenly.

"And your da?"

"William Chambers."

"And who am I?"

"My sister Mamie."

Just then, an older nun emerged from the classroom. "What's going on here?"

"I'd like to enroll my *sister* in school," Mamie said.

The older nun looked at the younger one. "Sister, you are dismissed."

"I am Mother Berchmans," the older nun said to Mamie. "I am happy to enroll this child in school."

"Thank you," Mamie said. "She is my younger sister, and she's newly arrived from County Mayo."

"You're the one living at the saloon a few houses away," Mother Berchmanns said. "Father Molony has spoken of you. I only wish you might convince Catherine Masterson to send her child to school."

"Kate's a stubborn one."

The nun bent down to Bessie. "What is your name?" she asked.

"Elizabeth Chambers. But people call me Bessie."

"Bessie Chambers, you begin school tomorrow."

Mamie felt her lips twitching into a smile, thankful that this old nun believed her, instead of barraging her with cruel questions. "Thank you, Mother," she said with genuine relief.

Forty-Three

Mamie still rose early to make oatmeal for the hungry in the Angle, and now she had Bessie to assist her. They worked side-by-side in the kitchen. The morning after their visit to the girls' school, a little girl about Bessie's age visited with her mother, looking ashamed as they took their bowls.

"You're my new classmate," the girl said to Bessie. "I saw you at the schoolhouse yesterday, no?"

"Yes, Bessie will attend school," Mamie said.

"Well, if you don't mind...please don't tell the girls you see me here," the girl said. "Not everyone's as kind as you."

Mamie walked Bessie to school before she went to work at the Hanna house. She had to trust Bessie to make the short walk home by herself, since the school was down the street. Still, Mamie worried.

"When the nuns dismiss you, come home immediately," Mamie said, leaning down to help Bessie lace up her boots. "Don't stop to talk to anyone. Don't accept an invitation to go anywhere." She thought of what had happened to Molly.

Kate Masterson went to visit Molly on Jay Avenue every few days. The walk was quick, especially now that winter had passed. One morning, Agnes greeted Kate at the door, looking anxious.

"Can Molly stay alone while we go to the Pearl Street market?" she said hurriedly.

184

"The Pearl Street market? I don't need anything there," Kate replied.

"Shh," Agnes said. "Please, Kate. Will you do me just this favor?"

Kate nodded, and she explained to her daughter where they were going. "Can you wait here?" Kate asked.

"Yes, ma," Molly replied, giving her a tight hug. "But hurry back soon."

When Agnes and Kate had rounded the corner on Pearl Street, Agnes broke the silence.

"The priest with whom I had an indiscretion goes to the market every week," she explained. "I need to see him one last time. I want him to acknowledge he was just as guilty as I."

Kate didn't doubt Agnes' motive. However, it didn't prevent her from being annoyed.

"Girl, that's why you dragged me here?" Kate complained.

Kate could smell the market already, with its rich blend of sweet pastries, herbs, and roasted meats. It almost blocked out the stench that emanated infernally from the streets. Immigrants from the four corners of Europe sold their wares here.

"My priest friend and I, we used to walk to this market together," Agnes said. For a moment she looked wistful. "But it was just a ruse, of course. We weren't shopping. We would instead walk down to Euclid Avenue, Millionaire's Row, where of course no one would recognize us..."

"I made the mistake of asking him to walk with me to the beach one day. I just wanted to see the water, and what it looks like away from the stench," she said. "But it wasn't far enough from St. Malachi, and we were found out."

Kate scanned the crowd for a priest in his black stole.

"No priests," Kate said, her voice flat but relieved.

Agnes said nothing as they went about their shopping for herbs and vegetables. As they waited in line for fresh butter, a ruckus broke out across the street.

Kate grabbed Agnes' shoulder, scaring her. "Look!" she exclaimed. "Priests!"

Men in black stoles, four or five that Kate counted, were gathered around the entrance to Cassie Chadwick's brothel.

Agnes, usually calm and collected, ducked behind Kate. "There he is!" she gasped.

Kate slipped her hand around hers. "If you wish to confront him, here is your chance."

He was berating a group of prostitutes, who hissed and sneered at him. These weren't the penniless women of the night that sold their bodies in Public Square. Those prostitutes often had missing limbs, and ugly, gnarled teeth. These women were painted with cosmetics and wore their hair in ornate curls.

Without another word, Agnes stalked the priest like a stray cat pouncing on a mouse.

"No peace for the wicked!" the priests shouted at a throng of prostitutes trying to enter its large, ominous-looking door.

"Casting stones, are we?" Agnes said. The young priest turned on his heel.

His eyes widened, and he stepped away from the small contingent of priests.

"Agnes!" he exclaimed. "Why are you here?"

"The same reason I always come here," she said, lifting her wicker basket with a defiant look on her face. "But food's a bit harder to come by these days. I go hungry often."

"Agnes, I have nothing more to say to you," he said. His eyes were the clearest blue, like drops of dye in water. He looked away.

"It looks like you have much to say about sexual sin, after all," Agnes said, observing the priests howling at the group of brothel girls.

"They're whores."

"So was Mary Magdalene, aye?"

"Please leave me," the priest said, and Agnes turned away, indicating to Kate it was time to go. But as they left, Agnes slipped her hand into her apron and produced a few coins. She handed them to one of the brothel girls who sat with her chin resting on her knees outside the door, looking despondent. She appeared no older than sixteen.

"Take this and go home for the night," Agnes said, dropping the coin as the girl extended her palm. She looked astonished.

"Thank you," she whispered.

"Ah, that's chump change, you idiot girl," a harsh, grating voice snapped at the young prostitute. "Get inside and get to work."

Kate looked up at the owner of the voice. Their eyes met. Kate recognized the woman instantly. And in an instant, she knew the woman recognized her, too.

It was Marie St. Jean, the saloon singer that had lured away Mamie's husband-to-be. At least, Kate *thought* it was Marie. But she wasn't certain, because this woman had a different accent: harsh, nasal, and definitely not French. She had a different appearance—she looked hardened, cruel, and anything but beautiful. Her cosmetics were garish. She wore her hair in a severe chignon, and it looked frizzy and matted around her temples.

She had the look of the devil in her eyes.

"Hey!" Kate called after her, but in an instant the woman was gone.

✝

Forty-Four

Kate didn't tell Mamie what she'd seen—or thought she'd seen—at the Pearl Street Market that day. Mamie looked distracted anyway, standing at the bar with a pen in hand, her eyebrows furrowing as she wrote a letter.

"Is that for your ma?" Kate asked.

"Yes," Mamie said with a sigh. "I would give anything to talk to her today. Mr. Hanna is acting strange."

"Strange? How?" Kate's heart sank. Taking advantage of their maids was a status symbol among rich men. They bragged to each other about their ability to coax sexual services from the women they hired—even the foreign women who were Catholic and raised in religious households. Mamie, with her gentle demeanor, was exactly the type of woman they preyed upon.

"I would like to think he's nervous about the presidential election," Mamie replied. "He's heavily invested, you know."

"Yes, I believe everyone knows that about Mr. Hanna," Kate said grimly. "Well, when you finish your letter, give it to me and I'll post it for you."

"Thank you, Kate."

Kate trudged upstairs, feeling weary and demoralized. She kept telling herself she hadn't seen what she'd thought she'd seen at the brothel. That the prostitute outside Chadwick's brothel couldn't possibly be the woman who had visited this saloon months ago. And yet...

"What's the matter with you, Kate?" Patrick asked. He was buttoning up his sailor uniform in front of the mirror, because he was leaving again tonight to sail to Michigan. He never knew when he would be back. It could be ten days, it could be twenty. It all depended on the weather—which, now that it was summer, was liable to change at any minute. It was oppressively humid this week, which told Kate a week of storms was on the horizon.

Although she had promised herself she wouldn't tell anyone, Kate blurted out, "I saw that woman today. The woman who disappeared with Peter Sweeny."

Pat lost interest in the mirror and whirled around to her. "Where?"

"Outside Cassie Chadwick's brothel," Kate said. "Except she's not French, and she's no saloon singer on Mississippi steamboats. She looks like a dime-a-dozen *hoor*, and a mean one at that. She speaks with one of those horrid Yankee accents. Like the New Yorkers when we got off the boat from Ireland."

"That's because she *is* a Yankee," Mad Annie piped up.

Mad Annie was kneeling on the floor of the attic, folding laundry. Her outbursts were less frequent now. Kate had taught her how to properly sort, wash, and hang the laundry. She wondered if Annie might be functional enough to get a job as a laundress somewhere.

Somewhere the master of the house wouldn't violate her, Kate thought to herself. And in this neighborhood, there was a fat chance of that. Austin Carney had shown the men they could molest Annie and no one would believe her.

"Have you seen her recently?" Kate asked, on the off chance Annie knew what she was talking about.

"No. Not since I've stopped roaming the streets at night," Annie replied. "Her story about being a saloon

189

singer is just that—a story. She's a con woman, like Cassie Chadwick."

Patrick sat on the bed on the men's side of the attic, resting his chin in his palm.

"I never told you, Kate, because I never imagined she would resurface," Patrick said, "But after that night Peter went missing, I felt certain I had seen that woman before."

"Where?"

Patrick's eyes wandered out the window. "I swore I've seen her at Satter's Tavern in the French Creek District, in the wilderness. That's where my shipmates always want to stop on the way home. I would bet my summer salary it was her. I just wonder how she goes between here and there, from the wilderness to the city."

Kate looked at Patrick. "Want to do some sleuthing?"

"I'm not patronizing no brothel," Patrick scoffed.

"I wouldn't ask you to," Kate said. "But you might sniff around Satter's Tavern. See if the people there know something."

Patrick got a twinkle in his eye. When he had seen Mamie collapse in the street that morning, wailing for her husband-to-be, he developed a hatred for Peter Sweeny that had never died. Even if Sweeny himself was dead.

"Sure," he said. "I'll do what I can."

Forty-Five

Seán Fada, the owner of the hotel across from the saloon, knew his days were numbered. He was well into his seventies, and his body was failing him. For a man who had survived the Irish famine and spent years toiling on the railroads before buying this hotel, he knew he'd lived an unusually long and lucky life.

Still, he felt there was so much left to do before his inevitable death. He had so many stories to tell. So many secrets he needed to share before they died with him.

So he made a list of things he wanted—nay, needed—to do before he passed. And the first thing he did was ask Mary Chambers to come see him after she left the Hanna mansion for the day.

"Sir, you wanted to see me?" Mamie asked, entering his empty hotel lobby shortly after dinnertime. Her cheeks looked rosy from her daily commute in the Ohio sun, and a few golden streaks had formed at the crown of her auburn hair. She had the same sad blue eyes that Seán Fada had seen many times before.

Seán Fada realized Mamie Chambers looked like a perfect composite of her mother and father.

"I know your parents," he said frankly, diving right into the heart of the matter. "It took me all these months to realize who they were, and who you are. There are many Chambers families in Cleveland. But certainly you belong to a line of Chamberses I shall never forget."

Mamie sat down in the chair across from him, realizing this conversation was taking a different direction than she'd anticipated. "I thought you were going to offer me a job cooking in the hotel kitchen," she said, voice flat.

"No," Seán Fada replied. "But perhaps I should, 'cause I shan't be running this place much longer. I believe I will depart soon for a world beyond this one."

She fluttered her eyes and let them close a moment, indicating she already knew he was dying.

"How did you know my ma and da?" she asked.

"Your father saved my hotel from the other William Chambers," Seán Fada said. "Black Willie."

Mamie waited for him to continue on, and he did.

"Your Da, we called him Tylor Mor," Seán Fada said. "It means..."

"The Big Man," they said in unison.

"What did he do to save the hotel?" Mamie asked.

"His gang fought a notorious street fight against Black Willie and his gang," Seán Fada said.

"Gang?" Mamie said, her eyes growing rounder.

"Oh, yes. He never told you? Your father was a Dead Rabbit."

Mamie almost choked on her own breath, thinking of the America Wake in Roskeen. She thought of how her father had beckoned Johnnie to come to him. *"What did I say about that Dead Rabbit talk?"*

"The two gangs clashed at the top of the hill above Whiskey Island," Seán Fada said. "As the fight culminated, the two men named William Chambers approached each other, and legend has it that after Black Willie fell to the ground, your father pinned down Black Willie's hand and put a knife through it. 'Next time, it will be your heart,' is what he told him, allegedly. I wasn't there. But I thought it showed your da had some compassion for people, even for his enemies...even for Black Willie."

192

"Black Willie and his men left Whiskey Island," Seán Fada continued. "They never tried to take another business there by force, because they couldn't. They were afraid. They also left certain businesses here in the Angle alone, including this hotel, and Dan Dyra's saloon. They wanted them—oh, how they wanted them!—but they knew they couldn't touch any business owners aligned with the Dead Rabbits. Even after the day Tylor Mor disappeared."

"What happened?"

"One night, your mother and father came in here to this hotel," Seán Fada said. "It was a dark night in the fall—very cold. Your mother was soaking wet. 'She tried to drown herself in the Cuyahoga,' Tylor Mor told me. 'Get me a room, will you, Seán Fada, and don't say a word—and I'll make sure you're repaid manyfold.' That was what he told me. I sent them upstairs, and in the morning, they were gone. But your father kept this word. The Dead Rabbits have helped protect me from the Angle Mob ever since, and they've never laid a hand on me."

"I intend to keep it that way," Seán Fada said. "Even after I depart this world. I'm to write my will soon. You and Kate will surely be in it. But no matter what becomes of me, just promise you won't let the Angle Mob take this hotel, as long as you have anything to do with it."

"I promise," Mamie said. "God bless you, Seán."

As Seán Fada sat down that night, fountain pen in hand, to start writing his will, he thought about how much he didn't tell Mamie Chambers. His conscience ate at him as he sat as his desk, wondering what he would want to know if he were a person in her shoes: a young bride-to-be in America, awakening to find her future husband...gone.

As Seán Fada wrote that night, he died, slumped over his desk with his pen still in hand. He had written letters to his friends and family, as well as a partial will. But God took him before he finished all of it.

Kate Masterson was the first person to arrive when she heard the hotel guests in the streets, shouting that the hotelier was dead. In a furtive move, she quickly folded up the letters strewn before the dead man, still seated in his chair.

No matter what happened next, his secrets would be safe with her.

Forty-Six

Mamie's mother, Bridget Chambers, was starting to worry when summer came and she hadn't heard a word from any of her children in America. She shouted with joy the day the mail carrier arrived at her cottage in Roskeen.

Baby Norah was a little older than six months now. She was smiling and cooing and scooting herself around the cottage on her belly. The sun shone between intervals of rain, and the wildflowers were blooming in the hills. To Bridget Chambers, it felt like a good day. She tore into the letter as she held Norah in the crook of her other arm, breathing a sigh of relief when she recognized Mamie's careful handwriting.

But her joy didn't last long. Slowly, her hands began to shake a little, and her already fair skin blanched white.

"Will!" she shouted, loud enough for her husband to hear her in his tailoring shop, which was attached to their cottage.

He rushed to her side, looking alarmed by the urgency in her voice. "Don't scream like that, Bridget," he said. "I thought something was wrong with the baby."

"It's just as bad," Bridget said. "Read this. Tell me it doesn't say what I think it says."

Will scanned the letter. He was a faster reader than Bridget, and soon enough, his face went white, too.

"She didn't marry Peter," Will said, sounding less surprised than Bridget expected.

"But that's not the worst part," Bridget said. "She's working for Mark."

"My Mamie is working for Mark," she whispered again.

Will folded up the letter, as if he couldn't bear to read any more. He searched Bridget's eyes.

"*That* Mark," Bridget said, answering his question before he asked.

Bridget sunk back into her chair, clutching baby Nora as if they might both wash away in a rushing river. "Do you remember that night I tried to drown myself in the Cuyahoga?" she asked Will.

He sat back in his chair, too, looking stiff, his mouth set in a straight line. "It was one of the worst nights of my life," he said.

It happened one night in the summer, 1867. Bridget had tried to sneak out of the Rhodes mansion to go see Tylor Mor at his apartment on Whiskey Island. He lived on the top floor of a four-floor building.

Bridget sat up in her bed and looked out the window. It was dark. She was afraid of the dark. The pale walls of the maids' quarters were now gray, and shadows were jumping around everywhere. All the residents of the Rhodes mansion were asleep. All except for Bridget.

She moved to the edge of her bed, prepared to slip her day clothes and boots on so she could leave again to see Tylor Mor.

Then, as she tiptoed to the stairs, she heard someone else's footsteps. A man's, and much louder and more aggressive than her own. Her mouth parted open.

"Don't explain yourself," Mark Hanna said. "I know you're going out whoring again."

"Mark—"

"Shh!" he hissed. "You may call me Mr. Hanna."

There was nothing she could do as he grabbed her wrist, led her downstairs and pulled her into the guest bedroom.

"I knew it. You've been out whoring, haven't you?" he said. "You want to be a whore? You'll be a whore for the men who pay you well. It's time to earn your keep."

What could she do? He was Mark Hanna, the brilliant businessman, the all-powerful, and she was Bridget, the help...his maid....nothing.

And there was nothing she could do as he forced her down, pinning her still, his hands feeling for the buttons of her nightgown. His pants were unbuttoned. She avoided looking, because she didn't want to see him naked. He pressed against her, thrusting harder and harder, but...she wouldn't give. Her body rejected him, and even he seemed to balk at the idea of forcing himself into her. Finally, he had to face the truth.

"You *are* a virgin," he said.

He tried one more time. Bridget straightened out her hand and slapped him, hard, across the face. As she rose from the bed, she stepped backward, accidentally overturning the sole lantern in the room. A small trickle of flames began to spread across the floor.

"You idiot!" Mark hissed, rushing to stamp out the fire. As he was distracted, Bridget fled down the stairs, running across town to Tylor Mor's apartment.

She pounded on his door, feeling the tear between her legs. It stung even worse than the tears gathering in her eyes. "Open up," she said.

"Tylor Mor isn't here," a mean voice on the other side of the door said, and then added, "Go away."

Bridget nodded, tasting the salt of a cold teardrop on her lip. "Tell him I'll go to be with God now," she said. When there was no answer, she ran.

She ran to the wooden bridge that stretched over the Cuyahoga River, a treacherous bridge that people only crossed when they must. Bridget had no concern for modesty. What difference did it make now? Without care, she hiked her skirts up to her thighs and threw one leg over the bridge. She couldn't swim, and when she looked down at the rushing waters of this wicked river, she wondered if she was really prepared to die...or not.

She was ready.

"Girl, what're you doing?" a man in the gathering crowd asked. They were gathering to stare and gawk, but not to stop her.

"Tell Tylor Mor I love him," Bridget said. "Truly." Then she let go and dropped into the void of black, hissing water.

Bridget knew she couldn't swim, but she wasn't prepared for the terror of drowning. As soon as her head sunk beneath the surface of the Cuyahoga, she realized how long it would take to die. Although she'd imagined submersion producing an instant death, she was still very much alive in the river. She was flailing, kicking, and trying to inhale air.

She wanted to scream, "Help me!" But instead her lungs were screaming for air. The world around her was black, silent, and cold...very cold, even though it was late summer.

Just as the intense pain of suffocation engulfed her, she felt a pair of arms engulf her, too. Maybe this was what the end felt like. Perhaps this was Jesus wrapping his arms around her and holding her like a child as he carried her to heaven.

Instead, as her head surfaced above the foul Cuyahoga, Bridget recognized the face of Tylor Mor as he dragged her to the riverbank. The only thing she would recall years later was Tylor Mor rolling her onto her side, smacking her back until she coughed up the putrid river water.

"Bridget. Bridget, wake up," Tylor Mor said, shaking her shoulders. He parted her lips with his fingers. "Bridget, breathe!"

Finally, she vomited the last of the foul, discolored water, choking and gagging.

"Mr. Hanna," she gasped. "He...he..."

"No," Tylor Mor said, shaking his head. "Don't tell me. I'll kill that man with my bare hands."

Tylor Mor glanced up at the crowd gathered to stare at them, who were leering and murmuring amongst each other. "What are you looking at?" He challenged angrily. "Get on with it! And leave my poor girl alone."

Tylor Mor scooped Bridget into his arms and carried her like a child to Seán Fada's hotel, on the street next to the river. It was chilly tonight, and the rain was beginning to pour, an August lightning storm rolling in over Lake Erie.

"Hang on there, Bridie girl," Tylor Mor said. "I'll get you inside before the lightning hits."

"Glory be," Seán Fada said when she answered the door. "Get her out of those wet clothes."

Seán Fada's woman friend drew hot water from the open kettle she kept over a wood-burning fire. She had a bathtub in one of the rooms for rent, in the same room with a small bed and an old nightstand. All the furniture in the loft looked like the discarded remains of old items from Millionaire's Row. Whiskey Island residents often plucked items from junkyards along the Cuyahoga River bank. As Bridget emerged from her shock, she noted what a beautiful little room it was, with its oversized quilts covering the bed.

"That's all the hot water I have," Seán Fada's woman friend said as Bridget undressed. She handed her a bar of homemade soap. "Wash the filth out of your hair."

Bridget stayed in the bathtub a while, listening to the clatter and the loud voices downstairs. Now it was silent. Everyone must be in bed for the night. A mighty roll of thunder shook the frame of the house, causing Bridget to gasp and grasp the bathtub with both hands.

"It's me."

Tylor Mor's voice cut through the dark.

Her hands flew over her breasts, and she hugged herself with both arms. "I'm bathing!"

He shut his eyes and clapped his hands over his face dramatically, shielding his view. He fumbled around for a blanket and held it out to her. The sight of it made Bridget laugh—for the first time in a long time. She climbed out of the tub and wrapped the blanket around her naked body as Tylor Mor stood there with his eyes closed.

"Say when I can open 'em," he said.

She took a deep breath and tossed the blanket aside, on the edge of the bed. Nearly twenty years of indoctrination—about heaven and hell, about virtue and virginity—flew out the window. The storm rumbled outside. "Open your eyes," she said, breathing deeply as he realized what she was asking for, standing there naked in front of him.

Bridget McGlynn woke early in the morning, listening to the rain still falling on the roof. Years later, she would look back and realize she knew right away she got pregnant that night.

✟

Forty-Seven

As Mamie walked up the hill to go to work at the Hanna mansion one morning, she passed two men standing along Pearl Street. They were shoving pamphlets into the hands of passerby.

"Hear, hear!" they called. "Read about why Grover Cleveland is the enemy of the Irishman!"

The President's name caught Mamie's attention. She reached out to take a pamphlet.

"Not you," the man said to her dismissively. "You can't vote anyhow. You're a woman."

"My brothers can vote," Mamie said, unsure whether it was true. In Ireland, there was no such thing as voting. They were ruled, without input, by the British crown, and the Irish hated Britain for that. She didn't know how Americans, especially new immigrants, went about voting.

"Och, well, if you have brothers, tell 'em we offer cash incentives for turning out to vote," the pamphleteer replied. "But only so long as they vote for Mr. Harrison."

"Mr. Hanna is paying Irish men for votes, is he?" Mamie blurted out. The man shot her a look of warning.

"I said nothing of the sort," he said. "Our benefactors will not be revealed."

Mamie put her head down and continued along Pearl Street, shoving the pamphlet into her apron pocket. She forgot it was there by the time she arrived several minutes late to work. She went about cleaning the breakfast dishes in a harried manner, hoping Charlotte Hanna wouldn't realize she'd been late.

"What do you have there?"

Mamie whirled around, surprised that Mark was home this morning. She held the tea kettle she was washing out in front of her as if it were a shield.

"Not that," Mark said. "You found one of my pamphlets."

"I passed a man handing them out on Pearl Street," Mamie said.

"Ah-ha. Very good. The campaign of 1888 is officially underway," Mark replied. "Mamie, I have a proposition for you."

She looked at him, but asked no questions and offered no reply.

"How would you feel about distributing these pamphlets at your saloon?" he asked. "You'll get paid for your trouble, of course."

"It's no trouble for me, Mr. Hanna," Mamie said. "But I must admit I know nothing about Grover Cleveland. Or Mr. Harrison, for that matter."

"You don't have to know," Mark replied. "But I will tack six dollars onto your weekly pay."

Mamie's heart fluttered at the proposition. The Irish men who worked on the docks earned six dollars a week for hard, often deadly labor. Something about Mark's offer stank. But like the obedient Catholic woman she was, Mamie accepted.

Besides, Mark's money would keep the saloon in Kate and Mamie's hands just a little longer.

"Also, Mary," Mark said. "I'll need you to go on a holiday with Charlotte and me to visit the summer estate of our friend."

He laughed when he studied her facial expression. "Don't look so alarmed," he continued. "It's about ten miles west, in Dover Township. My friend John Huntington owns an estate there on Lake Erie. Or perhaps I should say *former friend*. He was bitter when he ran for Cleveland municipal office and I thought he was unfit for the position. But we're repairing our friendship as the Republican Party moves forward to more victories."

Mamie looked at him, both of them knowing she cared nothing about the Republican Party. "When are you visiting?" she asked.

"Several weeks from now," Mark replied. "I'll give you notice so you can pack adequately. Do you have any summer dresses besides that one?"

"No, sir," Mamie said, looking down at the lightweight calico dress Kate had sewn for her, so that she wouldn't succumb to the summer heat walking to work. Summers were much hotter in Cleveland than in County Mayo, and Mamie had arrived unprepared.

"I'll see what Charlotte's dressmaker can do about that," Mark said.

Every night, with some reluctance, Mamie arranged Mr. Hanna's pamphlets on the bar at the saloon. And every night, she watched patrons pore over them with curiosity. Kate looked at them with growing disgust every evening. She finally swept them all into the rubbish, on top of damp scraps of bread and spilled beer.

"Kate!" Mamie cried. "What was that for?"

"Do you read the papers every morning, Mamie?" Kate asked. "You need to read the papers. Benjamin Harrison isn't on our side. He's on the side of the people who think they own us. The people who pay our men five dollars a week to get black lungs in their cargo holds."

"But Mr. Hanna says—"

"Mr. Hanna thinks we're stupid," Kate replied. "He thinks Irish men will vote based on some primitive, tribal hatred of the British. And many will. Have you seen those men distributing those same pamphlets on the streets? Mark

Hanna is paying this neighborhood to vote the way he wants."

Mamie frowned. "He's paying me six dollars a week to distribute these pamphlets," Mamie said, picking one out of the rubbish. "*Six. Dollars.*"

A tiny smile twitched at Kate's lips. "So you keep the six dollars," she said, "And throw out his pamphlets." She raised her eyebrows at Mamie.

Independence Day arrived soon after that day Kate threw Mark's pamphlets in the trash. Mamie had never seen anything quite like it. All throughout the city, people poured into the streets, carrying torch lights. They sang patriotic songs; War Songs they'd learned during the battle between the states. The thunder of explosives rattled the saloon as Mamie served German lager to her usual crowd: Germans, Poles, and Hungarians, and Irish men who weren't boycotting the place. The sight of torch lights in the streets gave Mamie an uneasy feeling. She remembered that night they found a kerosene-soaked rag beneath the shattered window. After dark, when firecrackers lit up the sky, Mamie watched Mad Annie pace around the kitchen. She was gripping her belly and grimacing in pain.

"Annie, what's the matter?" Mamie asked. Annie dabbed her brow with a damp cloth. Mamie reached out to touch her arm, and Annie jerked away.

"I'm fine!" she said. Ever since that terrible night in February, Mad Annie hated to be touched.

Mamie was speaking with a patron who spoke stilted English when she caught Annie out of the corner of her eye again. This time, Annie was leaning up against the wall, breathing heavily. Then, with a sound like a mop bucket overturning on the floor, a great rush of fluid dropped between her legs, pooling on the floor.

"Jesus, Mary, and Joseph," Mamie said, sweat gleaming around her hairline—and not just from the oppressive summer heat. "Annie, let's go upstairs."

Mamie grabbed Annie's arm as they brushed past Kate. "Take over the bar," Mamie murmured to Kate. "It's urgent."

"Annie, lay down," Mamie commanded, in a forceful tone that didn't come to her naturally. "You should be off your feet."

Across the attic, Bessie sat up in bed. "Mamie," she asked, "what's going on?"

"Nothing," Mamie replied. "Annie is sour of stomach, is all."

Bessie, who had seen the births of her younger siblings, including baby Nora, wasn't convinced. "Mamie," she said, tiptoeing across the floor, "is Annie having a baby?"

Mamie swallowed hard. "I'm not sure," she answered.

Bessie hugged her around the waist, hoping to reassure her. "Don't be scared, Mamie," she said. "We've seen lots of babies born, haven't we?"

"Yes, m'dear," Mamie said, "I was there when Ma birthed *you.*"

"And when she birthed Katie, and Johnnie, and Bridie…" Bessie said, reciting the long list of Chambers siblings. "Da said Johnnie came out feet-first, because he was born to bend the rules."

Mamie chortled a little, then wiped her brow. "Bessie, go find some clean cloths downstairs, and a piece of twine," she ordered, and the little girl nodded. "We'll make sure Annie's babe makes it safe into the world."

Annie labored all through the night until there were streams of blood and fluid pooling around her legs. Kate and Mamie were there the whole time, talking her through the crushing pain of contractions. As the first rays of morning sun peaked over Lake Erie, a bloody little head emerged. Mamie gently gripped it between her palms as she guided it out of Annie's body.

The baby fell between Annie's legs, and Mamie carefully turned the baby over as she swept the infant's mouth with her finger to clear the fluid. She couldn't remember the exact procedure, but she tried her best to mimic what she had seen the midwife in Roskeen do many times. The baby wailed, and that was how Mamie knew the baby had survived the birth, healthy and alive.

"You have a boy," Kate said as she placed the baby on Mad Annie's chest. "What shall we call him?"

The baby was lovely, with giant eyes and the first soft wisps of auburn hair. He didn't have Annie's candle-in-the-night shade of red hair; the baby's hair was a cross between red and a dark brown shade.

"Maybe I will call him Brian, after Brian Bóramha," Annie said, referring to the last High King of Ireland. "Or maybe I should name him after the Archangel, St. Michael. I like that...Michael."

"She conceived this babe before that night you found her in the snow," Mamie said flatly. "Someone's been violating her for a long time now." Her heart heavy at the realization.

Kate squeezed her arm. "Don't you dare tell anyone Annie had a baby," she said to Mamie. "Why do you think I tried to distract everyone, reassuring you it was all in her imagination? I've known all along."

Mamie looked at her, astonished.

"Keep it a secret for now," Kate reiterated. "Someone will be held to account when the time is right."

✟

Forty-Eight

Mamie didn't sleep well the week leading up to her trip to Dover Township with the Hannas.

When her brother Johnnie reappeared at the saloon with his dog, she demanded that he stay.

"Someone needs to walk Bessie to school," Mamie told him. "Your brother Tom is busy at the mortuary, and God knows Kate has enough on her plate here. You need to help your sister and not run off again."

Johnnie shrugged. "Will Pat Masterson stay here, too?" he said, swinging at an imaginary figure before him. "I want to practice boxing."

"I'm here now," Patrick said from the back door. He was helping to unload the latest shipment of Gehring lager. "But I ship out again soon, to Michigan. In the meantime, we'll box."

Patrick addressed Mamie next. "And you. You shouldn't go anywhere with that crusty old boss of yours."

"I have no choice," she said, unable to argue with his basic sentiment.

"Sure you do," Patrick replied. "Tell him you have a household to run and children to care for. Who is he to bring his maid to a home that's not even his?"

Mamie knew it was strange, too, but she was going anyway.

"And if I didn't go, he'd fire me and find someone more compliant," she said. "There are a thousand docile, hard-working foreign girls in this city, ready and willing to take my place."

And they weren't just Irish girls. Every day this summer, trains and ferry boats delivered immigrants fleeing East Europe. The old neighborhoods were becoming more condensed as the Poles, Hungarians, and Ukrainians built up their own neighborhoods. Their women wanted to work as domestics, too—although Irish women had the advantage of speaking English.

"That man don't want any woman to take your place," Patrick argued. "I wish you'd seen him through these eyes o' mine, that night at the theater. He's possessive of you. He behaves like a cross between a master lording over his favorite mistress and a father guarding his favorite daughter."

Mamie shuddered. "Enough, Patrick Masterson," she said sharply. "I'll be home in a week."

Mamie rode in the Hanna's carriage with Mark and Charlotte. She felt awkward as they chatted about their rich friends and the upcoming election. She stared out the window at the Lake Erie shoreline as the carriage moved past the clamor of the city and onto the long, winding road toward Dover Township.

It was a beautiful day, and the view of Lake Erie from the carriage reminded Mamie of Clew Bay on the west coast of Ireland. Her favorite thing about this season—August, she figured, although she wasn't sure of the exact date—was the chorus of crickets at night. It was a mesmerizing hum, one that distracted from the annoying buzz of mosquitoes. Kate burned basil leaves at night to keep the mosquitoes at bay.

Mamie imagined the crickets would be even lovelier against the silent backdrop of Dover Township.

When they arrived at the Huntington Estate, Mark helped Charlotte and Mamie out of his carriage. They stepped onto a block of stone placed there for the purpose. "Lovely, isn't it?" he asked Mamie with a wink.

"It's beautiful," Mamie said, looking at the cliffs that sloped down to an empty beach. "...It looks like Ireland."

In the parlor room of the Huntington estate, Mark insisted on introducing Mamie to his friends. There was John Huntington and his wife. There was another man with a thin face and a pinched nose, whom Mark introduced as John Rockefeller.

"You are newly arrived from Ireland, I hear. I'm an Englishman," John Huntington said. Mamie had already surmised it from his accent.

"I migrated here when I was a young man, about your age," added.

"So, Mary, what do you know about Grover Cleveland?"

"He's the Premier," she responded.

The men laughed as Mamie realized her mistake. "The President," she corrected herself. "Grover Cleveland is President."

"But not for long!" John Huntington said. "Benjamin Harrison will unseat him in November, just wait."

"Mary is assisting the campaign," Mark explained to his friends. "She distributes our pamphlets about the tariff issue in her neighborhood." The women rewarded her with stiff smiles. The men beamed, happy to see Mark's maid do his bidding.

"Mr. Hanna, may I take a walk to the lake before dinner?" Mamie asked, eager to excuse herself from the parlor. She had already put a tea kettle on for Mrs. Hanna. Mark himself rarely drank liquor, at least not in public. But Mamie knew it was customary for the rich to have drinks before dinner. She didn't want to be here when their inhibitions loosened and they started badgering her with presumptuous questions.

"Yes, of course," Mark replied. "Go ahead."

John Huntington's house sat on the cliffs above the beach. Mark and Charlotte referred to it as a "cottage" on the ride here. The word "cottage" brought to Mamie's mind the thatched-roof dwellings back home. Therefore, she laughed inside when she saw John Huntington's house. It was a mansion, with terraces and chimneys and a wraparound porch. Mark had also bragged about how John Huntington raised horses, and maintained orchards and vineyards of his own.

Mamie thought about old Mr. Mulchrone, her neighbor in Ireland, and his beloved horses. She wanted to see the horses.

She walked down a steep hill, where she spotted an enclosed pasture in a meadow full of dense, tall grass.

"Come here, sweet girl," she said when one of the horses trotted toward her. She held out some wild berries she'd picked on her walk, and John Huntington's horse ate it from her hand. She smiled unconsciously. She was thrilled to be standing here on this remote country estate, where she could look out over the lake and see rolling green cliffs on the horizon. It was easy to pretend she was back in Ireland.

She became so lost in the comforting fantasy that she didn't realize how many hours ticked by. She forgot that Mark was back at the house, wondering where she'd gone.

Meanwhile, Mark Hanna and his friends had moved to the porch, enjoying the view of the lake. The ladies stayed inside, declining to sweat. But Mark thought it was pleasantly hot today—not too humid, but bright and warm enough to feel the sun browning the skin on his hands.

The slightest hint of fall was in the air. Less than three months remained until Election Day.

"Your maid is a lovely girl," John Huntington said.

Mark agreed, of course, but he was surprised to hear Huntington say so. Mary Chambers, with her thick auburn hair, blue irises, and dash of freckles below her sad eyes, was quite lovely to Mark. But she didn't have the fussy beauty and prim fashion that the rich favored. Mary came to work at his house with horse manure on her boots and sunburn on her cheeks. Still, Mark admired her body. It had the natural hourglass shape that wealthy women mimicked with brutal corsets and other trickery.

"She is," Mark said, unsure of why John felt the need to comment on it. "She's been a loyal employee."

"You have a penchant for those Irish girls, don't you, Mark?"

Mark's chin jerked upward. "What do you mean?" he asked.

"I remember your father-in-law's servant on Franklin Avenue, during those dark days after the War Between the States," John said.

Mark laughed wryly. "Let's not revisit them," he said, hoping to avoid discussing the years he was a failure as a businessman. They were behind him, anyway.

"I can still picture her. Red hair. Small. Looked like if you picked her up, she'd feel like a sack of feathers," John said. "What was her name?"

"Bridget," Mark said. "Her full name escapes me. She disappeared on us one day."

John shrugged. "She had a good arrangement with your father-in-law," he said. "I'd wager she still rues the day she left. She probably went on to have a litter of babies, like those Catholic women do."

Mark's mouth settling in a stiff line. "I'm sure she did."

✝

Forty-Nine

There wasn't a soul in sight when Mamie finally returned to the Huntington house late in the evening. It was still light out, but the sun was fading and taking some of the heat with it. Mamie assumed the Hannas and the other couples were drinking wine in the garden. Maybe they took a walk to see Mr. Huntington's vineyards and exotic plants.

Mamie went to the small maid's quarters on the top floor of the house, where she was to sleep. It wasn't dark yet, but still, she was exhausted and sweaty from her walk. She stood in her undergarments, digging for her nightgown.

She nearly jumped out of her skin when the door opened without warning.

"Where were you all night?" Mark demanded, neither greeting her nor apologizing for intruding.

"I took a walk around the estate, sir," Mary said, crossing her arms over her breasts. She expected him to apologize profusely when he realized she was in her undergarments, but he offered nothing of the sort.

"Mr. Hanna, sir," she exclaimed, "I'm not dressed!"

"I've told you that you're to call me Mark," he said.

"Mark Hanna," she said, growing defiant, "please allow me to put my clothes on."

Mark took a long stride into the bedroom, forcing Mamie to back against the wall.

"What is your mother's name?" he demanded.

"Bridget Chambers," Mamie stammered.

"Chambers is your name," Mark corrected her. "Your mother married a Chambers. A man who was perhaps once known as…Tylor Mor?"

Mamie drew back in horror.

"My father's name is William," Mamie said, her heart pounding.

Mark put his hand on the wall, next to her head, but then he took a step back and looked at her, studying her eyes.

"I had a maid named Bridget once," he said, his usual charming, political façade fading. His voice sounded cold and sinister. "About twenty years ago, maybe a few more. She ran off with my tailor."

Mamie's first instinct was to blurt out that her father was a tailor, too. But then she remembered she had already revealed that—and Mark had reacted so strangely.

"I had an indiscretion with her," Mark continued. "I would have restrained myself if I'd known she was bedding my tailor as well. A few months later, after it became obvious she was pregnant, she ran away."

Mamie's lips parted, and she began to quake with horror. "What are you trying to tell me?"

"Does any of this story sound familiar to you?" Mark asked, his eyes boring into hers.

"No."

"You've never heard the name Tylor Mor?"

"I've heard it, but I never called my father that name," Mamie replied. As far as she knew, it was the truth.

"Because if you do, you cannot be trusted in my home," Mark said. "That man tried to ruin my career with outrageous accusations and slanders about my carnal appetites. Do you know what I'm saying?"

"No, Mark, I don't."

She looked away and corrected herself. "I'm sorry. No, Mr. Hanna, I do not."

Mark's shoulders relaxed, and he backed away from her, for the first time looking slightly embarrassed.

"I'm sorry, Mamie," he said, wiping his lips. "I feel foolish. Maybe the heat got to me, or the liquor. You know how seldom I drink."

"Yes, Mark."

"Go to bed and forget this conversation," he said. "There's nothing to it. I'm sorry to perturb you."

But Mamie lay awake half the night, staring at the moon through the sliver between the curtains. Despite Mark's commands, she knew she wouldn't forget the conversation anytime soon, no matter how hard she tried.

Fifty

Mamie tried her hardest to avoid Mark the next day, and she had an inkling that the desire was mutual. She served the Hannas and their friends their morning tea and pastries, their late-afternoon cocktails, and refilled the water pitchers, since it was still sunny and hot. Then she asked to be dismissed for the rest of the evening. This time, she asked Charlotte Hanna for her permission, not Mark.

"Do as you wish," Mrs. Hanna said. "We will be taking the carriage to the summer home of another friend tonight. We won't return until late. You'll manage yourself, right, Mary?"

"I will."

When they left in their separate carriages, Mamie took another walk around the Huntington estate. She peeled off her shoes and walked down the steep hills to the beach. It was empty, and the sand felt good between her toes. Eventually she removed her dress as well and waded into the water in her undergarments. The water in Cleveland was brown and full of sludge, but the water here was clear, and she could see the pebbles shifting below the water with each new wave. She dipped her hand into the water and collected a few white seashells.

In the early evening, storm clouds began to form over the lake, and Mamie all of a sudden felt spooked by the total absence of another human being here on this beach in Dover Township. This place was even more remote than the Clew Bay in County Mayo. She looked east, to the city of Cleveland, and saw the faintest outlines of buildings and a few ships on the docks. She looked west and saw nothing but rolling cliffs and beach. In the distance—what must be five miles away, she guessed—she thought she saw a ship, and a large bonfire burning on the beach.

Mamie shuddered. Who would camp out on a deserted beach? She knew just a little about Indians—the copper-skinned people who had lived in America before anyone else arrived. She wondered if they still lived in this area; if it was their campfire. Shuddering at the thought of encountering Indians all alone, she jumped back into her clothes and climbed up the hill to the Huntington mansion.

She made sure to shake all the sand from her clothing before sitting in the parlor room. Watching a storm roll in over the lake was eerie, especially when she was all alone. She curled up in a loveseat, grabbed a book from the bookcase, and tried to focus on the story as the rain hammered on the roof. She kept losing her focus every time she heard a noise outside—a swaying branch, a squirrel scurrying along the roof. She thought she heard footsteps.

She shook the thought out of her head, scolding herself. It was just her imagination.

Until, moments later, she heard a series of strong yet hesitant knocks on the back door.

"Jesus!" she cried, jumping out of her seat. It couldn't be the Huntingtons or their entourage—they had keys. Mary scurried behind the sofa and crouched there, watching the doorknob rattle. Whoever was out there, she would not answer the door.

When it finally opened, she almost fainted with relief.

"Jesus, Mary and Joseph," she breathed, clutching her chest. "Pat Masterson, how did you get here?"

He wore his sailor's uniform, which was wet through-and-through. His boots were caked with mud.

"I walked," he said without missing a beat.

She was so filled with the joy of relief that she ran into his arms and hugged him. For once, it was Patrick who looked taken aback by her forwardness—not the other way around.

"My ship is docked for the night in the French Creek area because of the storms," he said. "I could have spent the night at Satter's Tavern, over there in Xuema—er, Avon. I'm not sure what they call it these days. But when I realized I must be only two miles from you, I walked. You said the Huntington Estate was along the Lake Erie shoreline, aye? Well, I found it…and you."

Patrick looked around, taking in the elegant mansion that the Huntingtons called a cottage.

"Where's old man Hanna?" he asked.

"They're at the vineyard. But I expect them home soon because of the rain," Mamie said. She was still so nervous she was trembling. "You can't stay. I can't imagine what Mr. Huntington would do if he discovered an intruder."

"Intruder? Nonsense," Patrick said. "You let me in." He winked at her, and she knew he was just teasing.

"I planned on staying here a while and then walking back to my ship," Pat said. "We're docked a short distance away. I'll keep you company, and when Hanna arrives home, I'll bail out."

"What?! Pat, what's gotten into you?"

He took a fresh tomato from the fruit basket and bit into it, savoring the taste. "One thing you learn about rich people—they have so many things, they don't notice when a little thing is missing," he said. "Like this lovely tomato."

"You're mad," Mamie replied. But then she found herself reaching for a ripe, fire-red tomato, too.

"I'm mad for you."

Mamie paused, holding the tomato before her lips. "I beg your pardon, Patrick?" she said, her eyes meeting his.

217

"You heard me," he said. "Ever since that night you stepped off the boat. And even more so when I returned in the spring and saw you in that red gown…"

"Pat Masterson, don't burden me with this knowledge," Mamie said, her heart pounding. "A year ago—nah, a little less—I was betrothed. I swore not to love another man after Peter Sweeny. How could I?"

"Peter Sweeny is a fool," Patrick spat. "Or was. Who knows if he's still alive. But I'm no fool. I know a good woman when I meet one. A woman who's lovely, inside and out…"

"Stop. Please," Mamie said. "I'll hear no more of it."

Pat crossed his arms over his heart. "As you wish," he said. She looked at the floor.

"You have nothing to say to me, aye, Mamie?"

She shook her head.

"I know I drink too much, and I'm gone too often; I live a lonely life as a sailor," Patrick admitted. "But if I ever had a reason to quit this life, I'd make a fine husband. I'm no Peter Sweeny. Know that."

Mamie hid in her room until the Hannas returned, listening to them murmur to each other. When she heard Mark snoring she knew it was safe to sleep.

Fifty-One

Satter's Tavern was a beloved gathering place for sailors on the Great Lakes. Twenty miles west of Cleveland, in the middle of God-knows-where, Satter's Tavern was known for its rowdy upstairs entertainment. At the end of the night, the saucy women invited the sailors back to their boudoirs.

But Patrick wasn't interested in women of the night, and he was even less interested in visiting their boudoirs. The mystery his sister Kate had presented to him was burning on his mind. Was the woman Kate saw outside Cassie Chadwick's brothel the same woman who had lured away Peter Sweeny? The same men who visited women's boudoirs at Satter's Tavern were often the same men who patronized Cassie Chadwick's brothel. Whoremongers, the sailors called them. Patrick wasn't one. But he didn't look down upon them; he never saw the sense in judging people who sinned differently. And he was more than willing to dig them for secrets about Marie St. Jean. He thought here, in this tiny town on the Lake Erie shore, he might find some answers.

Patrick wasn't sure what this town was called. Some people called it Xeuma, its supposed Indian name. Others called it French Creek, or its most recent name: Avon-on-the-Lake. The Satter homestead was hidden in the woods a short distance from the lake. Patrick liked it out here, far away from the grime and noise of the city. One could breathe here, although it got quite lonely at night. Satter's Tavern backed up to wilderness. There was no organized police force or neighbors to count on in times of trouble.

At least no one out here had to answer to the Angle mob, Patrick thought grimly.

"Patrick Masterson!" one of the barkeepers shouted to him as he entered the tavern in his sailor uniform. "I haven't seen ya in a coon's age."

"A year," Patrick corrected him, taking a seat at the bar. "Say, do you still have them 'working girls' upstairs?"

The barkeeper lowered his eyebrows. Patrick saw his fellow patrons' ears prick up, and he knew he had their attention.

"Don't look so startled," Patrick said, tossing some coins down on the table to cover his double glass of whiskey. "I'm not looking to cozy up to anyone. I'm just wondering if you're familiar with a prostitute in the area."

The barkeeper looked at him with steely eyes, intrigued. "Describe her."

"Yeah, describe her," another patron chimed in. "We'll tell you if we done seen her."

Patrick conjured a memory of that fateful night in December. He had been drinking. It was an ugly night— and there was far more to it than Kate had ever suspected. Mamie, needless to say, was totally in the dark about what really happened.

The truth could not get out. That was why Patrick had to find out if the alleged "Marie St. Jean" was still out there, playing her dirty games.

"Dark hair, nearly black," Patrick said. "She's painted up with cosmetics. Crimson red lips. She sings— not very well, although she seems to think she possesses a rare gift. She speaks with a French accent, but it sounds phony. Least it did to me."

The barkeeper gnawed his lip and looked upward, as if he were looking back into time.

"There was a woman who took clients here last summer who matched that description," the barkeeper said. "A real rough woman who said she sang on Mississippi steamboats."

Patrick believed he'd seen Marie St. Jean here last summer, too. His stomach did a turn and he took another sip of his whiskey to settle it.

"She said she was from down South somewhere—Tennessee, or Kentucky. Somewhere like that. Said she was a Cherokee princess of some sort, came from royal Injun blood."

Pat nearly spat out his whiskey. "Say what?"

"I know, I know," the barkeeper said. "Hard to believe, considering the Injuns don't have no system of royalty, far as I know. But some of the men here ate it up."

"Do you know where she is now?" Patrick asked.

"No sir, I sure don't," he replied. "Nor do I care to."

"Thank you," Patrick said. "Now I'll take another whiskey."

Pat Masterson slept on his boat that night, too disturbed to spend the night at the Satter's tavern. He was certain the same Cherokee princess luring gullible sailors was the same woman who tried to seduce Peter Sweeny.

Fifty-Two

The night before Mamie returned from the Huntington Estate, Black Willie visited Kate at the saloon, just before closing time. His willingness to come here, instead of demanding she visit his home, said something about his desperation.

"I'll make you one final offer," he said.

She ignored him and went about her business. "You say that as if I'm interested," she said sarcastically. "You sent the man who tried to snatch my Molly."

"I did nothing of the sort," Black Willie shot back. "And where is that pretty little girl of yours, anyhow? No one's seen her of late."

Johnnie Chambers, the kid who had beat The Watcher unconscious, sat with his dog at his feet. Black Willie suspected it was one of the puppies his dog had borne, now grown. Johnnie stared at him with a defiant confidence that was unnerving. Johnnie had grown bigger that summer, and so had his dog. Willie glared at him.

He would love nothing more than to shank that kid in retaliation. But he couldn't breathe a word about what happened that night at his house, because then he'd have to admit he'd arranged the whole sordid affair.

"We'll pay you four thousand dollars for this building," he continued. Kate's face didn't move.

"This building is not for sale," she replied. "We're bringing in plenty of business since we switched to German lager. Your little plan to bankrupt me fell flat. Now go. The

Angle Mob shan't be turning this place into another brothel."

"We suspect there's enough whoring going on around here," Willie shot back. "Everyone knows you're a whore."

"I haven't lain down with a man since I conceived Molly," Kate said. "And we were married. However briefly, we were married nonetheless. Get your facts straight."

Black Willie was getting flustered. Usually, the worst thing you could call an Irish Catholic woman was a whore. But Kate Masterson wouldn't budge.

"You, and that crazy redheaded bitch, and that woman who ran her husband off," he continued. "You mean to tell me you're not paying the overhead with some upstairs entertainment?"

"My sister would never," Johnnie said. His dog emitted a low growl. "You better tread lightly, ye auld goat."

Willie's back stiffened. "Are you threatening me?"

"That's exactly what I'm doing."

At just the right moment, Annie's newborn began to cry.

"What's that?" Willie exclaimed. "Kate, did you drop another baby?"

"No," she said.

"What is going on here? Whose kid is that, now?"

"Why don't you get the hell out instead of nosing around where you don't belong?" Kate replied. "There's no sale taking place as long as I live. This is our saloon now. And I won't have my virtue questioned by people who steal children."

She slammed a beer glass on the bar and poured out a lager for herself. "Get out," she said.

Johnnie's dog growled again and rose to its feet.

"I'd be happy to go," Black Willie said, refusing to admit he had lost this argument. He dusted off his bar stool with a dramatic swipe. "After all, I don't want to sit on a bar stool that's come in contact with your nether regions, Kate Masterson."

Later that night, Black Willie met with other members in good standing of the Angle Mob.

"Why can't we just kill them?" The Watcher asked.

"Because Mary Chambers' uncle is a police officer, that's why," Black Willie said. "He might look the other way with some things we do. But he certainly won't stand for his niece getting killed. We'll face a serious investigation and possible hanging."

The Watcher threw his hands up, indicating he was out of ideas.

"Don't look so defeated," Black Willie said. "Sit down. I have another idea."

Fifty-Three

Mamie returned to the saloon the next evening around supper time. She'd spent a few long hours in the carriage with Mark Hanna and his wife. They chatted about the beauty of the Huntington Estate and how tired they were after the week's festivities. Mamie couldn't wait to go home.

A breeze whipped through the trees, and Mamie felt the slightest hint that the weather was changing. Autumn was arriving, and with it, Election Day. Mark Hanna would be on edge, and he would also expect results from Mamie's efforts at the saloon. She wondered how he would react if he knew his pamphlets were in the trash.

When Mamie reached the door, Kate was outside, switching the "open" sign to "closed."

"Shhh," she said, ushering Mamie inside. "Want to go on an adventure?"

Mamie cringed. She thought she'd had enough adventure for the week.

"We shan't leave Annie and the babe and Bessie here alone," Mamie replied.

"Annie and the babe are sleeping, and Johnnie said he'd keep watch," Kate said. "Bessie will join us. It'll be great fun for her."

Bessie came downstairs, her braids swinging, a sparkle in her eye.

"We're going to see the President," she told Mamie.

"What?"

"Grover Cleveland is visiting a house on Euclid Avenue," Kate replied. "He keeps a low profile, and he lets his vice president do most of his campaigning for him. But I have it on good word from a patron that he's in town. I thought it would be grand to get a glimpse of him, don't ya think?"

They took the long route to Euclid Avenue—over the bridge spanning the Cuyahoga, and up the hill to downtown Cleveland.

The city streets grew cleaner and greener as they approached Euclid Avenue. It was one of the wealthiest streets in the world. Kate led them to the gates of a palatial estate hidden behind overgrown trees.

"See how there's no gate on this side?" she said. "If we follow this row of bushes, we can peak into the garden."

"We could run into trouble with the law," Mamie said. She checked her surroundings. The highest-ranking police officers patrolled Euclid Avenue, where their only real job was keeping an eye out for riffraff.

Kate shrugged. "I don't see any policemen here. They don't come out 'til nightfall," she said. "Besides, you can run in those boots."

"You go first," Mamie told Kate.

They crouched behind the fence and peered through the bushes at a sprawling lawn. Several couples were seated at white tables around a fountain.

"There he is!" Bessie gasped. Her hand flew to her mouth as if to suppress her own voice.

"He looks just like the cartoons, aye?" Kate said.

Mamie squinted at the rotund Grover Cleveland, who was standing up with his hat in his hands. He had a more pleasant-looking demeanor than the man portrayed in Mark Hanna's newspapers.

"They say he has a son from an illicit affair," Kate said.

"Yes," Mamie said. "Mr. Hanna said so many times."

Kate snorted. "As if he has a right to sit in judgment," she said wryly. "He oughta remove that plank from his eye."

Mamie shuddered. She wondered if she should tell Kate about her bizarre encounter with Mark Hanna at the Huntington Estate.

"It's funny, isn't it?" Kate continued. "A woman like me has an illicit child and she's disgraced. A man has an illicit child; he becomes President of the United States."

As Mamie opened her mouth to respond, Kate gasped and shoved Bessie's head down. Mamie, slower to react, locked eyes with Grover Cleveland himself.

"Run!" Kate ordered. They snatched up their skirts and tried to free themselves from the bushes. But it was too late.

"Who's over there?" a voice called. "Stop where you are!"

Mamie froze. Kate grabbed her hand. "Are you mad? Run!"

But someone was already opening the gate that led into the garden, where the party hosting the President was underway. Mamie said a silent prayer as the man approached, beginning to tremble. Surely they would send for the police.

Suddenly, Bessie broke out in a wail: "I just wanted to see Grover Cleveland!" She started to cry, her rosy cheeks turning fiery red.

The man laughed. "It's three girls," he called to his guests, who laughed and smiled too.

He offered his hand to Bessie. "Would you like to meet President Cleveland, young lady?"

Bessie nodded, still looking petrified. "Aye," she said softly.

"You must be a new one." He motioned for Kate and Mamie to step forward. "You, too. Would you like to meet him?"

Mamie and Kate didn't say anything, but followed Bessie into the garden.

"Mister President," the man of the house said, "these girls were hiding in my bushes in the hopes of meeting you. What say you, sir?"

Grover Cleveland laughed a hearty laugh, the jowls beneath his fleshy face quivering. He didn't laugh with an air of sarcasm as rich people often did. He seemed genuinely amused at the idea of three girls hiding in the bushes, peeping at him.

"What's your name?" he asked Bessie, taking her hand like a true gentleman. She looked at her boots.

"Elizabeth Chambers," she whispered.

"Well, Elizabeth Chambers, tell your Pa that President Cleveland would be honored to have his vote," Grover Cleveland said. He reached into his pocket and produced a crisp new handkerchief adorned with the pattern of the American flag.

Bessie's eyes sparkled, and she twisted the handkerchief through her hands. "This is for me?"

"Yes, it's for you to keep," Grover Cleveland said. "Perhaps you should give it to your lady friends for safekeeping."

"My da lives in Ireland," Bessie blurted out. "I live with Miss Kate and my sister, Mamie." She looked up at Kate and Mamie for reassurance.

"But we tell our man friends to vote for Mr. Cleveland and the Democrats," Kate added quickly. Grover Cleveland looked charmed by her, looking over her pert beauty with a keen eye.

"Thank you, Miss Kate," he said, nodding to her like a proper gentleman. "It was my pleasure to meet you all."

They walked home to the Angle, their hearts light. But then Mamie wondered what nefarious motives Maggie Carney and her friends would invent, if they knew they'd met the President.

"Don't you dare tell anyone at school we met Grover Cleveland," Mamie said to Bessie as she tucked her into bed that night. "It must stay a secret between us, you promise?"

"I promise," Bessie said, looking sleepy.

Fifty-Four

One hot day in late summer, Maggie Carney and her tight-knit circle of women from St. Malachi gathered to prepare Annie Joyce for her upcoming wedding to Patrick Moran.

It was supposed to be a joyful event, in which the women showered Annie with gifts. The women brought everything from pots and pans to appropriate undergarments for a married woman. Annie's sister-in-law even brought a traditional Make-Up Bell, a metal bell that Irish couples kept in their homes to ward off evil spirits. The ringing sounded like a church bell's, and demons apparently recoiled from the sound. One half of the married couple could also ring the bell when they were ready to end an argument.

And, of course, when the party was ending, the married women would give the virgin Annie a basic education on what to expect on the wedding night.

But instead of glowing with joy, Annie seemed irritated.

"I was to be married in July," she said. She was pouting, her arms crossed over her midsection.

"We know, Annie," Maggie said. "But your house needs several repairs. Patrick has worked hard to provide you with a decent home. And we want it to be all ready, don't we?"

Annie brushed the other women away as her sister-in-law retook the measurements for her wedding gown, which several of Annie's relatives had worn at their own weddings. Annie Joyce had always been a slip of a woman; she had spindly legs and meager breasts that looked like cherries beneath her clothes. But today, as she tried to wriggle into the dress, it was clear she'd outgrown it.

"I'll let it out a few inches," her sister-in-law said, furrowing her brows.

"This is madness," Annie said, on the verge of a tantrum. "It fit just fine a month ago."

Annie's sister-in-law, trying to keep the bride-to-be calm, wound a ribbon around Annie's bust to see how many inches of fabric to let out.

"Don't pull so tight," Annie snapped. "I'm sore enough as it is."

Annie's sister-in-law dropped the ribbon, looking over her shoulder to see if the other women could hear her.

"Annie," she said, lowering her voice, "Is there any chance you're carrying a child?"

Fifty-Five

The saloon stayed full every night during those hot final weeks of August. The days were long, but fall was approaching. It seemed the men wanted to embrace the warm nights by drinking them away. The German lager flowed, and the dock workers, ship builders, and other immigrant men packed the bar.

Kate was usually the one who stayed awake until midnight or later to close down the bar. But Mamie's head was still humming from the whirl of activity that evening, and she couldn't fathom falling asleep.

"Why don't you let me close the saloon tonight?" she said to Kate. "You deserve a rest."

Kate squeezed Mamie's shoulder in gratitude and retired to bed, too proud to admit she was tired.

Mamie didn't know she was being watched. Outside the saloon, a man waited in the shadows across the street. He wanted to approach her in front of a crowd, making it hard for her to rebuke him. He planned to induce the greatest humiliation.

She looked quite a bit different now than last winter, when she was newly arrived to Cleveland. She had lost weight, the extra flesh that made her look matronly, leaving her well-shaped like an hourglass. She had shed her drab black skirt and simple bun for a fiery red saloon maiden's dress. It looked bold against her dark hair. Her hair was different, too—styled in long, loose curls, although he knew her curls were natural. Still, she looked like a scandalous and sinful woman—which made him feel not the least bit guilty about what he was doing to her...

Finally, it was time to move.

He walked slowly to the door, making sure to remain composed. He didn't want to give off the scent of fear. And was Johnnie Chambers there with his dog? He'd been warned about Mamie's brother, as well as the dog.

He hadn't seen the boy all night, although he would like to get his hands on him, too.

He swung the door open and put on a cool smile. Mamie looked up from her other patrons as he approached, towering over her. "May I help you?"

"Mamie," he said, "It's me. You don't recognize me?"

"Pardon me?" she replied, studying him from behind the bar, looking confused. He removed his hat to help her out.

"It's me, your husband-to-be," he said, holding his hat over his heart. "Peter Sweeny."

Fifty-Six

The crowd stopped to stare at the showdown playing out before them.

"No," Mamie said. "You're not Peter."

She felt dizzy as she examined this man standing in the saloon. He wasn't Peter Sweeny, but he did resemble him—in an eerie, terrible way. He was tall and lanky and had sable wisps of hair, showing the first signs of balding. And he had a small, sinister-looking scar that formed an ugly line through his top lip. It made her all the more certain this couldn't be Peter.

"It's been not even a year and you don't recognize me?" the man said. He took three wide, swaggering steps toward her, his hand closing around her forearm.

"You're not Peter," she said, trying to loosen her arm from his grip, which made his fingers coil even tighter. She grabbed his hand with her own, digging her fingernails into the back of his hand. She had small hands, but her nails were long and sharp, and it caused him to hiss with pain.

"You're not Peter," she said again. "Don't touch me, you hear?"

"You promised to marry me," he replied. "You know there are legal consequences to breaching a contract to marry."

"I didn't promise to marry you," Mamie replied, backing up slowly toward the stairs. "You're a stranger."

Mamie stared at him, wondering if she were trapped in one of her many dreams about Peter Sweeny.

Was this an especially lucid dream—or, more accurately, a nightmare?

"Please go," she said, her voice quiet and frightened.

"I'll be back to discuss our vows to marry," the man said, reaching for the doorknob. "This isn't over, Mamie."

"Peter called me Mary."

"This isn't over, Mary," the man hissed, slamming the door behind him.

The patrons, the ones who understood what had happened at least, buzzed among themselves. Mamie saw what was happening already. There was no way to stop this terrible rumor from spreading through the neighborhood like swamp fever. She tried her best to stay calm, refilling beer glasses for men who gawked at her, watching her reaction.

When the last patron left, Mamie locked the door to the saloon, but it didn't seem like enough. She dragged a heavy chair and forced it against the door, then another. She awoke Kate with the noise.

"What in God's name is going on?" Kate asked, appearing in her nightgown.

"A man came in tonight," Mamie explained frantically, "saying he's Peter Sweeny."

"What do you mean, saying he's Peter Sweeny?" Kate repeated. "*Was* it Peter?"

Mamie stopped in the middle of dragging another chair to the door and stared at her. "I don't know," she said. "I don't think so."

"What? Mamie, did Peter Sweeny come in here or not?"

"He looked like Peter, but he wasn't Peter," Mamie said. She felt tears sting the corners of her eyes. "I know from the scar on his lip."

"Dear God," Kate grumbled, shaking her head.

"I'm leaving to find my brothers," Mamie said, trembling. "Tom and Johnnie…they'll know whether this man is Peter Sweeny."

Kate grabbed her shoulders, steadying her, and looked straight into her eyes. "You're going nowhere," she said. "Mamie, listen to me. You don't need a man—any man—to judge whether this man you saw is Peter Sweeny. You know he isn't, because you saw with your own eyes, aye?"

Mamie nodded.

"Second, this is our saloon, and we're gonna learn to protect it," Kate said. She went behind the bar and pulled a large butcher's knife from its resting place on a hook in the wall.

"Keep this near," Kate instructed. "If that man returns, you give him a good slash across the face. Put another scar on his lip. You wouldn't hesitate to do so, right?"

Mamie stared at the knife, remembering the story Seán Fada had told about her own father putting a knife through Black Willie's hand. A year ago, when she was still living in Roskeen, such an action would be unthinkable. But now she understood why her father did what he had to do.

Mamie was finally seeing had a large part of her father's spirit in her, too.

Mamie nodded to Kate, and they proceeded, silently, to bed.

✝ Fifty-Seven

Despite the nightmare of the night before, Mamie still had to rise early in the morning. She was duty-bound to walk Bessie to school and then report to her job at the Hanna mansion. Bessie had slept through the chaos last night, and Mamie had no intention of telling her what had happened...yet.

When they reached the schoolhouse doors, Bessie looked up at her, her rosy cheeks a bit paler than usual, her blue eyes round with worry. "Mamie, what's wrong?" she asked.

"Nothing's wrong."

"Then why are your hands shaky?" Bessie asked, and Mamie folded them behind her back where Bessie couldn't see them. She paused for a moment before she knelt down to Bessie's level.

"Bessie, do you remember Peter, my sweetheart from Roskeen?" she asked.

Bessie nodded. "I remember him."

"And if you saw him, you would recognize him right away?" Mamie asked.

Bessie squinted, thinking for a moment. "I would."

"Thank you, Bessie," Mamie said. "Now be a good girl at school today, you hear?"

Mark Hanna was spending more time away from home as the election drew closer. As soon as she cleared the supper table, Mamie asked Mrs. Hanna to release her.

But Mamie didn't return to the saloon. Instead, she went to see the only person who solemnly swore to keep her secrets safe: Father James Molony.

"Forgive me, Father, for I have sinned," she said, rushing through the all-too-familiar introduction. "It's been…too long since my last confession. I can't even remember the days, let alone the date of my last confession."

"It's the sixth of September, a Thursday," Father Molony said. "What happened? This isn't the Mary Chambers I know."

Mamie took a deep breath.

"My husband-to-be, Peter," she said. "Someone claiming to be Peter…is back."

For once, Father Molony—always a reservoir of peace and serenity—was the one to look shocked. "What do you mean, claiming to be Peter?"

"I've heard that question many times since last night," Mamie said, her shoulders slumping.

"Good God, Mary," Father Molony said, emerging from the confessional. "Follow me. I'll go to the saloon with you."

Everyone on the Viaduct was familiar with Father Molony. They fell quiet when they saw the earnest look on his face as he walked beside Mamie, leaning on his old staff. A small crowd was already gathered around the entrance to the saloon. Men sat on the stoop outside the door, or leaned against the brick building, escaping the summer heat inside the saloon.

Mamie's brothers, Johnnie and Tom, were already waiting for Mamie to get home. They ran to her as she approached.

Kate, too, came outside when she spotted them through the window. A group of men walking home from work stopped in the middle of the street to gape at the scene, smirking at the possibility of drama unfolding.

Mamie noticed Patrick Moran and Austin Carney among them.

"Catherine," Father Molony said to Kate, "Send someone to fetch this man calling himself Peter Sweeny. Where is he?"

"He's staying at an inn near the river," Kate said, beckoning Mamie and Father Molony to come closer to her so no one could hear her. "Word sure travels fast in this neighborhood. Peter—ah, the man who says he's Peter—arrived there a few days ago. He's telling people some form of amnesia struck him after your brother Johnnie beat him about the head. He claims he was traveling around for months. Until he recovered his memory and bought his passage back to Cleveland."

Johnnie stared at her, open-mouthed. "That's horse shit," he said. "Amnesia? ...How could anyone believe such rawmaish?"

"People in this neighborhood believe whatever they want to believe," Tom said. They all looked to Father Molony for guidance, and the priest looked incredulous as well.

They all knew it was lies. A pack of lies—but that wasn't enough to convince the mob gathering outside the saloon...

One of the men went to retrieve the alleged Peter Sweeny. They returned some twenty minutes later with the tall, lanky man with the scar on his lip. Tom Chambers gasped.

"He does look just like Peter," Tom said.

The man with the scarred lip smiled. "You hear that?" he said to no one in particular. "Tom Chambers recognizes me."

Tom crossed his arms over his wide chest, setting his jaw. "I didn't say I recognized you..."

"It looks like Peter, but it ain't Peter," Johnnie said, crossing his arms as well. "I knew the real Peter Sweeny for years. I sat behind him in church. I slept in the bunk below him when we sailed the Atlantic, all the way to New York. And I remember the look in his eyes—that devil-look on his face when his eyes started to wander that night. He's not Sweeny, but he's a decent imposter." He kicked at the dust with his boot in the man's general direction. "So who are you, anyway? And what do you want with my sister?"

At just the wrong moment, Mad Annie stumbled out of the saloon, nursing her baby at her naked breast. "I've seen Peter Sweeny, too," Mad Annie said, "and I know that isn't him." Her red hair was disheveled, and her eyes looked clouded.

Everyone gathered around the saloon was now transfixed on the sight of Annie and her infant, staring in astonishment.

"Hey," someone said. "When did Mad Annie Kilbane have a baby?"

Fifty-Eight

"Mad Annie dropped a bastard child."

Austin Carney looked up at his wife, Maggie, who looked like she was dressed to go to church. Austin shrugged at the news, a bit bored with the revelation. The woman Austin married never ran out of gossip, although she usually saved it to share with her women friends from St. Malachi when they gathered on Saturday nights before church the next morning.

"It should surprise no one," Austin said. "I assumed that's how she fed herself, by whoring. A child results from the act eventually."

"It hasn't for us," Maggie said.

Austin cringed, wondering why she had to remind him. He and Maggie had been married long enough now to have more than one child, but instead, they'd produced none. They were uncertain whether his seed or hers was to blame. In any case, it was a source of growing bitterness between them.

"I heard her baby is a boy," Maggie said. "It would be so tragic for a boy to grow up amid all those whorish women, those bar maids. Kate's daughter Molly has it bad enough, but she's a girl. You know what they say about boys..."

"An inch of a lad is better than a foot of a girl," they both said at the same time.

"Yes, it would be tragic," Austin agreed, and went back to reading his newspaper. Maggie walked over and snatched it out of his hand.

"Do you hear what I'm saying?" she demanded. "That poor child should be taken from Annie. I'm going to alert the Ursuline nuns that something must be done about it."

"I wouldn't," Austin said. "Haven't we tired of trying to punish them? Pat and I were lucky to escape suspicion over the arson."

"No one knows you and Pat set the fire," Maggie snapped.

"Exactly," Austin replied. "So what do you say we lay low and stay out Kate Masterson's business a while? I'm sick of hearing her wretched name."

Maggie huffed. "I care about this neighborhood, and I'll do what I must to protect it from her seedy influence," she said as she threw the door open.

✠

Fifty-Nine

Seeking out the nuns at their convent was verboten, so Maggie found them at the girl's school. She was shrewd enough to avoid Mother Berchmanns. Mother Berchmanns had a bleeding heart; she was soft on sin. Maybe it was because Mother Berchmanns was born in the most vulgar and obscene of countries—France. In any event, Maggie and her friends knew to go around the soft-hearted Mother and approach her underlings instead.

"Sister Teresa," Maggie said as she waved her hands at another Ursuline nun, a youngish but mean-faced woman who taught at the school. "May I speak with you? It's of the utmost urgency."

"Yes, Missus Carney," the nun said. "What troubles you?"

She ushered Maggie into the empty classroom, where the last stragglers were gathering their books for the walk home. Maggie leaned in, putting on her best expression of righteous indignation.

"It's Kate Masterson," she said.

Mother Teresa rolled her eyes. By now, many of the nuns were aware of Kate Masterson and the moral threat she posed to the Angle. Working as a saloon madame was scandalous enough. But Maggie hoped that harboring unwed mothers was an outrage the Catholic nuns wouldn't abide.

This ought to be the final straw, Maggie thought to herself.

"I've gotten wind that Annie Kilbane just gave birth to a baby," Maggie said. "Sister, I just cannot stand by and let that poor, innocent little lad grow up that way...at a saloon, with a mother who should be committed. No father to guide his moral development..."

She could tell Sister Teresa agreed.

"It is a travesty what has happened to Kate Masterson's sweet young daughter, growing up fatherless," Maggie continued. "And speaking of that, no one has seen Kate's daughter in months. I shudder to think of what might have befallen her."

As the nun blinked in horror, Maggie managed to coax a few tears to her eyes.

"Could you please intervene? I've approached Father Molony, and he won't do a thing about Kate," Maggie said. She let a tear roll down her cheek, although it was really for herself and her empty womb.

Sister Teresa nodded emphatically. "Of course something must be done," she said, and from the look on her face, Maggie knew the meeting had achieved her ends.

Sixty

With her brother Tom keeping watch outside, Mamie marched up to the hotel where Peter Sweeny's imposter rented a room. This wasn't a nice hotel—it was old and the lobby smelled of mildew. It was the only other hotel in this neighborhood besides Seán Fada's. This one was known to be more accepting of prostitution and other seedy activities.

But Mamie marched forward anyway. She was too angry to be afraid.

"Wait here for me," she said to Tom. "If I don't return within the hour, go in after me."

She walked up to the check-in desk. The owner kept the name of guests and their room numbers scrawled in a leather-bound book.

"I'm looking for Peter Sweeny," she said.

She half-expected him to give her a dirty look, or question why she was visiting a man at his hotel room unescorted. But this innkeeper had seen it all before, and he barely looked at her.

"Mr. Sweeny is on the second floor, the last room on the right," he said, sounding bored.

"Ah, Mary," the imposter said when he opened his door. "I'm glad to see you've reconsidered. I take it you've decided to honor your vows to marry me?"

Mamie stepped into the room, arms folded across her chest. She thought of sticking her foot out behind her to keep the door cracked, but to her dismay, he shut it behind her.

"Why are you doing this?" she asked, patience wearing thin already.

"Doing what?"

"I know you're not Peter," she said. "You know you're not Peter. Who put you up to this?"

The imposter didn't answer. Instead, he looked out the lone window in the hotel room. As if the goings-on in the street below were so much more important than her questions.

"Chambers," he said, his tone curious yet nonchalant. "It's a Scottish name, no? It's not Gaelic."

"I don't know," Mamie replied. "My family lived in Ireland for all the generations we can recall, that's what I know."

"Perhaps they were gallowglasses," the imposter said. "Do you know who they were?"

"No."

"They were fierce warriors from Scotland brought to Ireland to defend the Catholics," he replied. "The Mastersons must descend from such people, as Masterson is a Scottish name. Fighters. You're a fighter too, Mary, but it's to your own detriment. You can resist me all you want, but the law favors the man in these matters. And we all know public opinion is on my side. Your neighbors already think you are a scandalous woman, defying the man she promised to marry."

"I know," Mamie said.

The imposter turned away from the window and took several broad strides toward her. He had long legs, like the real Peter.

"You know," he said, "the Scottish also perfected the art of burning heretic women at the stake. To make the unseemly process easier, they strangled the women first."

He reached out and grabbed Mamie around the neck. She gasped. Before she could react any further, he dropped his hand and laughed.

"Don't look so frightened. I'm not going to personally execute you for heresy," he said. "You'll be your own worst enemy in that regard."

"Are you going to answer my question?" Mamie asked. "Why are you doing this? If you tell me what you want—like money, I presume—it ups your chances of actually getting it from me."

"I don't want money," he replied. "I want your saloon."

"Ah, now we've reached the heart of the matter," Mamie replied. "Did the Mob put you up to this?"

"I want you, too," he said.

"No, you don't," Mamie replied.

Again, the imposter ignored her comment and changed the subject.

"Mary, are you familiar with Sigmund Freud?"

Mamie harrumphed, growing annoyed. Sigmund Freud and his scribblings on psychology were something pompous people dwelt upon. It was something Mark Hanna and his friends pretended to care about to impress each other.

"I've heard the name, but I've no interest in his work," she replied. "But—"

Suddenly the imposter threw up her skirts. He thrust his hand between her legs, manhandling her. She jumped. Then, afraid of what else he'd attempt, she slashed him across the face with her fingernails in one swift motion.

"Get out of my hotel room, you immature hoor," he said, suddenly angry. "Go back to your tavern, you slattern! You'd make an unsatisfactory wife anyhow."

Mamie yanked her skirts back into place and calmly turned to the door.

"That's another reason why I know you're not Peter," she said with a bemused smile. It seemed to enrage the imposter even more. "Peter Sweeny knew nothing of Dr. Freud. He didn't care to."

✝

Sixty-One

Mamie met Tom outside the hotel. Fall was approaching, and a strong wind blew some papery brown leaves around their feet. "He wants the saloon," Mamie said, crunching a dead leaf with her heel. "There's no doubt the Mob put him up to this, whoever he is."

"I could have told you as much," Tom said. He pushed his eyeglasses up his nose, shielding his tired eyes. He looked like he hadn't slept in weeks.

The usual crowd gathered around the saloon, now that it was supper time and the men had finished work for the day. Austin Carney and his friends were sitting on a stoop on the opposite side of the street, heckling the crowd as usual.

"Feckin' Polacks," Austin sneered. "Crazy Kraut kids. I can smell 'em from over here."

Mamie pushed past them to the front door.

"Don't give 'em the time of day," Tom said, shooting the men a hateful glance. But underneath his steely demeanor, Tom was tired. Mamie could see the constant hatred was eroding Tom's soul, making him question why he came to this country. He could have lived a quiet life as a tailor in Roskeen. But now...

Johnnie was sitting near the front window of the saloon with his dog. Now that Seán Fada was buried and gone, and Patrick Masterson was on the lakes, Johnnie had become their protector. He stationed himself at the front door every night. Johnnie's presence did seem to scare off some of the hecklers.

But Mamie wasn't prepared for the Devil to come knocking at the saloon door that night. He came in the form of several Ursuline nuns led by a young priest.

"Mamie, why is my teacher outside?" Bessie asked. Mamie looked up from the bar, alarmed.

Kate knew why the nuns were there before they knocked.

"Turn them away," she said to Mamie, rushing to the door. "They're coming for Annie's child."

Annie sat in a chair near the kitchen, nursing baby Michael. Kate motioned for her to leave the room—but it was too late.

"Catherine Masterson," the meanest nun said. "We're here to take Anna Kilbane's baby into our care. I'm sure you understand this is not a suitable environment for a child?"

Kate stood in the doorway, blocking the entrance with her arms. "No, I don't understand," she said. "Where were you when Annie was violated? Do you believe for one second she chose to lay down and make that baby?"

"That is irrelevant," the lone man in the group, the priest, said. He pushed Kate aside and allowed the nuns to barge into the saloon. "She is an unwed mother."

"I know you," Kate said, jabbing a finger in the priest's face. "You're the priest who had an affair with Agnes, the former nun."

"You're talking nonsense," the priest said. "I know nothing of which you speak."

One of the nuns marched up to Annie and, without a word, ripped baby Michael from her arms. Annie screamed.

"My baby! They're stealing my baby!"

Annie ripped off the nun's veil and pulled at her hair with a violence that could only come from a mother whose child had been snatched away. She clawed at her face. The priest gave Annie a decisive shove, causing her to reel back and trip over the chair.

"Hey, don't you push her!" Johnnie said, jumping to his feet.

With one hand, Johnnie snatched the baby from the nun's hands. Then, holding the infant under one arm, he pummeled the priest, his closed fist pounding his eye socket. *Crack.*

Baby Michael began to squall. His little face was blotchy and red.

"He's assaulting us!" the nun shrieked, running into the street. "Send for the police!"

"They're trying to have us arrested," Kate mumbled. "And of course they are. None of their other attempts to scare us have worked, so why not jail?"

"You shouldn't have struck the priest," Mamie said to Johnnie. "You knew he'd run screaming to the authorities."

"So be it," Kate replied stubbornly. "Perhaps they can also arrest Annie's rapist, finally. If only they cared enough to investigate."

A short time later, Father Molony arrived at the saloon.

"Girls," he said, and there was a fatherly pain in his voice when he called them "girls."

"Yes, Father Molony," Kate replied.

"Why did no one come to me when Annie had a baby?" he asked. "You know someone should have told me."

"Because the neighborhood harpies would summon the nuns to take the babe, that's why," Johnnie replied, sounding annoyed. "Why do you think Kate sent her girl away?"

Father Molony crossed his arms. "Kate, for God's sake, where is Molly?"

"I'm not telling," Kate said defiantly.

The police rapped on the door. "Open up," a stern voice commanded.

Mamie answered the door and found her uncle, Michael, and his partner there. "Uncle Michael," Mamie said, "you're not really going to arrest your nephew because the nuns summoned you out of pure malice. Are you?"

Michael grimaced, plainly uncomfortable with the dispute he had no choice but to address. Mamie could read his body and face clear as day, and he wanted nothing to do with this scene. But it wasn't up to him.

"They claim Annie and Johnnie assaulted them," he said.

"They tried to take Annie's babe," Kate replied.

"That isn't what I asked."

"Uncle Michael, no one here assaulted that two-faced, ne'er-do-well priest or those cold-hearted harpies," Johnnie said indignantly. "Only reacted after they started the shite. So go on and do some real work, will ya? Like finding the man who raped Annie and left his seed in her."

Uncle Michael's partner took visible offense. "Finally," he said, taking a long stride toward Johnnie. "You're the kid who's been pilfering shit down at Whiskey Island. If I had a dollar for every report about you..."

"I only pilfer coal to make sure my people survive, sir," Johnnie replied. "Wouldn't you do the same?"

"Check his pockets," the officer barked at Uncle Michael, pointing at Johnnie.

Michael brushed the sweat from his forehead. "He's my nephew," he said.

"Family relations don't trump the law. Check his pockets."

Mamie pressed her first two fingers to her eyebrow like a shield, afraid of what she might see. She half-expected Uncle Michael to pull some scrap metal or pilfered coins from Johnnie's pocket. But what fell onto the saloon floor was worse than she could ever imagine.

"Hey, whose wallet is this?" Michael's partner demanded, picking the expensive piece of leather from the floor. "It's not yours. That's a given."

He opened the wallet. "Ah, you're pick-pocketing the high rollers," he said. "An address on Euclid Avenue, of all places. I'll be damned."

The officer turned to Uncle Michael. "Take him to the jail," he barked.

Mamie gasped. "No!" she whispered, burying her face in her hands. Her brother Tom put his hand to her back, attempting to soothe her.

"I'll deal with you later," Michael's partner said to Kate.

They watched helplessly as their own uncle loaded Johnnie into the police wagon and rolled away to the squalid city jail.

Sixty-Two

Johnnie showed no fear as he entered the jail, which seemed to antagonize his captors. But it didn't mean he didn't feel it. He did—especially when the police officer led him to the putrid-smelling cesspool that housed prisoners. The only thing worse than the smell was the noise—men yelling, leering, spitting, and clanging the metal bars that entrapped them.

"What's your name, boy?"

"Chambers," he said, watching a puddle of urine stain the toe of his boot.

"What's that?"

"Chambers!" he yelled, and the men laughed.

Uncle Michael's partner stuck his key in the padlock that kept the iron fence shut. He opened it and gave Johnnie a forceful shove inside.

"So you're a Chambers, eh?" a scraggly man, who appeared to be in his forties, said. When he spoke he revealed a row of discolored teeth, and the skin on his face had the yellowed appearance of a heavy drinker. His clothes still smelled of alcohol. Still, Johnnie could tell that this man had been strapping and handsome in his younger years—and still was, if only he'd take a bath.

"I knew a man named Will Chambers back in the day," the jaundiced drunk continued. "The fiercest Dead Rabbit there ever was. We called him Tylor Mor."

Johnnie stared at him.

"You know him?"

"Aye, I know him," Johnnie said. "He's my da."

Johnnie wondered what his father would think of him if he knew he was here, in this dank jail cell.

It was impossible to know what time it was when a guard came to retrieve Johnnie sometime the next morning. It could have been five o'clock or seven. There were no lights in the jail, making it impossible to know if it was day or night. Johnnie reasoned it was morning because he had finally gone to sleep a few hours before.

The guard yanked him by the shirt collar, like a disgruntled housewife picking up a kitten by the scruff of its neck.

"Get up. You're a ward of the Children's Aid Society Now. You're going to the Industrial School," the man said.

He didn't have to explain to Johnnie what he meant. Johnnie knew about the Industrial School—a place worse than jail. It wasn't so much a school as a workhouse for juvenile delinquents, who were forced to do hard manual labor and learn religion. Protestant religion. The Englishman's religion. Catholic priests weren't allowed to teach to the young boys at the Industrial School or even hear confession, even though many of the inmates were Irish boys.

It was where a Catholic boy's soul went to die.

✝

Sixty-Three

The morning after the nuns tried to take Annie's baby, a man with red hair walked into the saloon.

"Kate Masterson, where is my sister?" he asked. Mamie should have guessed he was Annie's brother.

When he noticed Mamie standing there, he made a harried introduction. "I'm Anna's brother, James Kilbane," he said. "But most people call me *Coinneal*."

Coinneal meant "candle" in Gaelic. Mamie took one glance at his flame-red hair and didn't wonder why the name was bestowed upon him.

Kate brought Annie out of the bedroom, holding baby Michael.

"What're you doing here, Coinneal?" Annie asked, clutching Michael closer to her chest. "I haven't seen you in months."

"You've avoided me," he replied. "And you didn't tell me you were with child." He motioned for Annie to leave the room while he talked to Kate and Mamie.

"First, I want to thank you for what you did last night," he said to Kate. "I had no idea...until the rumor mill was up and running, of course. You've always looking out for my sister, no matter how unraveled she becomes. There's many in this neighborhood who don't give a damn what happens to her; would let her be raped and left for dead any night of the week."

Kate nodded silently, knowing it was true.

"People don't know her," Coinneal continued. "They don't know she was normal until she nearly died of a fever when she was young. My Da said it cooked her brain. She was never the same after that. Still, is she a woman or no? You'd never know she was a child of God like the rest of us, from the way this neighborhood treats her. But you're an exception."

Kate bit her lip.

"That said, I'm taking Annie and the baby to live with me," Coinneal said. "Annie won't like it much; she says I try too hard to control her. She wants her freedom. But if she gets it, that baby will disappear, and God knows where he'll end up."

Kate harrumphed, laughing in her usual wry manner. "A bassinet at Maggie Carney's bedside, that's where," she said. "I'm sure they'd give him a good Christian upbringing."

"Speaking of the Carneys, I also came to warn you, Kate," Coinneal said. "They're spreading a rumor that your daughter is missing."

"I know," Kate snapped.

"...And that you killed her," Coinneal added, searching her eyes until she understood how serious he was. "They're not accusing you directly, of course. But once the seed of such an ugly rumor is planted..."

Kate looked quietly furious. "Maggie is on her high horse again, eh? She won't have Father Molony's blessing for her little crusade. Holier-than-thou is what she is. Tell her Molly is alive and well...and she won't be laying a hand on her. Or on baby Michael."

Annie's brother nodded, in plain agreement with every word Kate had spoken. "I'll never forget what you did. God protect ya, Katie," he said as he departed.

Coinneal's words gave Mamie just enough courage to visit Johnnie at the Industrial School the next day.

The Industrial School looked and smelled like the worst kind of prison. Mamie had never seen a place like this. She knew they had workhouses in Ireland for the urban poor in cities like Dublin and Galway, which functioned as debtor's prisons. But she'd never actually been inside a workhouse. And the Industrial School looked far more ominous than she had imagined.

"School, my arse," she whispered to Father Molony as they approached the entrance.

Everything inside looked gray and dusty, and it smelled of mold. A guard stopped them at the door. He informed them that women were forbidden to enter.

"She's an inmate's sister," Father Molony protested.

"She can wait by the door," the guard barked. "Who are you here for?"

"John Chambers."

"Which one? We have a lot of Chamberses here."

"He's a spirited boy, just turned sixteen, likes to box..."

That was all Father Molony had to say. A few minutes later, the guard led Johnnie by the arm to the iron gate, throwing him against the bars.

"You have two minutes," the guard said.

Johnnie was freshly bathed, but his eyes looked sad and defeated. He was pale, like Patrick Masterson's ghosts along the road in Castlebar. It had only been a week and his face looked thinner, hollow.

"Father," Johnnie said, "you have to get me out of here."

Disobeying the guard's orders, Mamie went to the gate and held Johnnie's hands through the bars.

"They're going to force me to become a Protestant," Johnnie said. "They said my only way out is to learn a trade. Then maybe, when I'm eighteen, they'll consider letting me out. But I'll die in here before I turn eighteen. I'm sure of it."

"I'll see what I can do," Father Molony said, his mouth turning down at the corners. "You should at least have access to Catholic instruction."

When she returned home, Tom was waiting for Mamie at the saloon. She told him what had happened, and how the Industrial School could keep Johnnie until he turned eighteen. Maybe longer.

"It's no use," Tom said, looking utterly defeated. "The only way out of that place is in a casket."

Mamie's mind snapped to attention. Memories flashed before her: The America wake. The eulogy her father had given as she laid there, pretending to be dead. The coffins.

"Hold that thought," Mamie said to Tom. "You've given me an idea."

✝

Sixty-Four

After a long month in Michigan, Patrick Masterson was going home. He wondered what new trials-by-fire had befell his sister's saloon while he was gone…literally. The fire someone had started on purpose there had gone unpunished.

At this point, Patrick was prepared to take justice into his own hands. Which was why, when he stepped off his ship, he went to see Kate at the saloon for updates on their situation.

Johnnie Chambers was in jail. Patrick was disheartened but not surprised—with that boy, it was only a matter of time. And most bizarre of all the events that had transpired this year, Peter Sweeny had reemerged. The Peter Sweeny everyone believed was dead or long-gone.

The man had to be an imposter, Kate and Patrick agreed. But who had sent him? And what did they want?

Behind the bar, Kate repeated a rumor she'd heard on the street. A saloon singer who claimed she sang on Mississippi steamboats was performing tonight. She'd take the stage at the very hotel where a man calling himself Peter Sweeny stayed. Patrick planned to attend the singer's performance.

Patrick had always steered clear of this hotel. It was as much a venue for prostitution as it was for housing travelers. There was a lounge on the first floor near the lobby. It was the type of lounge where guests wooed ladies of the night with cheap drinks and even cheaper banter.

And there were lounge singers. This hotel had a carousel of lounge singers that performed here. Tonight, they were advertising a woman calling herself Zia. She claimed to be a Cherokee princess now making a living as a singer.

Zia. The woman who had lured away Peter Sweeny had dropped the charade about being French. She'd chosen another exotic name and another dramatic biography.

Patrick caught a look at himself in the smeary front windows of the hotel as he entered. His beard had grown out while he was in Michigan, and his hair, once close-cropped, was wild and curly. The summer sun had browned his face, to the point it looked copper and leathery, making his eyes look green as grass. He looked rough, like a burly seaman. He felt confident his new appearance would allow him to blend in to the crowd. The erstwhile Marie St. Jean wouldn't recognize him from that December night when Peter disappeared.

He went to the bar and bought a drink.

"Who's singin' tonight?" he asked the barkeeper, trying to make his interest sound casual and fleeting.

The barkeeper shrugged. "A Spanish woman," he said. "I hear her voice ain't nothing to write home about, but at least she's easy on the eyes."

A Spanish woman? The name Zia sounded more Italian than Spanish, but Italians were out of favor these days. Italians were once revered Renaissance men in American imaginations. But now, they were just another despised ethnic group pouring into the country, like the Irish a generation ago. Patrick began to wonder if this saloon singer was the same woman as the mysterious Marie St. Jean. If not, he was wasting his time, drinking cheap gin, which he hated. He considered leaving.

But then he thought of Mamie, wailing on her knees in the street that morning in December. It was worth waiting just to bring her some closure.

Patrick watched Zia take the stage, which was really just a raised platform a few inches above ground. She might have changed her name, but she had done nothing to change her appearance. She was definitely the same woman who had visited Kate's saloon. Her accent, this time, was a vague European mélange, neither English nor Spanish nor French. Patrick sucked in his chest and tried to identify the feeling within it, something he didn't feel very often…

Maybe, he had to admit, it was fear. He pretended to watch her sub-par performance. But silently, he was plotting how to approach her afterward.

He turned again to the barkeeper. "Do you have any coffee and sweet cream?"

"I have both," he replied. "I can't promise the coffee's fresh, but we have it."

"Pour some whiskey in it and give it to me," Patrick said.

When Zia finished singing, Patrick approached her, holding out the steaming coffee. "A sweet drink for a sweet lady," he said.

She wrinkled her nose. "What's this?" she asked, taking it and holding it up to her nostrils. "I hate coffee."

"It's an Irish coffee, m'lady," he said, bowing a little.

"I don't work for drinks," Zia said, handing the drink back to him.

"Well, what do you say we discuss your work in your boudoir?" Patrick asked, feeling he had no time to waste.

She put her hands on her hips and looked at him. "How do you make your living?" she asked.

She was trying to gauge how much money he might have before she went upstairs with him.

"I'm a sailor," he said. "I travel between here and there on a ship called the *Belle Chase*."

"A sailor?" she said, flaring her nostrils again. "You don't *smell* like a sailor."

"I'll take that as the highest compliment."

"Do you have money to burn?" Zia asked, cutting to the chase.

"I do," Patrick replied. "I'm a bachelor with a steady job and no cherubs to provide for."

"Perfect," she said. She looked him over like a housewife inspecting produce at the market. "Well, I'm on the third floor if you want to visit me when the lounge closes. I picked the most isolated room in the hotel so I could maintain complete discretion." She winked. "If you know what I mean."

"I know exactly what you mean," he said. And as the barkeeper closed the lounge for the night, Patrick slipped up the staircase to the third floor.

He knocked three times on the door—light knocks, so as not to draw attention to what they were doing.

"Enter," Zia's brash voice ordered. He did.

She was already stripped down to her petticoats and lacy underthings. "What?" she said as she studied his expression. "You've never been in a girl's boudoir before?"

"I have," he said, sitting tentatively on the edge of the bed. "I'm no virgin."

It was true, although he wasn't proud of it. He'd had a rough go of it as a sailor. He went through a stretch of time where he drank too much—and maybe he still did, come to think of it. Away from home, sailing the Great Lakes, he spent far too many lonely nights in camps and boarding houses. He'd had one woman he wanted to marry, when he was twenty-two, but in the end she rejected him.

He was twenty-six now, and starting to grow tired of his sailor lifestyle and bachelorhood. It was exhausting.

Zia held up a medicine bottle. "Try a drink of this," she said.

He wanted to tell her that pigs would fly before he sipped a mysterious elixir she had mixed. But instead, he feigned interest.

"What is it?"

Her eyes looked black, and her mouth twisted into a closed-lip smile that made her look evil. "Opium," she said. "It should help with your...performance."

Patrick stared at her. "Bathe for me," he said.

He noticed when he walked in that there was a bathtub behind a privacy curtain in the room, and it was full of water. He could practically smell the boiled water on the other side of the curtain. Zia looked a little insulted.

"Not that you're dirty," Patrick added. "I just like my girls smelling of soap."

"Done," she said, and stepped behind the curtain to undress.

It was really Patrick's opportunity to talk to her when she was relaxed and unable to react quickly.

Against his better judgment, Patrick threw aside the curtain and looked down at this naked woman in the bathtub. She smiled a lusty smile, lowering her chin and gnawing at her lip. Her body was uninviting. She had many scars and moles and what looked like a tattoo, ugly and twisted.

Everything about this woman was ugly.

"I think I may have met you before," he said as Zia rubbed herself with Castille soap.

"Where?" she asked. "You don't look familiar to me."

"I was at a saloon one night before Christmas, nearly a year ago. I believe you might have left with a man," Patrick said.

"Oh, I remember that night now," Zia said with a laugh. "My husband and his brother were trying to rob somebody. They use me for bait. I really haven't seen 'em since. We believe in free love, you see. My husband went out West for a time. And I certainly never saw that poor dumb chap again."

"What happened?"

"Nothing that I saw firsthand," Zia said. "My husband cracked him over the head and stole his money. When we came back in the morning to get rid of the body, he was gone. We assumed he woke up and went stumbling home like the drunken fool he was."

She started to slither out of the bathtub. "What are you staring at?" she demanded, standing in front of him naked. "Are we going to do this or what?"

"I'm sorry," Patrick said without thinking. "Whiskey dick."

Then he turned to leave.

"Hey!" she shouted, her coy smile disappearing. She was angry. She snatched her clothes with one hand and Patrick's collar with the other.

"Don't fret. I'm still paying you for your troubles," he said, whipping a paper bill at her. With that, she looked satisfied. Happy, even, that she could take his money without actually performing for him sexually.

"I'll be back," he told her.

He raced down the stairs, not realizing he was still holding the bottle of Zia's elixir.

✝

Sixty-Five

Father James Molony went to see Johnnie Chambers at the Industrial School. Johnnie whispered his confession to the good priest, and the priest whispered back. He murmured as he rested his hand on Johnnie's head, blessing him. Then Father Molony left. He nodded a silent thanks to the guards as he stepped out of the dankness of the prison into the sunlight.

Overnight, a cough ravaged Johnnie Chambers. A hacking, violent cough that filled many of the seasoned guards with dread. They had seen this kind of cough before, and all they knew was this: they didn't want to catch it.

"Put him in isolation," the headmaster said. "The last thing we need is an outbreak."

"Will I see a doctor?" Johnnie asked.

The headmaster sneered as he shut the door to the sick bay on him. "You're at the Industrial School," he said. "If you live, you live. If not, well...good luck to ya."

The cough grew worse, and two days later, Father Molony returned, asking to grant Last Rites.

"If you insist," the Headmaster said with a shrug, as if part of him was relieved that at least one inmate would soon be off his hands.

Father Sweeny reappeared some hours later. He told the Headmaster to leave Johnnie where he was, lest he infect anyone with consumption posthumously. Johnnie's brother Tom, who worked for the morgue, would fashion a casket for the teenager. He was working overnight with slabs of cheap lumber to build it. Tom and the other morgue employees would return to pick up the body tomorrow.

Later that day, Father Molony gave a formal notice to the family. A little more than sixteen years after he'd entered the world, Johnnie Chambers was dead.

Patrick Masterson helped Tom Chambers and his uncle, Joseph McGlynn, work through the night to build the casket. They knew time was of the essence. Patrick was leaving in a few days for another trip across the Lakes. As they hammered and sawed through the wee morning hours, Patrick didn't breathe a word about Peter Sweeny, or "Zia." He would address that all later. For now, their sole focus was on burying Johnnie.

Kate helped Mamie with the arrangements for the wake. Agnes, Mamie's cousin who was taking care of Molly, offered to host the wake in her parlor room. Mamie accepted. It was deadly important that the funeral take place some distance away from the Angle. Father Molony would be there to bless the body.

Mamie got Bessie dressed before the wake, in the simple dress she had worn on the trip from Ireland. She braided her hair. She secured it with Bessie's favorite blue ribbons. Bessie cried intermittently, grappling with the idea that Johnnie was dead.

As evening approached and they were preparing to leave for Agnes' house on Jay Avenue, Mamie leaned down and whispered in Bessie's ear. She nodded and smiled, agreeing to stay quiet on the trip and remain close to Mamie's side at the wake. Then the smile evaporated and her little face filled with fear.

Bessie wrapped Mamie in a hug. "I hate wakes," she said, burying her chin in Mamie's shoulder.

"I hate them, too," Mamie said honestly. "But we'll get through this one together."

"Are you ready?" Kate asked, appearing in the doorway, also dressed in black.

Mamie took a sharp breath. "Ready as we'll ever be."

It was supper time when they made the walk to Jay Avenue, and Mamie was thankful that few people were out. It was a gorgeous autumn evening. But the ever-increasing piles of dead leaves in the streets reminded Mamie that the Earth was dying, too. It would soon be cold and shriveled. It wouldn't come to life again until April, at the earliest. Mamie thought of how bitterly cold it had been last winter. Johnnie wouldn't be here to steal coal anymore, for the sake of keeping his neighbors alive.

What a crime, she thought bitterly. She thought of the Hannas and all the unnecessary luxuries they afforded. They would never worry about freezing to death.

Agnes had bathed and dressed Molly, who looked older by the day.

"The men are coming with the casket," Agnes said, watching the procession through the front window. Then she warned them, "The police are outside."

Mamie's eyes widened. "Why?"

She looked outside and saw Uncle Michael and another officer waiting across the street. They kept their eyes on the pallbearers marching Johnnie's casket into the parlor room. Before they shut the door to Agnes' house, Uncle Joseph stepped outside to talk to them.

"You really have to do this, aye, brother?" He asked Uncle Michael. "Your family hasn't suffered enough?"

"I don't make the rules," Uncle Michael said.

"You've become a real turncoat," Joseph said to Michael. "You don't give a rat's arse about our people anymore, do ya? You're just another tool of the people who think they own us."

"I've done more for Bridget's children than you'll ever know," Michael said defensively.

Joseph stared at him. "Like what?"

Michael's partner spoke up. "We don't trust you," he said, jabbing a finger in Uncle Joseph's chest. It was a mistake, because the tall and imposing Joseph jabbed him back, harder.

"Tell you what," Joseph said, "I'll give you half my week's wages to go away. Michael will come with us. That boy in the casket is his nephew."

Joseph threw a few dollars at the police officer, who stared at it for a moment. Then he looked at Uncle Michael.

"This is your problem now," he said.

The police officer hovered around Jay Avenue a bit longer, watching. To entice him to leave, the keeners began to wail. Mamie hated keening, the Irish custom of having older women wail throughout the wake with an eerie, haunting, incessant cry. Apparently, Uncle Michael's partner hated it, too. When Uncle Joseph stepped outside again, he was gone. Dark was approaching, and while some lights were on in the homes along Jay Avenue, nobody was out.

When the keening was over and Father Molony had blessed the body, they all knelt in prayer. Father Molony led them in praying for Johnnie's soul, that he would be accepted into heaven.

"In the name of the Father, Son, and Holy Ghost," Father Molony said, and the whole room responded with, "Amen."

Kate and Agnes extinguished the candles, and the room fell silent as it was dark. Nobody moved, although Bessie cried quietly.

When several minutes had gone by, Uncle Michael got up. "I'll check the street," he said. "If I don't return in ten minutes, it's safe."

Ten minutes ticked by.

269

Tom got up, noiselessly, as did Patrick Masterson. They gently pushed the lid of the casket open. Johnnie's foot poked out from it, followed by his head.

"That wasn't bad for a fake wake," Johnnie said, and the room burst into hushed laughter. They needed it, after several days of dread. They had no idea whether they'd pull this off—or whether they'd be sent to jail right along with the boy who played dead.

"We're off to Michigan," Patrick Masterson said. "We have no time to waste. My ship leaves at dawn."

Johnnie was going with him, to hide out in Michigan for a while until the law forgot he existed.

Mamie and Bessie laughed as they hugged him, still incredulous that they'd gotten away with it. Johnnie hugged his brother and uncles too, and Kate.

"I'll be back," Johnnie said. "Cleveland hasn't seen the last of me."

Patrick Masterson didn't look quite as cool as Johnnie. He leaned into Kate as she helped Mamie and Agnes stuff the casket with burlap sacks of vegetables and old linens. Anything to make it look—and smell—like a real body was inside. When they finished, Tom would nail it shut. No one would question it once the casket was in the ground tomorrow morning.

"Hold down the saloon while I'm gone and stay out of trouble, ya hear?" Patrick said to Kate before he spirited Johnnie away in the night. Kate didn't answer, knowing she could promise nothing.

Sixty-Six

"Peter Sweeny has filed a lawsuit against you."

Mamie Chambers stared at the man in front of her, knowing what he was saying but not comprehending it. She was in her work clothes, and had been walking out the door with Bessie to take her to school.

"Why?" she asked, sounding exhausted. She was at her wit's end with the imposter's game. Every day it was a question of what new humiliations this man would visit upon her.

"It's all in this document," the man said, offering it to Mamie. She reluctantly accepted.

"You know he's not Peter Sweeny, don't you?" she said, annoyed. "And I can prove it in a court of law."

"Mr. Sweeny invites you to try."

The man talked over his shoulder at her as he walked away. "You know, he's willing to settle, if you'd move out and give him this building," he told her. "After breaking your promise to marry him, it's the least you could offer."

Mamie slammed the door in his face.

At the Hanna home, Mamie threw herself into her work. She couldn't afford to get fired now. And since she had started this job, there had been nonstop trials at the saloon.

The days were getting shorter now. Before dinner, when a chill permeated the air, Mark Hanna called Mamie into the sitting room and shut the door.

"What is it, Mr. Hanna?"

Mamie usually never addressed a man of Mark Hanna's position first; she waited for him to speak. But she realized that the longer she lived in America, the less interested she felt in abiding by the rules.

"Have a seat," he said. She sat, holding her thighs together tight.

"How are your patrons receiving my pamphlets at the saloon?" he asked first.

She nipped at a loose fingernail. "Well, a good part of my neighborhood will vote for Mr. Harrison. So I suppose they've been received well," Mamie replied.

"Very good," he said. "Well, I don't know how else to say this, but your behavior has been...strange lately."

"Has it?"

"Yes, Mary, it has," Mark replied. "I hope that our conversation at Mr. Huntington's estate didn't disturb you."

Of course it did, Mamie thought to herself. How could it not? But she sat with her hands on her knees, waiting for him to continue.

"More important," he said, "I hope you would never reveal the details of a very private conversation. You wouldn't do that, would you, Mary?"

"I would never have such a discussion with anyone," Mamie said.

"Then I would hope that you might reveal to me what's troubling you," Mark said. His eyes searched her face, looking for clues.

The words that came out, slow and deliberate, were, "I need a lawyer."

"A lawyer?" Mark repeated, looking stunned. Maybe he assumed Irish people fought their battles via street justice, and not in the courts. And for the most part, that was true. Except now—Peter Sweeny's imposter was trying to legally take the saloon.

"Yes," Mamie said. "I know you're a lawyer yourself. My former husband—ah, husband-to-be—is taking me to court."

Mark Hanna pressed his index finger to his lip. "It's hard to imagine any man having a quarrel with a kind-hearted woman like yourself."

"He wants my saloon," Mamie said, staring at the tops of her hands. Her fingers gripped her knees.

Mark leaned back in his chair, and she looked up at him, finally. It was like they made a silent agreement. She would never breathe a word about his relationship with her mother, and he would find her an attorney—and a good one, at that.

"Consider it done," he said.

✝

Sixty-Seven

Mamie didn't meet her lawyer until the day she had to report to court. His last name was Rhodes, and that was all she could commit to memory. Daniel Rhodes was Mark's father-in-law, and Mrs. Hanna had been born Charlotte Rhodes. This young lawyer, who looked about thirty, must be Mark's nephew, or a cousin of some sort.

As she walked to the courthouse, Mamie thought for the first time it was unjust that women couldn't practice law. The thought had never occurred to her. Just like only women bore babies and only men became priests, only men became lawyers. That's just the way it was. But now she was realizing the unfairness of this situation. Only a fellow woman who had been a sacrificial lamb for this social system they all lived in—a woman like Kate or Agnes, or even Annie—could understand what it was like to be Mamie right now.

The lawyer Mark had hired for her recognized her as she walked toward the courthouse with her brother Tom.

"Mary Chambers," he said. It was a statement, not a question.

"Yes, Mr. Rhodes," she replied.

"Mark briefed me on your case," the lawyer said. "I've read the lawsuit. Utter nonsense, but this judge is a wild card. We must play our cards right. I suggest you keep quiet and let me do the talking."

Of course, Mamie thought to herself glumly. Because why would an American judge, a highly educated man of stature, care what she had to say? Her word seemed to count for nothing—no matter how nonsensical the imposter's demands.

Just as her attorney instructed, Mamie sat quietly on the bench before the judge, refusing to look across the room at the imposter. But this room was small enough that she could see him out of the corner of her eye, staring at her. She refused to turn.

She let Attorney Rhodes present her case, listening with a certain degree of numbness. She drew a pattern in the dust on the bench with her finger, her attention to the attorney's words fading in and out.

The judge caught her by surprise by addressing her directly.

"Miss Chambers," he said, and she snapped to attention. "Do you have any witnesses who might support your claim this is a case of stolen identity?"

"Yes," Mamie said, her voice small. She glanced at the back of the courtroom, where Kate waited with Annie. As she'd promised, Kate helped Annie arrive at court groomed, her red hair secured in a neat chignon for once.

"Catherine Masterson and Anna Kilbane," Mamie said, trying to maintain a steady and confident voice. "Both were there the last night we saw Peter, and they will testify that this man is not Peter Sweeny."

"Objection!" the imposter's attorney barked. "These women have no credibility as witnesses, none whatever. That red-haired woman...well, she's known about town as 'Mad Annie.'"

"And therefore they are unable to identify this man?" the judge asked, peering at the attorney over his eyeglasses.

"Their testimony cannot be trusted."

"Let us hear it anyway," the judge said. "Anna Kilbane, you may go first."

Kate held Annie's baby as she took the witness stand, looking as lucid and composed as Mamie had ever seen her. Mamie whispered a silent prayer, hoping Annie's mind wouldn't wander into a dark wilderness of wild conspiracies.

"Miss Kilbane, have you met the man in question, Peter Sweeny?" Mamie's attorney asked.

"I can't say I've met him," she replied, and Mamie cringed. "But I've seen him."

"When?" Attorney Rhodes asked.

"The last night anyone saw him," Annie replied. "He had just arrived in Cleveland that morning, I hear, although I don't know the specifics. I saw him enter Kate Masterson's saloon with Mamie and her brothers earlier that night. I was across the street, at Seán Fada's hotel. He had given me a room for the night…"

Annie paused, as if she were waiting for him to ask why she was homeless and sleeping in a hotel. But he didn't.

"Later that night, after everyone had gone to bed, I saw Peter Sweeny cross the street to the hotel. He walked slowly, and kept looking around, like he was watching for someone. I saw him come in through the front doors of the hotel. It was always open late, you know—people came looking for rooms late at night, so the bar in the lounge stayed open. Seán Fada allowed it."

"And then what?"

"A short time later, I heard people outside in the street again. I was just getting ready for bed, but I went to the window. And I saw him, Peter Sweeny, with the woman. The woman who claims to be a singer. She's been around this area for years, and rumor has it, she seduces men to rob them. That was when I knew he was in danger. So I went outside and followed them at a distance…"

"Do you know whether Mr. Sweeny ended up in the Cuyahoga River?" Attorney Rhodes asked. "What did you see?"

"I saw him walk away with the woman, that's all I know. I saw Kate and I tried to warn her, but she wouldn't listen."

Annie gazed across the courtroom at Kate, who quietly rocked Annie's baby but showed no reaction.

"So I went back inside the hotel to find Seán Fada. I told him that the newcomer was in grave danger. He ordered me to go upstairs to bed."

"And then what?"

"And then...nothing," Annie said. "That was the last anyone ever heard from auld Peter Sweeny. But the woman...she's still here, working the streets."

Mamie's attorney stopped pacing and stopped to look at Annie. "How do you know?" he asked, as the courtroom sucked in a collective breath.

✝

Sixty-Eight

"Your Honor, give me one reason we should trust this woman," the imposter's attorney said. "They call her 'Mad Annie.' She has not a shred of legitimacy."

"Better question," Mamie's attorney interrupted. "Does the opposing council have any witnesses of his own who can vouch for the alleged Peter Sweeny, who has no identification and no proof for his claims?"

Mamie breathed a sigh of relief...until the attorney spoke.

"Yes, in fact, I do," he replied. "I would like to call Patrick Moran as a witness."

Mamie felt her pulse rushing in her temples. Behind her, Kate looked ready to combust. *Patrick Moran?*

"My witness, Patrick Moran, has known Peter Sweeny since they were neighbors in Burrishoole Parish," the opposing attorney said. "He can vouch for his identity."

Mamie turned around and watched Patrick Moran approaching the bench. In the back of the room, Annie Joyce, her brothers, and her gang of St. Malachi matrons were huddled together, watching. They looked smug.

Now that Annie was holding her own baby, Kate jumped up from her seat.

"Interesting you should call Annie Kilbane 'illegitimate,'" she said, walking toward the judge. She began to pull something from her skirt pocket; a piece of paper.

"Sit down," the judge ordered. But Kate refused.

278

"I received this in the mail last week," Kate said, her voice rising. "You might want to review it before you accept Patrick Moran's testimony."

The bailiffs began stalking after Kate, prepared to grab her and drag her from the courtroom. But before they could reach her, she slapped the pieces of paper down on the judge's bench.

"It's our certificate of matrimony," Kate announced. "My mother sent me a copy from our church in Mulrany, where Patrick Moran lived his whole sorry life...until he ran off. The second document is my daughter's baptismal certificate, dated five months later. Her birth name was Mary Margaret Moran."

Mamie heard a scream as the bailiffs grabbed her. But the sound wasn't coming from Kate. Instead, Mamie looked behind her and saw Annie Joyce falling to her knees. She has fainted—and hit her head against the bench in front of her.

The back of the courtroom erupted in chaos as the judge hastily adjourned them until further notice.

✠

Sixty-Nine

Letters from people in the Old Country to their loved ones in America traveled faster these days. But for Bridget Chambers, it couldn't be fast enough. By fall, she was eagerly awaiting mail from Mamie. She wanted to know how Bessie was faring in America—and how Mamie was holding up after her marriage to Peter Sweeny had fallen through.

That summer, Bridget had responded to Mamie's letter. In careful handwriting, Bridget told Mamie the truth she and Will had been keeping from her all these years.

Bridget went back to the Rhodes mansion after that awful night when she jumped into the Cuyahoga. She mumbled an excuse about how she had been ashamed about almost starting a fire when she knocked over the lantern.

Mr. Rhodes made Bridget sit in the parlor as he dressed her down. He upbraided her for her disobedience and warning her that if she ran off again, he'd fire her.

But it didn't matter, because she and Tylor Mor had already plotted their escape. On an uneventful night in late November, Bridget got up and dressed in the middle of the night. She had been through this routine many times, but she knew it would be her last. She stuffed her few belongings into a burlap sack and made her bed in the moonlight. She considered leaving a note for Mr. Rhodes telling him why she was leaving, but then trashed the idea.

It was better to leave them wondering whether she would return again.

By the time they went looking for her, she would be on a ship to Ireland with her lover, Tylor Mor.

Leaving America to return to Ireland was not the usual course of things for immigrants. But it wasn't unheard of, either. It was most common in Bridget and Tylor Mor's circumstances. The exploitation they encountered in America had become too much to bear. Either that, or they had run afoul of the law--or both.

After two soul-crushing years here, Bridget couldn't wait to go home. She ventured into Cleveland's dank streets toward Tylor Mor's Whiskey Island apartment. Her heart burst with joy at the thought of seeing Ireland's rolling green cliffs and moss-covered hills again.

But before that happened, Bridget had a secret she had to share with Tylor Mor.

As always, he met her at the door so he could guide her through the dark bottom floor to his second-floor apartment.

"It's late," he whispered to her as they slipped behind his door. "Are you ready to sleep straight away?"

"Yes," she replied, stripping down to her undergarments so she could sleep. She slid under the shabby blankets next to him, immune to the guilt she used to feel about sleeping in sin. Before he extinguished his lamp, he pressed two tickets for passage to Ireland into her hand.

"I bought them today," he said. "We leave in two days."

"I hope I can hide out from Mr. Rhodes and Mr. Hanna for that long," Bridget said.

"Neither man owns you."

"Aye, true that. But it's important they never track my whereabouts," Bridget said. She inhaled a deep breath of the chilly November air.

"I'm going to have a baby," she whispered.

It was cold in this room, but Tylor Mor's big body felt warm underneath the blankets. In the light of a half-moon, he gazed out the window. Then he turned his face toward the heavens--uttering a curse. Or maybe it was a prayer.

"Say something," Bridget coaxed, wrapping her arms around his neck. She wanted to say she was sure he wouldn't abandon her. She'd been abandoned enough times in her life that she never ruled out the possibility.

"I had a feeling you were," he finally replied. Then he looked at her, the whites of his eyes shining in the moonlight.

"Well, that changes things," he said at last. "You'll have to marry me tomorrow."

She laughed a little. "You can't be serious."

"Oh, but I am, darling," he said. "You underestimate me. I'd not let you become a mother before you're a bride."

Tylor Mor kept his promise, and the night before they left Cleveland, Seán Fada's lover was helping Bridget into a white wedding gown. Other brides had worn this dress. It was a little piece of communal property among Irish girls who couldn't afford their own dresses. It was a bit long on Bridget, but it was clean and crisp and white as bone. Late that night, when the church was otherwise empty, Bridget and Tylor Mor stood before the young priest, James Molony.

They were in St. Mary's church on the west bank of the Cuyahoga River. The Irish population had swelled since the famine, and they were laying the foundation of a new church named St. Malachi. But it wouldn't open for another month at least. So Bridget and William Chambers were marrying at the altar of St. Mary's.

In the hours leading up to the wedding, Bridget kept glancing over her shoulder. She half-expected to see Mark Hanna or Daniel Rhodes standing there, demanding to know where she had been. But as she approached the altar, all her fears melted away. She slipped into a dreamlike state as Father Molony read the vows, and Tylor Mor repeated them. Then it was her turn.

As she lifted her veil and received her first kiss as Tylor Mor's wife, she knew this man would keep his promises.

As Bridget composed her letter to Mamie, she reflected on her wedding night, and the days and months that followed. They escaped Cleveland and journeyed across the sea. They disembarked at Galway, a port city south of County Mayo. They were home. They made another short journey to Roskeen. That was where Bridget's family—the still living ones, anyway—resided. They welcomed their first child, a girl named Mary. They called her Mamie to distinguish her from all the other Marys. Bridget had grown up feeling neglected and invisible, and she wanted her own daughter to feel special.

Mamie was grown up now, the same age as Bridget when she gave birth to her. And Mamie needed some motherly advice.

"My dearest Mamie," she wrote slowly. "Forget Peter Sweeny. I never told you, but your father and I never liked him much anyway. Find the man who adores you..."

She recounted how Tylor Mor had rescued her from the Rhodes house. Mamie needed to find a man like her father. A man who'd do anything for her, not a man who could take or leave her, like Peter Sweeny.

Mamie received the letter the day after she went to court. She tore into the envelope and read it, absorbing the secret Mark had already revealed. She was disheartened, but no longer shocked. She dwelt upon the last few paragraphs. Her mother instructed her to find a man who would move mountains for her. And who was Mamie to disobey her own mother?

As she set the letter down on her bed, she knew she'd already met that man. He hadn't moved mountains yet, but he'd trudged through the rain to Dover Township to check on her.

The man she was looking for was Patrick Masterson.

✝

Seventy

The first frost of autumn 1888 fell on the night Tom Chambers and his uncle Joseph set out to dig up Peter Sweeny's grave.

Since he worked in the morgue, Tom had knowledge of the burial process and had access to a directory of gravesites. The body he'd been asked to identify last December had never been claimed, and the city had dumped it in a pauper's grave with no headstone. Tom had made a mental note of the grave's location, though--just in case he had been wrong, and the body really was Peter's.

Now he was certain: he was wrong when he said the body with the gunshot wound to the head was not Peter Sweeny. Part of him had hoped Peter would come to his senses and come crawling back to Mamie. Or that his disappearance had merely been an awful misunderstanding. But now he was sure Peter was dead, and the Irish Mafia knew it--which was why they sent an imposter.

"This is it," Tom said, clutching a shovel in front of the unmarked grave. It couldn't be very deep. In fact, he could still see the outline of the hole that had been dug hastily, and the gravediggers hadn't done much work to cover it well.

Without another word, he thrust the shovel into the ground and heaved the first heap of dirt beside the gravesite.

"I had to do it tonight, before the frost sets in and the ground gets hard," Tom said, frowning.

Uncle Joseph shrugged. "I'll keep watch," he said, his eyes scanning the area to make sure no one was watching. Grave robbery wasn't uncommon in this area, with all the poor people living in close vicinity. These were pauper's graves, so the police generally turned a blind eye.

"They care, but not that much," Michael McGlynn told Tom and Joseph when they let him in on their plan. "I don't know what good it'll do, but I won't stop you."

Tom didn't know what good this would do, either. Maybe he just wanted to know, once and for all, that it was Peter in the grave, and the man taking his sister to court was an identity thief. Tom was looking for a piece of evidence—anything at all—that could end the madness.

"Help me pry this casket open," Tom said, and Uncle Joseph complied. It barely took any work, since the crude coffin wasn't even nailed shut.

Their hands flew to their faces as the lid popped open. They instinctively turned away from the evil smell.

"Good God," Joseph said, turning his head away. "He stinks to the high heavens. Even worse than he did in life."

Tom snorted a little, relieved to get a laugh in the midst of this morbid scene. "Give me your lamp, please."

The skin on the face was rotting away. The area around the jaw was black and leathery, leaving the large, discolored teeth exposed. The city had dumped this body in the grave wearing the same clothes that had spent nearly two weeks in the filthy Cuyahoga River. The clothes were in just as bad shape as the body; tattered, molding, and nondescript.

"I give up," Tom said. "This sack o' bones could belong to anyone."

"Why don't you check the pockets?" Joseph suggested with a shrug.

This suggestion was so simple, so glaringly obvious, that Tom felt foolish for not thinking of it himself.

But what could possibly remain in these pockets after ten days in the Cuyahoga and nearly a year in the ground? Besides, the morgue workers would have checked them immediately for identification.

He checked anyway. In the two side pockets, there was nothing.

"It looks like one of the morgue workers took the gold watch for himself, though," Tom said. His hand wandered to the breast pocket, inside the jacket. He shuddered as his hand made contact with the mummified skin on the man's ribs.

A sturdy slip of paper remained there, wrinkled and badly faded, but still readable after eleven months.

It was a steerage ticket from the *Britannic*, issued to Peter Michael Sweeny.

Peter Sweeny had been dead all this time, probably within hours of going missing.

✝

Seventy-One

"I need you here on election night to keep watch on my house," Mark Hanna told Mamie the day before the polls opened. Tomorrow, America would decide whether to keep Grover Cleveland or cast him aside for Benjamin Harrison. Mamie hadn't told Mark yet that she wanted to quit, so for now, she planned to do what he asked.

"Where will you be?" Mamie asked.

"Downtown at a hotel with the missus, with the rest of the city's Republican Party," Mark replied. "There could be unrest on election night, and I want this house occupied. My groom and butler will be here as well."

Mamie didn't know either man very well, but she trusted Mark's groom and butler enough.

"The guest bedroom is ready for you," Mark said. "I trust it won't be an issue for you to stay overnight. I know you've been distracted by your legal troubles."

"Yes," Mamie said with a resigned shrug. "But not today. I'll prepare for election night."

"Thank you, Mary," he replied before he left the room. In the doorway, he paused.

"It is a shame about your case," he said. "Charlotte and I will see what we can do to right the situation."

"You found me an attorney, and that's more than enough, sir," Mamie said.

The polls opened early on Election Day. Through the front window of the saloon, Mamie could see a steady stream of men walking up the Viaduct. They were going to vote before work.

"Benjamin Harrison is expected to win Ohio with some ease," Kate mused over the morning's bland oatmeal and tea.

"Of course he is," Mamie replied. "The Republicans are cheating."

Kate looked paler than usual. "Will you manage on your own tonight, Kate?" Mamie asked. She had never experienced an American election night. But from Mark's description, it sounded like a prime night for mayhem. Mamie shuddered, thinking about the night someone tossed a burning rag into the saloon.

"I'll be fine," Kate replied. "I'm more concerned about you. How do you feel about staying at the Hanna's place alone?"

"I don't have much choice," Mamie replied. "Mark's butler and groom will be there, that's all I know. And it's a big enough house, with plenty of locked doors to shut myself in if there's trouble."

"Well, my brother Patrick promised he'd be home tonight. So don't worry about me," Kate said.

Mamie nodded and slipped out the door, donning the coat she had worn on the ship from Ireland for the first time in many months. It was cold, and the morning air had a wintry bite to it. It would only get colder from here.

✝

Seventy-Two

Patrick was definitely going to check on Mamie at the Hanna mansion that night. But first, he was stopping at the hotel on the river to visit Zia. Or Marie St. Jean. Whatever she was calling herself these days, he had gotten wind that she was still living there. Mamie Chambers was due to go to court again tomorrow with the fake Peter Sweeny.

"Who goes there? Pat Masterson!" the barkeeper said when Patrick opened the door, letting in a whoosh of cold air. "Do you want your usual whiskey?"

"Aye, and make it a double," Patrick said. When the barkeeper passed him the drink, he leaned in to speak to him.

"You have girls upstairs?" Patrick asked.

"A few."

"A girl named Zia, aye or nay?" Patrick asked. "The one I asked you about the last time I was here, remember."

The barkeeper's eyes glowed with knowledge. He agreed to keep quiet about the discussion they had.

"She's here," the barkeeper confirmed. "Visit her as the night winds down."

As the men returned from voting, the hotel saloon grew crowded with men grabbing a drink and a bit of warmth. There was a celebratory feeling in the air, but also an air of hostility. Politics made for mayhem in this city. The police were always prepared for riots on Election

Night, especially in the ethnic neighborhoods. The Angle was Ground Zero.

The barroom filled up with smoke and men pounding whiskeys and ales. Patrick slipped upstairs and knocked on the door bearing the correct number. The barkeeper told him which room he'd find her.

"Enter," Zia's voice purred, and Patrick twisted the knob. When Zia saw him, her demeanor shifted in an instant. The saucy façade slipped away to reveal a hardened, angry woman.

"Jesus Christ and General Jackson, what do you want?" she demanded.

"A confession," he said.

"Me? Confess?" Zia emitted an obnoxious laugh, conveying that she found the idea preposterous. "To what?"

"You lured that man away with the intention of killing him," Patrick said. "It was late last year. When I asked you about it, you remembered."

"I wasn't going to kill him," Zia said. "Maybe my husband intended to kill him, but me? I care about getting my money. I told you they cracked him over the head and left. Whatever happened next, I just don't know. But I do know he cried out for his beloved when he realized his fate."

Patrick winced thinking of Mamie, and how, on that night at least, she would have done anything to save Peter from his fate...but now...

"What's your real name, then?" Patrick asked.

"I guess you'll never know."

When Patrick turned back to Zia, a large knife was in his face.

He lunged at Zia as she tried to swing this time. "Oh no, you don't!" he said. "You picked the wrong man this time."

In one swift move, he twisted her neck. He had never applied so much brute force to a living person before.

Even he was surprised by his own strength, the force of his hands snapping the bones in her neck.

He left Zia dead on the floor with a knife still in hand, in case anyone questioned whether this murder had been committed in self-defense. It was. There was no doubt. But it turned out not to matter, because no one came looking for Zia—not until a week later, when a guest occupying the next room complained about the smell.

✝

Seventy-Three

"Going to court wasn't part of the plan, dammit," Peter Sweeny's imposter said to Black Willie, the head of the Angle Mob. "I'm fixin' to get found out. We all are."

Black Willie leaned back in his chair, staring and stroking his long black beard. They were all gathered here. Black Willie, The Watcher, and the man they had hired to impersonate Peter Sweeny. They had hoped Mamie Chambers would cave in and pressure Kate Masterson to abandon the saloon. But neither woman was budging. Instead, the shameless tart had her employer, Mark Hanna, hire an attorney.

No, it wasn't part of the plan.

"That girl is just like her father," Black Willie spat. He pictured Will Chambers twenty years ago, shortly before the girl was born. The dark hair, the serious demeanor, the fiery spirit.

Like father, like daughter.

"I'll tell you what," Black Willie said. "We're going to pay her a visit tonight. She's at the Hanna house, and Mark Hanna and the wife are out for the night."

"A visit?" the impersonator asked.

"Yes," Black Willie said. "I'll even join you myself. We'll see if we can provoke her into assaulting us. If she goes to jail, like her brother, she'll have no remaining credibility."

The other members of the Angle Mob stayed silent, as if they were awaiting further instructions.

"We've nothing to lose," Black Willie said. "You're due in court in the morning. We need to delay it from happening."

✝

Seventy-Four

Darkness came early on Election Night. Until the Winter Solstice passed, these next few weeks would be the darkest of the year.

Mamie sighed heavily when she realized the Winter Solstice was approaching again. It had been a whole year since she'd left Ireland. A long, hard year.

As dusk fell, Mamie shut all the curtains on the first floor of the Hanna house, as if it would ward off evil. At the same time, she turned all the lamps on, feeling a bit of comfort without having to walk past darkened rooms.

As men returned from the polls, Mamie could hear people chanting.

"Ma, ma, where's my pa?"

That was the Republicans' chant to jeer Grover Cleveland. Almost on cue, another group of men replied, "Off to the White House, ha ha ha!"

After they ate a simple meal Mamie had prepared, the groom and butler had gone to bed for the night.

Mamie didn't want to sleep yet. She felt more in control when she was awake and vigilant, instead of lying unawares in bed. Even though the voting had gone off without a hitch so far, Mamie was consumed with dread. Every scratch of a tree branch against a window made her jump out of her skin.

As she sat in the Hanna's library, she heard a crash at the back entrance of the house.

"Who goes there?" She shouted into the darkness. Part of her was steadfast in assuming it was a falling branch, or even a drunkard at the wrong house. She never expected her worst fear to appear in the form of Peter's imposter. She couldn't see him, but she could hear him stalking towards her through the foyer.

"Hello, m'dear," he called. "I see you stayed up waiting for me."

Mamie threw open the window of the parlor and jumped through it, landing in the Hanna's bushes. She lost a boot on the way down. Instead of searching for it, she tore off the other one and ran, in her stocking feet, down Pearl Street. She didn't realize until she saw St. Malachi rising on the corner that she had been too scared to scream.

She pounded on the door of the church, but she knew it was no use. It was just before midnight and no one with legitimate business in this neighborhood was still awake. Instead, a vagrant who'd been sleeping outside the rectory grabbed at her.

"Hey there, little lady," he said, and she recoiled from his grasp.

She cut through the church yard and ran down the hill to the saloon. She tried to get in through the front door, but it was locked. Kate and Patrick weren't expecting her home until tomorrow.

"Kate!" she cried, knowing it was futile.

The roof. She could get in through the roof, the way Kate had told her when she first arrived. She had never done it before, but now she climbed the back stairs to the roof, where she could climb in, perilously, through a window.

But when she steadied her stocking feet on the roof, she saw Peter's imposter right behind her, climbing the stairs behind her, right on her heels. She whirled around to face him.

"Go ahead and kill me," she said, refusing to move her eyes from him. "But first, just tell me who you are. You're not Peter."

"I'm not," he finally admitted. "I'll give credit where it's due—you weren't as easy to fool as we imagined. And you've proven yourself surprisingly hardy. If the real man weren't presumed dead, I'd ask him why he left you. I find your persistence rather…stimulating."

He reached out and grabbed her around the neck again, just like he had in the hotel room. The force of his grip overwhelmed her; his hands felt strong for a tall, lanky man who was a poor imitation of Peter Sweeny. She shut her eyes, pretending she was giving in and letting him strangle her. And then, when he relaxed a bit, she slashed his hand with her nails.

"Eeeow!" he shrieked, just like the phantom in Patrick Masterson's ghost story. And suddenly there was another arm around the fake Peter's neck, trapping him under the crushing weight of a strong upper arm.

"I've been waiting for this moment," Patrick Masterson said, choking the man with all his might. What he lacked in height, he more than bested this fraud of a man in sheer brute force. "I just didn't think I'd be lucky enough to find you on my roof." And with that, he backed the fake Peter to the edge of the roof, where he pushed him to his death with a single shove.

✝

Seventy-Five

Mamie's uncle was the first police officer to reach the scene where the fake Peter Sweeny was lying dead.

"He tried to break in. Then he slipped and fell from the roof," Uncle Michael explained to Patrick and Mamie, holding their gaze to make sure they all agreed on the story. "At least it will be written up that way."

While he investigated, he found proof the man was no Peter Sweeny, anyhow. Tom Chambers had the ticket he'd recovered from the real Peter Sweeny's grave.

As morning broke, a crowd gathered around the saloon to gape at the scene, fueling wild speculation about what had happened there. As ordered by her uncle, Mamie stayed inside. Then, shortly before the work day began, Mark Hanna himself appeared outside the saloon. He stood out like a sore thumb in this ragtag crowd of ethnic workaday folks.

"Pardon me," he said as he moved through the crowd, not used to the jostling of the more densely packed streets. "I'm here for my maid. When I got home this morning, the windows were open and my parlor was ransacked…and I found this."

He held out Mamie's discarded boot.

Mamie stepped outside.

"Mark," she called, "I'm right here. I'm so sorry about…"

He shushed her, knowing already she wasn't the one to blame. "Who trespassed into my home last night?"

The crowd grew a little quiet.

"This man," Uncle Michael said, motioning toward the dead body. Mark recoiled from the sight of it. "And others. He wasn't acting alone."

"I want them arrested," Mark said. "Don't make a big production of it. I just want them off the streets."

And with that, Mark Hanna put a stranglehold on the Irish mafia, and it wouldn't have happened if Mamie Chambers weren't his maid. The Angle Mob was powerful in its own neighborhood, but there were far more powerful men in the city of Cleveland at large. The police, including Uncle Michael, finally had an excuse to arrest them. People didn't say no to Mark Hanna.

For now, in her generation at least, Mamie Chambers had finished what her father started and put a chokehold on the Angle Mob.

✞

Seventy-Six

Groups of people wandered past the saloon for days after the imposter died and Black Willie was carted off to jail. They wanted to know what happened, and they talked in low voices among themselves, spinning theories. One of them was Annie Joyce, and she was alone this time.

"You're lucky things never went too far with Peter Sweeny," she said to Mamie, her eyes looking sad and tired. "I conceived a babe with Patrick Moran, but after that day at court, I lost her. 'Twas another girl, like Molly, so she's lucky to be in Heaven anyhow, instead of having a father like…him."

"I'm sorry," Mamie said, stopping in her tracks. This was the first real conversation she'd had with a woman she'd known her whole life.

"I thought of returning to Roskeen to be with my ma and da, but I have no money of my own," Annie said. "And I met another man. He's over there. He delivers the newspapers; you've surely seen him?"

"Yes, I have," Mamie said.

Annie shrugged. "His name is Patrick Masterson, too, if you could believe that. There are fourteen Patrick Mastersons in the Cleveland directory. Some of them are white, but most of them are negroes. His grandfather was a Negro, but you can't tell, can you?"

Mamie looked at the other Patrick Masterson, surmising he got the name Masterson as the descendant of a slave owner. Son of the Master.

"I can't," Mamie said, "But it doesn't matter. It only matters that you're happy, Annie."

Kate was on the front stoop getting the milk delivery for the day. "Least you know what it's like now," she said.

One of Annie's friends overheard the conversation and snapped at Kate. "How dare you judge her?" she hissed.

Kate raised her eyebrows. "I never did," she said, before she went inside and didn't slam the door for once.

✝

Seventy-Seven

In early December, when the snow started, Kate finally told Mamie what Seán Fada had written in the letter he wrote to Kate before his date. It was the first time both of them knew what really happened that night.

After Mamie went to bed, Peter Sweeny came to the hotel to meet Marie St. Jean, a mulatto woman whose real name was Alice Biggs. Presumably one of her parents was born a slave, but Biggs herself had grown up in relative comfort in New York, enjoying the privileges of a light-skinned woman who made a living seducing, and robbing, men.

"I overheard Peter talking about how he was leaving his wife-to-be, how he had decided on the voyage over that his mind was made up, and he would take off," Seán Fada wrote. "The son of a bitch had it plotted out, and then he saw his opportunity. He thought of going back to Ireland, but not if it meant facing her family. So he took these strangers up on an absurd offer to dig for gold."

At the hotel, Alice Biggs and her accomplices sold Peter Sweeny a fake gold watch to convince him of what was waiting for him out West.

"You know why they call it Fool's Gold," Seán wrote. "Back in the day, in the Middle Age, the Arabs traveled around Europe, hocking fake gold that was no more than cheap hunks of rock. It was also tainted with leprosy. The Irish encouraged their British enemies to travel on the road and find the gold merchants—we call them *leper cons*—and the bastards fell for it."

But Seán Fada knew the woman who had lured him away was a con artist, so when they left the hotel together, he followed them at a distance, watching. When he found Peter Sweeny lying on the ground, unconscious and robbed, and pulled out his shotgun and put him out of his misery. Peter Sweeny didn't even flinch when the gun went off, and that was the end of him. He was probably going to die anyway, but Seán Fada couldn't risk him coming to and following through on his evil plot.

"Perhaps I'll go to hell for it, but I'm not so sure," he'd written. "I can't imagine a more heartless act than abandoning a woman in a foreign country and taking off with her father's money."

When Seán Fada went back at dawn to check on the body, seeing if it was still there, he looked up to find Michael McGlynn standing over him in his police uniform. Seán Fada tried to blurt out an explanation, but instead, Michael asked, "Do you need me to cover for you as you get rid of him?"

Seán couldn't move the body on his own, so he went to retrieve Patrick Masterson at the saloon. While Mamie's uncle acted as the lookout, prepared to distract anyone who came by and saw the blood, Patrick and Seán dragged Peter Sweeny to the Cuyahoga River and dumped the body.

"Good riddance," Patrick said as he used his foot to push him under the water. "Now he'll have no chance to abandon any children he creates."

He hoped the giant underwater panther he'd learned about from Ojibwa Indians in Michigan, the *Mishipeshu,* would come swallow up Peter Sweeny when he saw him with that gold watch about his wrist. That was what the Mishipeshu did—guarded the precious metals of the Great Lakes, and attacked anyone who threatened his reserves.

Michael McGlynn told no one about what he'd seen, not even his brothers. Tom and Johnnie were in the dark. Michael took Tom to the morgue to see if he would catch on, but surprisingly, he had no inkling of what they'd done.

And maybe they shouldn't have done it. Maybe they really were going to Hell. But, as Seán wrote, if nobody stands for what's right and good, we'll all meet the Devil—someday.

✞

Seventy-Eight

Christmas Eve in the year 1888 was quite a bit different than the Christmas Eve just one year before. The only tears that would fall from Mamie's eyes were happy ones. Her mother and father and three of her younger siblings—Bridie, Frankie, Georgie and the baby, Norah, were in Cleveland. They had arrived on the same ship that ferried Tom, Mamie and Johnnie across the sea last year. Ma and Da hadn't decided how long they were staying— maybe forever, maybe not. Life was hard in Ireland, and there was only room for one tailor in Roskeen. Da had trained the new husband of the third Chambers child, eighteen-year-old Katie, to assist him in the tailor shop. Da wasn't sure if he needed to return home, or if he should keep his family in America.

"You'll decide in time," Kate Masterson said as she passed around a tray of breads. "For now, you're here."

Molly was sitting next to her, having returned to her mother's care after the Angle Mob was vanquished. She was getting older now, but for the first time, she was going to school.

They were in the saloon, where Mamie still worked but no longer lived. Mark Hanna had paid off their mortgage. Kate and Mamie co-owned this place now, although it remained registered in Patrick Masterson's name.

Mamie had taken her savings and purchased a modest house on Jay Avenue. It had a bedroom downstairs and a loft where Bessie slept. For now, Mamie slept alone in the downstairs bedroom—but she wouldn't be alone for much longer. She was engaged again.

Patrick Masterson planned to retire from the lakes after one more summer of sailing. Then they'd get married. Peter Sweeny was nothing but a distant memory, one that Mamie could look back on with some bittersweet fondness. But now that a year had passed, she realized she'd left him behind in County Mayo with everything else she used to know. Peter Sweeny never really made it to America. Patrick Masterson was the man of her American dreams now.

"When we have a baby, I think we should name her Mamie, too," Patrick joked to Mamie's parents as they watched a light snow dusting the Viaduct outside. "Or if it's a boy, Grover."

"Mr. Cleveland lost the election," Kate reminded him.

"Aye," Patrick said. "But it's not over yet for ol' Grover Cleveland. I wager he'll be back again, even if his two terms aren't back to back."

"Grover, aye?" Mamie repeated. "I like it well enough." He had been the first American president she'd lived under, and the only one she'd been lucky enough to meet. She still worked for Mark Hanna for now, so maybe one day she'd meet Mr. Harrison as well. But Patrick told her to plan on quitting the Hanna house when they married. It wouldn't be long.

"You know, mad as it sounds in this world, I hope my first one is a girl," Mamie said, biting into a sweet piece of bread.

Raising girls in this world wasn't easy—for now, Mamie couldn't even own this saloon in her own name. But she suspected progress were on the march. Women were fighting back, in small ways, and things had improved just in this generation. Mamie wondered what

Cleveland would look like for her daughters and granddaughters, and great-granddaughters after that. Different, she hoped.

"A girl?" Patrick said, sliding his arm around her. "I certainly hope so, m'dear."

Author's Note

In the spring of 1890, my great-great-grandparents, Mamie Chambers and Patrick Masterson, got married at St. Malachi Church and had one daughter and three sons. Their first child was a girl they named Mamie. Their second child was a boy they named William Grover after President Grover Cleveland, who did go on to be re-elected in 1892. William Grover Masterson was my great-grandfather and the father of my late grandmother, Regina.

After Patrick Masterson's tragic death in a work accident in 1899, Mamie Chambers married again, this time a man from Westport in County Mayo named Michael O'Grady. They had one daughter together. Mamie Chambers kept the saloon until shortly before her death in 1937.

Mamie Chambers Masterson O'Grady, her two husbands, and her siblings are survived by dozens of great-great-grandchildren, including me.

My great-aunt Mary Jane Masterson, who was nine years old at the time of her death, always recalled Mamie sitting in her rocking chair, recalling her days of fighting off the Angle Mob.

Made in the USA
Monee, IL
26 June 2021